'In the hour of mankind's greatest triumph, the seeds of heresy are sown.'

Battle for the Abyss – *Neil Roberts*

THE HORUS HERESY®

VISIONS OF HERESY
BOOK ONE

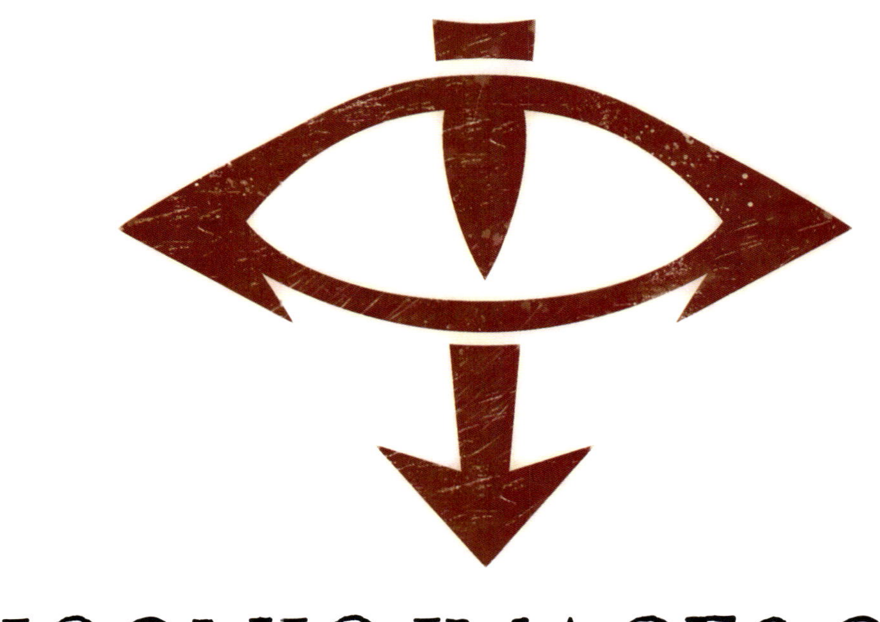

ICONIC IMAGES OF BETRAYAL AND WAR

BY ALAN MERRETT

Credits

Written by .... Alan Merrett
Compiled and edited by .... Laurie Goulding
Concept art by .... John Blanche
Cover art by .... Neil Roberts
Book Production & Layout by .... Adrian Wood

Featuring art by .... Abrar Amjal, Steve Belledin, John Blanche, Steve Boulter, Alex Boyd, James Brady, Paul Carrick, Kevin Chin, Kari Christensen, Ed Cox, Daarken, Paul Dainton, David Deen, Adam Denton, Chris Dien, Wayne England, Al Eremin, Carl Frank, David Gallagher, Mark Gibbons, John Gravato, Des Hanley, Andrew Hepworth, Paul (Prof) Herbert, John Hodgson, Neil Hodgson, Ralph Horsley, David Hudnut, Paul Jeacock, Hugh Jamieson, Nuala Kinrade, Cos Koniotis, Karl Kopinski, Sam Lamont, Kenson Low, Chuck Lukacs, Colin MacNeil, Thomas Manning, Dave Millgate, Torstein Nordstrand, Justin Norman, Dominik Oedinger, Pat Oliff, Jen Page, Tony Parker, Jim Pavelec, Ben Peck, Michael Phillippi, Rachel Pierce, Eric Polak, Mark Poole, Rhys Pugh, David Rabbitte, Eric Ren, Karl Richardson, Neil Roberts, James Ryman, Rick Sardinha, Dan Scott, Phil Sibbering, Adrian Smith, JD Smith, Anne Stokes, Ian Strickland, Tiernen Trevallion, Chris Trevas, Andrea Uderzo, Franz Vohwinkel, Dan Wheaton, John Wigley, Brad Williams, Sam Wood and John Zeleznick

'Macragge's Honour' by .... Dan Abnett & Neil Roberts

A Black Library Publication.

Thanks to John Blanche, Ben Douglas, Christian Dunn, Steve Horvath, Jervis Johnson, William King, Graeme Lyon, Rick Priestley, Edd Ralph, Demetris Tampakoudis, all at Games Workshop, and of course all of the wonderful artists whose work is featured in this book.

Special mention must go to all of the many people who have worked on the story over the years: writers, artists, plotters, planners, model makers, managers, editors and all the other backroom staff without whose tireless and dedicated efforts none of this would have been possible.

First published in Great Britain in 2013 by
Black Library, Games Workshop,
Willow Road, Lenton,
Nottingham,
NG7 2WS.

British Cataloguing-in-Publication Data. A catalogue record for this book is available from the British Library. Pictures used for illustrative purposes only.

UK Product Code: 60100181227 US Product Code: 70100181227 UK ISBN: 978-1-84970-215-7 US ISBN: 978-1-84970-216-4 Printed in China

Games Workshop website: www.games-workshop.com
Black Library website: www.blacklibrary.com

Contents

FOREWORD

The story of the Horus Heresy had its origins in a small piece of text presented in the very first Warhammer 40,000 miniatures gaming supplement that Games Workshop published, a long out of print book entitled *Chapter Approved – The Book of the Astronomican*. Published in early 1988, this snippet of text gave a tiny glimpse of what was to follow:

> *'The Horus Heresy is reckoned by many to rate as the greatest single disaster ever suffered by the Imperium. The specific details of the Heresy are known only to the Emperor, but its broader history is the stuff of popular legend. According to one version of the tale, Horus was once the most trusted servant of the Emperor. But in his heart there dwelt a hidden evil, and he became seduced by this evil, and came to nurture demons and other forces of destruction. Horus marched upon Earth with a third part of the hosts of the Imperium which he had seduced to his purpose. For seven days and seven nights the hosts battled until the Emperor caught Horus by the heel and cast him to the Eye of Terror and with him the third part of the hosts of the Imperium.'*

Later that same year Games Workshop published the miniatures game Adeptus Titanicus and the seminal Warhammer/Warhammer 40,000 supplement *Realm of Chaos: Slaves to Darkness*. Both of these featured expanded histories and background information about the Heresy, firmly establishing it as the most important and evocative story within the Warhammer 40,000 mythos. Since then the story has been embellished, added to and utilised as a wellspring of ideas – dozens of different products featuring the story have been published by Games Workshop and its subsidiaries during the intervening years.

The Horus Heresy has, quite rightly, acquired legendary status amongst Warhammer 40,000 fans, but until the publication of the *Visions* series of artbooks the story had never before been collected together as a single narrative. The four volumes plotted the entire story arc, from the ending of the Great Crusade through to the seminal final battle aboard Horus's battle-barge *Vengeful Spirit*. This new edition combines the four original volumes and also includes some brand new texts and yet more lavish illustration, drawn from the Black Library's best-selling Horus Heresy novel series.

Alan Merrett
January 2013

Timeline

Millennia	Age	Notes
1-15	Age of Terra	Humanity dominates Earth. Civilisations come and go. The Solar System is colonised. Mankind lives on Mars and the moons of Jupiter, Saturn and Neptune.
15-18	Age of Technology	Mankind begins to colonise the stars using sub-light spacecraft. At first only nearby systems can be reached and the colonies established on them must survive as independent states since they are separated from Earth by up to ten generations of travel.
18-22	Age of Technology	Invention of the warp-drive accelerates the colonising of the galaxy. Federations and Empires are founded. First aliens encountered and first Alien Wars are fought. First human psykers scientifically proven to exist. Psykers begin to appear throughout human worlds.
22-25	Age of Technology	First Navigators are born allowing human spaceships to make even longer, quicker warp-jumps. Mankind enters a golden age of enlightenment as scientific and technological progress accelerates. Human worlds unite and non-aggression pacts are secured with dozens of alien races.
25-26	Age of Strife	Terrible warp-storms interrupt interstellar travel. Sporadic at first, the storms eventually prevent any warp-jumps being made. The incidence of human mutation increases rapidly. Mankind enters a dark period of anarchy and despair.
26-30	Age of Strife	Human worlds ripped apart by civil wars, revolts, alien predation and invasion. Human psykers and other mutants dominate some worlds and these rapidly fall prey to warp-creatures. Humanity is on the brink of destruction.
30-present	Age of Imperium	Earth is conquered by the Emperor and enters an alliance with the Mechanicum of Mars. Finally, the warp storms abate and interstellar travel is possible again. The Emperor builds the Astronomican and creates the Space Marine Legions. Human worlds are reunited by the Emperor in a Great Crusade that lasts for more than two hundred years.

The Age of the Emperor

The Emperor – *Adrian Smith*

It is a time of legend.

Mighty heroes battle for the right to rule the galaxy.

The vast armies of the Emperor of Mankind have conquered the galaxy in a Great Crusade – the myriad alien races have been smashed by the Emperor's elite warriors and have retreated to their lairs to lick their wounds.

The dawn of a new age of supremacy for humanity beckons.

Gleaming citadels of marble and gold celebrate the many victories of the Emperor. Triumphs are raised on a million worlds to record the epic deeds of his most powerful and deadly warriors.

First and foremost amongst these are the primarchs. These superhumans have led the Emperor's armies of Space Marines in victory after victory. They are unstoppable and magnificent, the pinnacle of the Emperor's genetic experimentation. The Space Marines are the mightiest human warriors the galaxy has ever known. Each one is capable of besting a hundred normal men in combat. They are legion!

Organised into vast armies of tens of thousands called Legions, the Space Marines and their primarch leaders now rule the galaxy in the name of the Emperor.

Chief amongst the primarchs is Horus, the first and strongest and to the Emperor like a son. He is the Warmaster, the commander-in-chief of all the Emperor's military might, the subjugator of a thousand thousand worlds and conqueror of the galaxy. He is unmatched as a warrior, save by maybe the Emperor himself. His star is bright and his troops are devoted to him. But their trust is about to be shattered!

Unbeknownst to his troops or the Emperor, Horus has been corrupted by the secret powers of the warp. Chaos has whispered in his ear and Horus has listened to its guile and wickedness. Why should Horus do as the Emperor bids? Was he not the one who led the Space Marine Legions to countless victories? Does he not bear the scars of a thousand battles? Was the Emperor there to shed a tear as brave Space Marines died horrible deaths at the hands of their alien foes? No, it was Horus who fought and bled and cried! Horus who planned the wars and the victories. Horus who has earned the loyalty of the Space Marines. Horus who should be acclaimed Emperor of Mankind!

The Emperor sits on his throne on Earth and dreams of the future. He has single-handedly created the most awesome military force ever known. His genius mapped the genes and artifice of the primarchs and their Space Marine progeny. His brilliant mind conceived the Grand Plan: the marrying of the great Empires of Terra and Mars and their Great Crusade to rescue mankind from the thrall of aliens and warp-beasts. It was the Emperor who helped realise the full potential of the Navigators and enabled humanity to travel vast distances through the warp without peril. But his work is not finished and now he dreams his dreams and his vast intellect calculates the destiny of mankind. Time is against him. His precognitive powers are fading; the pressure to maintain the galaxy-wide signal of the Astronomican grows daily; the future has become clouded and dark. He is aware that others like him are aborning, but weaker than he, less able to fend off the seductive embrace of the Warp and the unknown horrors within.

It is upon these emerging psykers that the Emperor has focused his attention. Now is the time for him to order the fabrication of the Psy-Engines and Occullum Test Stations, the devices that will search out the inert psyker genes within the populace. Emerging and latent psykers can thence be trained and purified, protected from the dangers of the warp and the malignant entities therein. Mankind's destiny is a fragile thing and only the Emperor can guide it well and safely forward.

The Emperor's great armies have served their purpose. Now is the time for the Legions to be disbanded and the Space Marines set to other tasks guarding the worlds of humanity and policing the new regimes. The warrior lords that are the primarchs are to become the rulers of worlds and administrators of the Grand Plan.

Horus seeks vengeance! He wants to rid the galaxy of mankind's alien foes utterly. Not a single alien should remain alive to threaten humanity. The Legions must hunt them down and eradicate them all! The glorious armies of the Imperium should not be forced to put down their guns and swords. They must not be emasculated and converted into mere policemen and gatekeepers! The daemon argues a clever and compelling case in Horus's ear and the Emperor should beware the serpent!

Unity – *Adrian Smith*

The Emperor of Mankind – *John Blanche*

Imperial Palace – *John Blanche*

The Age of Strife

This terrible period of history lasted for over five thousand years. During this time, the worlds of man were isolated by searing warp storms that made interstellar travel virtually impossible. Earth was totally cut off from its colonies and allies. Across the galaxy, the human worlds fell into anarchy and war. Mankind was torn apart as local factions and empires fought for control.

As human civilisation fragmented, hundreds of alien races seized their chance to plunder unprotected worlds and enslave their populations. Planets were sacked and their peoples slaughtered. Those that survived the alien onslaught rapidly reverted to barbarism. Worse still was the threat from the warp.

The existence of warp creatures and the dangers they posed to the human mind were not fully understood. On worlds with large concentrations of psykers, these creatures were able to breach the barrier between the immaterium and realspace. Entire worlds fell prey to the indescribable horrors that burst forth. Some worlds were devoured whole and have been permanently lost in the warp.

Humanity was on the brink of annihilation. Alone and beset by internal strife, under incessant attack by aliens and facing the peril of warp incursions, the human worlds that survived were pitiable shadows of what they had once been. It would take a superhuman effort to save humanity and free it from its hellish bondage.

During the Age of Strife, the Earth was in a terrible state. Generations of war made the planet a virtual wasteland and the inhabitants a mass of degenerate, feral nomads. Insane prophets and religious demagogues led the warring tribes of Earth and the world was wracked by one religious war after another. Earth was isolated from its former empire in the stars. Only Mars was still in intermittent contact and the arcane tech-priests of the red planet were deadly foes of the mad rabbles of old Terra.

From out of this doom a powerful leader emerged. He was the Emperor and his power lay in his rationality and foresight. Few suspected him of being the mutant he was. The Emperor conquered great swathes of the Earth and instituted many social changes. Out went fear and blind faith, in came practicality and rationality. The Emperor started to experiment with genetics to stabilise the population and to recreate the race of mankind as it was before the radiation storms. The Emperor formed his War Council, comprised of his most able generals and a number of high-ranking administrators who hailed him as divine.

The Great Crusade

From the ashes of the Age of Strife there arose a mighty leader, the man who would be known only as the Emperor. His origins are unrecorded and unknown, but it was on Earth that he started to forge an empire that would unite the myriad worlds of humanity. The Emperor quickly conquered the Earth and reunited the warring factions.

From the outset, the Emperor employed the genetically modified warriors who were to become the Space Marines. These superhuman troops dominated the Unification Wars, easily defeating all their Terran opponents and forcing the tech-priests of Mars to sue for peace. They fought with righteous zeal and it was they who first referred to their mission as a crusade.

Just as the conquest of Earth was complete, a mighty cosmic event occurred. A massive shock blasted across the warp, clearing the warp storms that had raged for five thousand years.

The Solar System was the first region of space to be conquered by the Emperor and his Space Marine Legions. Alien invaders were flushed from the moons of Saturn and Jupiter and their wretched enslaved human inhabitants repatriated to Earth.

Mars had evolved a strong culture based around worship of the Machine God and was devoted to the study and construction of engines and machinery of all types. The Mechanicum of Mars, a parliament of technocrats, ruled this powerful world. The Emperor did not attack the red planet, but instead struck an alliance with the Mechanicum.

Access to the giant factories of Mars enabled the Emperor to vastly increase the power of his Legions with improved wargear. In addition, the tech-priests of Mars supplied the vast warp-engined battleships that could transport the Emperor's Legions across the galaxy and the mighty war machines known as Titans.

So it was that the Emperor led his Legions of Space Marines on a great mission to free humanity from the aliens and warp creatures that had nearly destroyed it – the Great Crusade had begun. World after world was reconquered. Alien oppressors were routed or annihilated in a series of epic wars. Worlds infected with warp creatures were cleansed with powerful virus bombs and vortex missiles in apocalyptic orbital barrages.

During the Great Crusade, the Space Marine Legions were reunited with their primarchs. Many of the planets upon which the primarchs had been raised, and which they now dominated, became the Legions' home worlds and they established permanent bases on them. From these new bases, the Legions could launch assaults on almost any enemy.

The power of the Imperium was at its zenith. Nothing could stand in the way of the Emperor and his mighty army.

Promethean Sun – *Neil Roberts*

Expeditionary Fleets

During the Great Crusade, the vast forces of the Emperor were organised into a number of different formations which became known as the Expeditionary Fleets. At first there was but one fleet – commanded by the Emperor himself – but as the Crusade spread across the galaxy more and more were launched. Trusted and powerful generals were appointed to lead these new fleets.

In order that they could be effectively supported and their movements across the galaxy tracked with some degree of accuracy, each of the Expeditionary Fleets was designated a number by the War Council. As the Great Crusade drew to a close, there were nearly 5,000 primary expeditions and more than 60,000 secondary deployment groups operating throughout the Imperium.

The composition of each of the fleets was not fixed. The various fleet groups, Imperial Army regiments, auxiliary troop formations and even Space Marine Legions that made up a fleet could come and go over time, as prevailing strategy dictated. But the designation numbers remained and, while most never held any particular significance, some became famously associated with specific primarchs or other prestigious leaders of the Imperium.

The numerical designation of an Expeditionary Fleet was also applied to worlds conquered by its forces – for example the Imperial world initially known as 63-19 was the nineteenth discovered by the 63rd Expedition. It was therefore possible for the Imperium's administrators to plot the movements of a specific fleet by the worlds it encountered, in chronological order.

The Expeditionary Fields – *Kevin Chin*

The War Council

The Great Crusade was a mammoth operation involving millions of troops and thousands of ships. Imperial armies fought campaigns across the broad sweep of the galaxy. Tens of thousands of worlds needed to be saved.

The Imperial military of this time comprised the entire force of the Space Marine Legions, thousands of auxiliary regiments drawn from the freshly reconquered worlds, gigantic war machines supplied by the Mechanicum and their forge worlds, foremost amongst these the mighty Titans of the Collegia Titanica, and a host of other smaller organisations and armed formations. The most significant of these was the Custodian Guard, the Emperor's bodyguard.

All of these were supported by a bewildering array of battleships, drop-ships and troop transports variously commanded by the Space Marine Legions, the Mechanicum and the other Imperial Commanders and leaders.

To manage the execution of the Great Crusade, the Emperor convened the War Council. This effectively became the ruling body of the Imperium during the Great Crusade – and through it the Emperor's law – was brought to hundreds of thousands of human worlds.

The Emperor sat at the head of the Council; at his right hand was Malcador. Each of the primarchs had a seat on the Council, as did the Chief Custodian. When the Emperor made his alliance with Mars, the Fabricator-General of the Mechanicum was offered a seat. Supporting the Council was a team of astropaths who provided communication between the members, since it became increasingly impractical for the group to physically assemble, given the size of the growing Imperium and the inherent difficulties of travel through the warp.

Null-Mistress – *John Blanche*

Malcador the Sigillite

During the conquest of Earth the Emperor gathered about him trusted lieutenants and gave to them tasks and duties befitting men of status. Most of these servants were drawn from the ranks of his bodyguard and Space Marine Legions.

Malcador was an exception. He was not a warrior, but a man of learning with the bearing of a priest. From the early years of the Unification Wars he was ever-present at the Emperor's side. His origins were unknown to all save perhaps the Emperor. He wore the hooded robes of a simple Terran administrator.

Malcador was appointed to run the Emperor's Palace and through it he managed the administration of newly conquered Terra. As the Crusade progressed, Malcador's power and influence grew as he became overseer of the Imperial Tithe and chief of the Imperial Adminstratum.

Blessed with unnaturally long life, there were many rumours about the true nature of this enigmatic figure. Some say he was a psyker, the first to have undergone the soul-binding ritual. Other rumours say that he was distantly related to the Emperor.

Malcador the Sigillite – *John Gravato*

The Gclden Palace – *John Blanche*

Departmento Munitorum

To cope with the ever-increasing workload of managing the Expeditionary Fleets and all of their attendant logistics and communications, a new division of the Administratum was created on Terra. Its remit was the total control of all supplies to the fleets of the Great Crusade, though in time this control was extended to troop requisitions and the supply and maintenance of all munitions, transports, vessels, war machines and wargear. As it was, the Departmento Munitorum was formally dedicated just prior to the great Triumph at Ullanor.

The task facing the Departmento Munitorum was immense and it quickly grew in size to meet this challenge. Many hundreds of thousands were recruited into its myriad divisions and sub-sections from the ranks of the Terran-based Administratum. As its size increased, so did its status within the Imperium, and so too did its power and authority.

Within a few short months of its establishment, the Departmento Munitorum no longer restricted its activities to the mere task of resupply and maintenance, but also became enmeshed in the mire of politics surrounding the great fleets and their military leaders. They were tasked with ensuring adherence to central strategy within the Expeditionary Fleets and with bringing the more wayward elements of the Imperial military back in line. This led to mistrust and unrest amongst the fleets themselves, as many within the military saw this as bureaucrats trying to take over and run the war effort – a view shared by several very notable individuals who resisted the interference of the Departmento Munitorum as much as they could without directly refusing to comply.

Field Adjutant – *John Blanche*

Urslavik 12th Infantry – *Cos Koniotis*

Contrador – *David Deen*

Origin of the Space Marines

Research and development leading to the creation of the Space Marines of the Legiones Astartes began during the Age of Strife whilst Earth was isolated from the rest of the galaxy. The Emperor gathered about him a team of master scientists and constructed a secret genetics laboratory in the vast dungeons of his Terran fortress.

Within these dark vaults the first super-warriors were created. The Emperor hand-picked men from his personal bodyguard and then subjected them to surgical and psychological modification. These warriors were not only immensely strong, but also had bred into them incredible willpower. With rigorous training and appropriate mental conditioning, they became an unstoppable force whose loyalty to the Emperor was unflinching.

The early Space Marines were organised into regiments, each comprising no more than a few hundred warriors. The Emperor named each one of the twenty regiments. These names became synonymous with the power of the Emperor and struck fear into the hearts of their foes. These super-warriors formed the Emperor's army, and with it he conquered the Earth and subjugated the myriad warring factions to his will. For the first time in unrecorded millennia, the Earth was united under the rule of one man. The number of Space Marines quickly increased as the Emperor recruited men from amongst the newly conquered tribes of Earth. By the time Terra was totally under the Emperor's control, each of the Legions could muster several thousand warriors.

For the Emperor! – *Des Hanley*

Devoticn – *Michael Phillippi*

The Crusader Host

The Space Marine Legions were clearly the most powerful military organisations in the Imperium, if not the galaxy. It was therefore deemed appropriate that they maintain some form of representation at the seat of Imperial power whilst the Great Crusade progressed. To this end a select group of Space Marines, drawn from the ranks of all Legions, was seconded to the Crusader Host on Terra.

The Crusader Host was based in the Preceptory. Within its hallowed halls they kept tally of their brothers' glorious victories, mourned the dead and acted as their primarchs' proxies in the Solar System.

Legiones Astartes

The Space Marine Legions and their Primarchs

The I Legion 'Dark Angels'
Lion El'Jonson

– ERROR #CDIV –
file not found

The III Legion 'Emperor's Children'
Fulgrim

The VII Legion 'Imperial Fists'
Rogal Dorn

The VIII Legion 'Night Lords'
Konrad Curze

The IX Legion 'Blood Angels'
Sanguinius

Legiones Astartes

The Space Marine Legions and their Primarchs

The IV Legion 'Iron Warriors'
Perturabo

The V Legion 'White Scars'
Jaghatai Khan

The VI Legion 'Space Wolves'
Leman Russ

The X Legion 'Iron Hands'
Ferrus Manus

– CENSORED –
by Imperial decree

The XII Legion 'World Eaters'
Angron

Legiones Astartes

The Space Marine Legions and their Primarchs

The XIII Legion 'Ultramarines'
Roboute Guilliman

The XIV Legion 'Death Guard'
Mortarion

The XV Legion 'Thousand Sons'
Magnus the Red

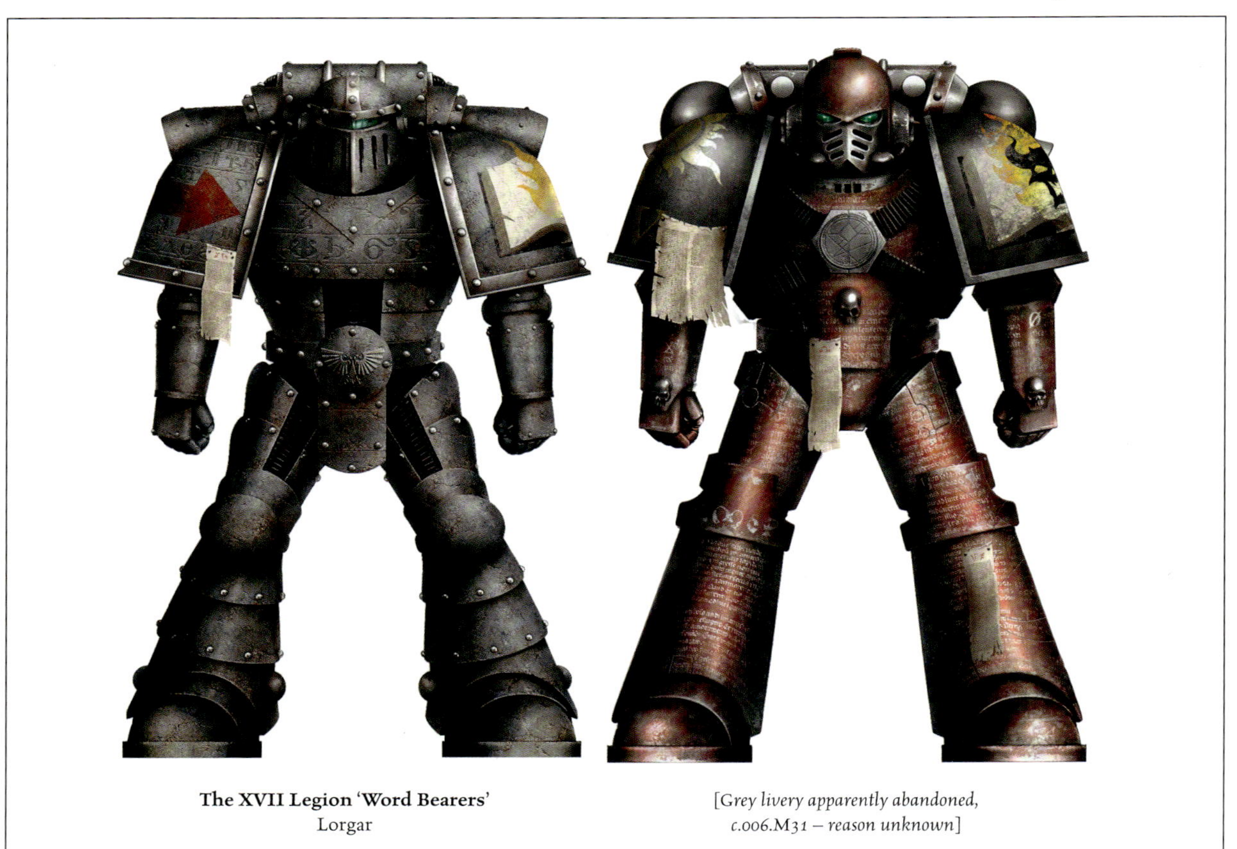

The XVII Legion 'Word Bearers'
Lorgar

[Grey livery apparently abandoned, c.006.M31 – reason unknown]

Legiones Astartes

The Space Marine Legions and their Primarchs

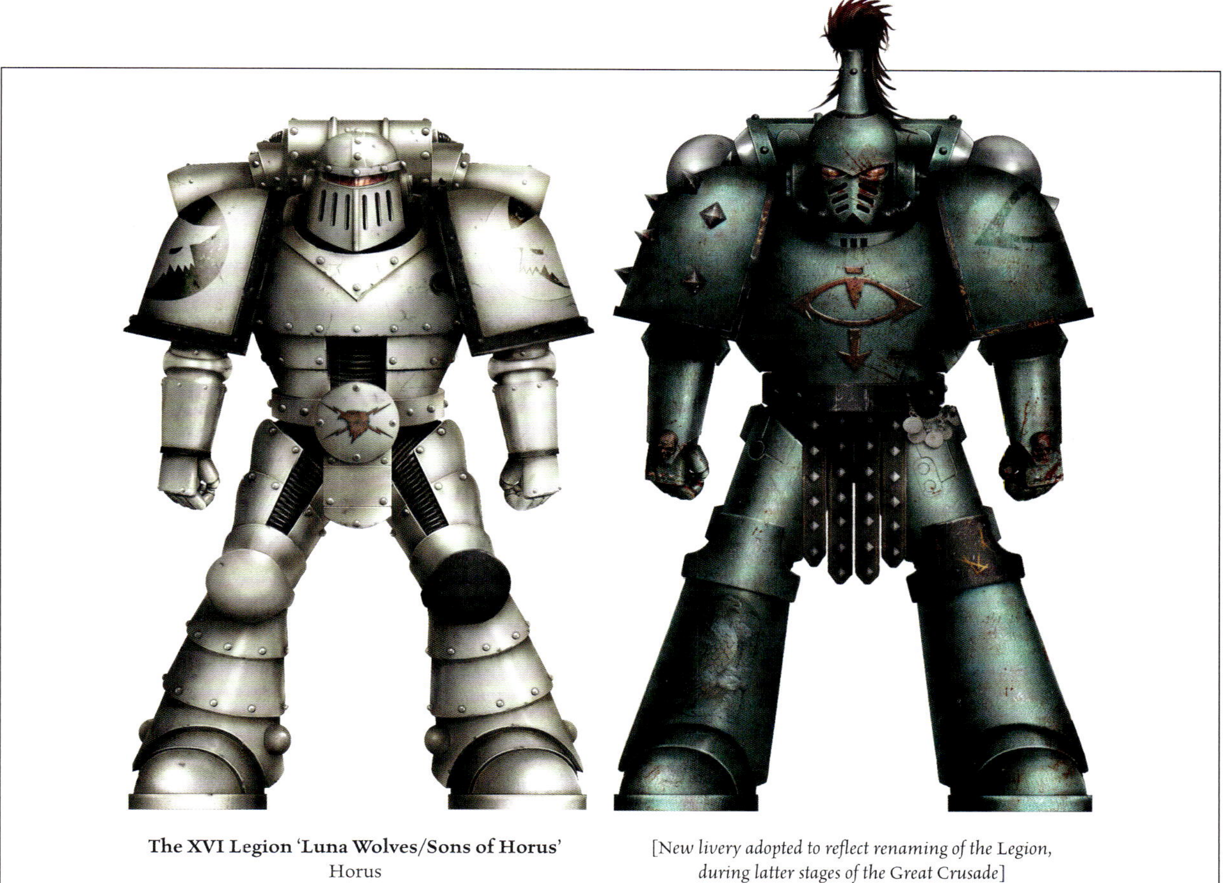

The XVI Legion 'Luna Wolves/Sons of Horus'
Horus

[New livery adopted to reflect renaming of the Legion, during latter stages of the Great Crusade]

The XVIII Legion 'Salamanders'
Vulkan

The XIX Legion 'Raven Guard'
Corax

The XX Legion 'Alpha Legion'
Alpharius

Death Guard Space Marine – *John Blanche*

Phoenix Guard Champion – *John Blanche*

Emperor's Children Space Marine – *John Blanche*

World Eaters Space Marine Veteran – *John Blanche*

Phoenix Guard – *John Blanche*

Space Marine Veteran – *John Blanche*

Cataphractii Terminator – *John Blanche*

Luna Wolves Space Marine – *John Blanche*

The Primarchs

During Earth's isolation in the Age of Strife, the Emperor was already planning ahead. In preparation for the reconquest of the galaxy, he conceived of and created the twenty primarchs. These extraordinary characters were to be his generals – great leaders who would conquer millions of worlds in his name. Each primarch would have powers and skills beyond those of any other human, possibly rivalling those of the Emperor himself.

The Emperor's ambitions for the primarchs appeared to be ruined by a cataclysmic event. A strange warp vortex snatched the still-foetal primarchs from the Emperor's laboratory and cast them across the galaxy. They were cast onto separate worlds where they matured. As the years passed they came to dominate their worlds and became powerful warriors and leaders.

During the Great Crusade the Emperor was reunited with the primarchs in turn, their superhuman skills and physiques having allowed them to rise to positions of authority within their adopted cultures.

That there is such a strong link between the primarchs and their Legions suggests that they were crucial in the invention of the Space Marines. Certainly the Space Marines share genetic material and some physical and mental traits with their primarch. So strong was this link that as the primarchs were encountered, in turn they each became the natural and obvious leader of the Legion with whom they had so much in common.

In many cases the primarch's adopted world became the new base of operations for their Legion and was known henceforth as the Legion's home world. Often the primarchs recruited their loyal followers from their home world into the ranks of their Legion.

Supposition and theory abound about the true nature of the primarchs, the most powerful of all of the Emperor's creations. Like gods they bestrode the battlefields of the Great Crusade and their names and legends would endure forever.

Some say that the primarchs were created from the Emperor's own genetic stock, each engineered to be a leader of men, a warrior and a hero, each a mighty warlord whose martial prowess was only matched by his charisma and mental prowess, each with special powers that set them apart from normal men.

Was it the Emperor's plan that they would be the ones to lead Mankind away from the powers of darkness and into a new golden age? Or were they merely a by-product of the experiments that resulted in the creation of the Space Marines?

What was the mysterious force that scattered the infant primarchs across the galaxy? The few records that exist of this event are vague and unclear. Tradition has it that it was a warp vortex – a swirling maelstrom that opens a portal or doorway between distant planets. The truth will likely never be known.

The Primarchs – *Neil Roberts*

And what of the scattering? Was it devised by the Emperor so that the primarchs might learn to live a life beyond the laboratory within which they were spawned? Was it so they might carve a destiny for themselves and prove their worth? Or were darker forces at work? Was this some devious plot by the Dark Gods to foil the Emperor's dreams and dash his hopes to save humanity? Stranger still was the theory that the primal psychic energies employed in their creation could not be contained in their foetal forms, and its release created the vortex.

The Custodian Guard

The Space Marines were not the only super-warriors created by the Emperor. The first group of genetically and psychologically modified troops he created were his own personal bodyguards – the Legio Custodes. Their duty was simply to ensure the safety of the Emperor at all times.

Stronger than Space Marines, the Custodians are fearsome warriors and have an unbreakable devotion to the Emperor. They are his most loyal and trusted servants. A detachment of the Guard always accompanies the Emperor, even when he retires to his private chambers.

During the coming years, the Custodians are also tasked with duties that now extend beyond those of guarding the Emperor's person. Small detachments of Custodians are frequently ordered to accompany the Legiones Astartes to ensure that the Emperor's will is followed.

The Custodians have access to all of the myriad types of weaponry and wargear that are used by the Space Marines, including transport and fighting vehicles. They also have access to the Emperor's personal transports and battleships so that they can always be at his side.

In addition to the Space Marines' wargear, the Custodian Guard also has access to a variety of weapons only they can use. An example is the Guardian Spear: a combination of boltgun and power axe, which is the standard armament for a Custodian Guard squad.

> *'These men are my bodyguards, their lives forfeit to the guarantee of my physical safety. Of their loyalty to me there shall be no question nor doubt. I, and I alone, shall have the authority to stand in judgment over them. No other commander shall they have in battle nor in service. None shall bar them from me and none shall hamper or stall their mission. So it is decreed!'*
>
> – *The Emperor*

Custodian – *John Blanche*

Aquila – *Sam Wood*

Neron – *Chris Dien*

Trajanar – *Hugh Jamieson*

Primarus – *Andrea Uderzo*

Valdor – Adrian Smith

Ascetum – *Adrian Smith*

Custodian Command Squad – *Adrian Smith*

Constantin Valdor – *Neil Roberts*

Lentum – *Sam Wood*

Ares Guard – *Sam Wood*

Agricolus – *Adrian Smith*

The Immortal Guardians

The Legio Custodes was the Emperor's personal bodyguard. They first appeared at his side during the Age of Strife, and since then have maintained a constant vigil over his person. In battle, a double-strength company always fights alongside him, and a detachment of the Guard even accompanies the Emperor when he retires to his private chambers within the Imperial Palace.

Each Custodian is an awesome warrior, stronger and more resilient than a normal human, or even a Space Marine. They are without peer in battle and have unshakeable devotion and loyalty to the person of the Emperor. Although they do not appear to have any psychic powers of their own, their willpower is such that they can resist assaults from the most powerful of psykers, save perhaps the Emperor himself.

There are reckoned to be only a thousand of these elite warriors in total, although this is highly speculative. Only the Emperor and his inner circle know their exact number. Certainly no more than a thousand have ever been seen together at any time, and then only once at the famous Battle of Gyros-Thravian, fought during the Great Crusade against the ork warlord, Gharkhul Blackfang and his vast greenskin horde.

The primarchs Horus, Rogal Dorn and Mortarion and their Legions were vastly outnumbered and close to defeat when the Emperor led an assault from his golden battle-barge. At the head of a thousand Custodians, the Emperor struck at the very heart of the ork horde, confronting Gharkhul himself. As the Emperor decapitated the giant, black-skinned ork, the Custodians laid waste to the warlord's prime warriors. It is said that within moments over a hundred thousand greenskins died and the Waaagh! was broken. Legend has it that only three Custodians fell at the battle, their names enshrined forever, engraved on the Emperor's armour.

The origins of the Custodian Guard are shrouded in myth and legend. During the Age of Strife, the Emperor came to dominate the Earth. At the forefront of his armies of conquest were the Space Marines. At some point, the Emperor conceived of and created the primarchs. It is unclear if the primarchs were created to provide the gene-seed required to produce the Space Marines, or were instead manifestations of the Emperor's experiments.

Whatever the case, the emerging primarchs were ripped from Earth by a mysterious force and scattered across the galaxy. Only later were they reunited with their kindred Space Marines to become leaders of their respective Legions. That the primarchs share genetic, physiological and psychological traits with their Space Marine Legion is indisputable.

Some say that the Custodian Guard are to the Emperor what the Space Marines are to the primarchs; that the Emperor's own genetic matrix was used in their creation and through this, their loyalty to him is assured. Others argue that the Custodians are not like the Emperor in the way that a Space Marine is like his primarch, and that some other source was used as a template for their physical and psychological form, a source that was lost during the anarchy of the Age of Strife. The truth will likely never be known.

Aquillon – *John Gravato*

Imperial Commanders

The galaxy is a big place and travel through the warp is, at best, unpredictable. Time flows strangely in the immaterium and communications are the biggest problem of the fledgling Imperium. As the Great Crusade progressed, a new class of human psyker was slowly introduced to the reconquered worlds – the astropath. Even so, messages transmitted by them through the warp are not certain to arrive at their destination, nor are they sure to be correctly interpreted if they do. There was no practical way to institute galactic-wide rule of the human worlds.

Newly conquered worlds are therefore handed to the rule of Imperial Commanders. Some of these new leaders are military men rewarded for their service by being given a planet to rule in the Emperor's name. Others are the indigenous rulers of worlds who now swear allegiance to the Emperor.

Imperial Commanders have important responsibilities. They are expected to pay tithes to the Emperor by way of supplying troops and materials. They must provide shelter and succour for his armies and fleets. They must cleanse their population of mutation, especially psykers. They are told to expect great black ships to visit them and transport their psykers to Earth. This is the Imperial Tithe.

Imperial Commanders are also charged with protecting humanity and must not harbour enemies of the Imperium. These are variously listed, but always include aliens, mutants and those that would treat with them. Daemons were not recognised at this time, but it is doubtful if any could make the distinction between a daemon, an alien or a monstrously mutated human in any case.

There is some degree of righteousness about the Great Crusade, and many reclaimed worlds are grateful to have been rescued from the anarchy they faced. Some worlds immediately venerated the Emperor. This was especially true on the many worlds that had developed myths and prophecies that spoke of their deliverance from evil by the 'Emperor of the Stars'. The hidden demagogues throughout the new Imperium were quick to fan the religious flames. The more strongly the Emperor denied his divinity, the more strident were their demands that he should embrace it.

Marshal Militant – *John Blanche*

Imperial Noble – *John Blanche*

Military Hierarchy of the Imperium

The vast organisations known as the Legiones Astartes – the Space Marine Legions – form the core of the Imperium's military might and constitute the main strength of the Emperor's armed forces. The primarchs who led these Legions were superhumans, blessed with abilities and fortitude beyond the imagination of normal men. They were the Emperor's generals, and each commanded a mighty host of warships, tanks, guns and warriors. The Warmaster was the most senior primarch, and held overall command of the Emperor's fighting forces at the outbreak of the Heresy.

There was no limit on the size of a Space Marine Legion and most of them could muster at least 100,000 combatants. The Ultramarines Legion was by far the largest, and its primarch, Roboute Guilliman, could call upon the services of over 250,000 Space Marines. New recruits were drawn from the Legion's home world, or any of a hundred feral worlds famed for the warrior prowess of their indigenous people.

The structure of a Space Marine army varied slightly from Legion to Legion, but at the core of all of them was the company of fighting men led by a captain. Companies were usually grouped into battalions, normally five companies strong and led by a lieutenant commander. Battalions were brigaded together in pairs. These were variously known as 'regiments', 'wings', 'chapters' or 'great companies'. A Space Marine with the rank of commander, or in some cases lord commander, led each of these units. Upon his promotion to Warmaster, the primarch Horus became overall commander of all the Emperor's armies and Lord of the Primarchs.

Subordinate to the Space Marines were the regiments of the Imperial Army. As the Great Crusade progressed, the need for more troops increased beyond even the capacity of the Space Marine Legions. Thus, it was decreed that each world of the Imperium was to supply men-at-arms to the command of the primarchs. Certain worlds, like the Space Marine home worlds, the forge worlds of the Mechanicum and those of the Solar System were exempt from this tithe. Even so, the decree provided the primarchs with millions of additional warriors. Although not as powerful as Space Marines, the soldiers of the Imperial Army could be stubborn fighters and their sheer numbers made them ideal for siegework, mass invasions and garrison duty.

The forge worlds of the Mechanicum were exempt from traditional tithes, but were obliged by their pact with the Emperor to supply his armies with war machines of various types. Chief amongst these were the great Titans – huge bipedal war engines crewed by tech-priests and armed with an array of devastating weaponry. Additionally, the Mechanicum supplied regiments of battle-robots and various grades of artillery, from small portable field pieces up to enormous barrage-cannons the size of a building. In battle, the Mechanicum forces reported to, and were commanded by, the primarch or his senior commanders.

Space Marine Captain – *John Blanche*

Administratum Scrivener – *John Blanche*

The Duality of the Space Marine Legions

The original Space Marines had all been recruited on Earth. During the Age of Strife, the ancient world of Terra was wracked with incessant warfare as the competing tribes of Earth fought for dominance. One man was to prevail in these wars, and he was to become the Emperor. His victory was in no small part due to the ranks of superhuman warriors he had created – the Space Marines.

When the Emperor launched his campaign to the stars – the Great Crusade to free humanity from its alien bondage – the twenty Legions could each muster many thousands of Space Marine warriors. Even so, their numbers were small compared to the Herculean task ahead of them. Millions of human worlds needed to be rescued and protected from the many dangers that beset them. To this end, the Emperor instructed the Legions to recruit warriors into their ranks from amongst the populations of the reconquered worlds.

The process of creating a Space Marine was not simple or quick, and potential recruits had to be exhaustively tested. The best new recruits were drawn from especially warlike cultures, men who had been raised for battle, physically strong and mentally tough. The failure rate amongst new recruits was high, and only a small percentage were successfully assimilated into the Space Marines' ranks.

When the Emperor was reunited with his primarchs, he found that each one had come to dominate the world to which he had been sent. There was great affinity between the primarchs and their adopted worlds. Most had become mighty kings, rulers of their worlds and leaders of fanatically loyal armies.

In many cases, the primarchs' armies also bore uncanny similarities to the Space Marine Legions from which they had been sundered many years previously. The warriors that comprised these armies would prove to be particularly suitable for recruitment into the ranks of the Space Marines. In the ensuing years, many tens of thousands of new Space Marines were created from these men, and many of the Legions enjoyed a massive expansion of their fighting strength because of this. For some Legions, their primarch's adopted world became their sole recruiting ground, such was the bond between them and the planet's indigenous culture or the success of the recruitment thereon. It seemed that for some of the Legions, they had found not only their primarch but also a world that they could indeed call home.

As each of the Space Marine Legions was reunited with its lost primarch, their efforts to pursue the Great Crusade increased dramatically. Under the leadership of their primarchs, the Legions became unstoppable and world after world was reclaimed from captivity. Within a few years, many of the Legions had also recruited tens of thousands of new Space Marines, created from the warrior-peoples of their new home worlds.

The integration of these huge numbers of new Space Marines into the ranks of the Legions appeared to be a fantastic success.

Legion – *Neil Roberts*

These warriors of the home worlds shared many characteristics with the Space Marines who had been recruited on Terra, and they made ideal recruits.

Each of the Legions established its own policy as to how these large numbers of new Space Marines would be added to their fighting complement. In some Legions, the new recruits were used to bolster the existing formations, acting as replacements and reinforcements. In other Legions, the primarchs simply added new regiments of home world Space Marines to their organisation.

The Imperial Army

As the Great Crusade progressed and more worlds needed to be liberated, the Imperium's need for more troops increased dramatically. Even the mighty armies of the Space Marine Legions could not alone complete the task at hand. It was therefore decreed that each of the liberated worlds would supply men-at-arms to bolster the war effort.

Each world was assessed and a census taken of its population. From this, the Emperor's administrators calculated the tithe that each was to pay in the form of regiments of soldiers and war materials. The numbers of regiments raised from each world varied enormously. Sparsely populated worlds would be tithed to supply only a handful of regiments each year, whilst the overcrowded hive worlds near to the galactic core would have to supply hundreds of regiments annually. This huge body of soldiers became known as the Imperial Army.

The indentured troops of the Imperial Army were assimilated into the command structure of the Space Marine Legions, and fell under the direct authority of the Space Marines. Space Marine transports would arrive at each world and carry the regiments of the Imperial Army away to fight on distant battlefields across the galaxy.

The sheer size of the Imperium, the whimsical nature of warp travel and the vast numbers of liberated worlds defeated any attempt to standardise the Imperial Army, and there was wide disparity in the wargear, drill and discipline of the various regiments.

Each of the tithed worlds supplied troops as best they could. Those from developed industrial worlds were kitted out with sturdy flak jackets and newly minted, standard issue lasguns. Soldiers from primitive worlds were fortunate if they had a pair of boots and a gun. Some worlds supplied troops that were well-drilled and organised into squads, companies and regiments. Others supplied what amounted to little more than loosely ordered mobs or warbands. Despite this, the soldiers of the Imperial Army proved their value in hundreds of campaigns and across thousands of battlefields.

To instil discipline and loyalty in the regiments of the Imperial Army, it was common practice for the primarchs to appoint special officers to the role of commissar. These veteran warriors ensured that the Imperial Army was unwavering in its duties to its Space Marine overlords.

Although not as powerful as the Space Marine units under the primarchs' command, the Imperial Army regiments were nevertheless useful additions to the expeditions' fighting strength. A Space Marine Legion sometimes had hundreds of auxiliary Imperial Army regiments fighting under its command. These troops were used to reinforce the Space Marines and were frequently deployed in sieges or mass invasions, and to garrison newly conquered planets.

The Imperial Army was rarely deployed within the home system of the regiments that comprised it. In fact, this was actively avoided by the primarchs to ensure that the soldiers' loyalties lay first and foremost with the primarch and the Space Marine Legion to which they were attached, and alongside which they fought.

Catachan 2nd Irregulars – *Wayne Reynolds*

Discipline Master – *John Blanche*

Battle Psyker – *John Blanche*

Fasadian 4th Infantry – *Andrew Hepworth*

Catachan 9th Infantry – *Eric Polak*

Gryphon – *Dan Scott*

Sallan 11th Infantry – *James Brady*

Imperial Emissary – *John Blanche*

The Warp

The warp is a separate or parallel dimension of energy that co-exists with the material world. Every point in space and time in the material world or true space has an analogous reference point in the complex energy pattern of the warp.

Where the material world is a place with familiar physical laws and the steady march of time, the warp is a place of anarchic, random energy. This energy swirls and oozes and is subject to eddies, currents and tides. The energy of the warp is distorted by massive shocks that reverberate through it – these are commonly referred to as warp storms. Time flows strangely in the warp, if it flows at all.

Human scientists discovered that a spacecraft could enter the warp from one point in realspace and after a few days travel leave it at another point, light-years distant from the first. By using the warp in such a way, a vessel could traverse the galaxy – journeys that at sub-light speed would take generations to complete could be accomplished in a few months.

Ships in warp space do not navigate as such, but move from one energy stream to another, cruising the flow of energy until they reach their jump point back into true space. Short trips through the warp, whilst by no means safe, can be made with a degree of reliability and precision. Longer jumps are unpredictable and very dangerous.

The tides of the warp move in complex and inconsistent patterns; ships attempting long journeys often end up wildly off course or are lost permanently within its complex weave. Furthermore, such vessels may suffer bizarre time shifts. It is not unknown for ships to arrive years after, or even years before, they had originally planned.

Warp storms and other disturbances within the aether can block navigation completely. Ships must simply avoid such regions, or be lost forever or destroyed by the rampant energy of the maelstrom. This means that it is impossible to reach some points in the material world through the warp. A world may be cut off for days, weeks or centuries. During the Age of Strife, massive warp storms shook the entire immaterium, preventing any interstellar navigation for the best part of five millennia.

Few, if any, humans understand the precise nature of the warp and its relationship to the material world. Countless philosophers, scientists and psykers have tried to explain it, but none have succeeded in revealing its secrets, or if they have, they have been unwilling to share such knowledge with the rest of humanity.

Psykers have a special affinity to the warp and can interpret some of its energies. These revelations most often take the form of visions and dreams. Few realise that the energy of the warp is the well from which all psykers draw their powers.

It is also widely known that the warp is home to predatory monsters collectively referred to as warp-creatures. These ravening beasts prey on the unwary psykers who commune with the warp too frequently, and on those whose warp-ships are becalmed within the energy weave.

Endurance – *Justin Norman*

Tides of the Warp – *Nuala Kinrade*

Psykers and the Warp

The Emperor is the first and greatest of all human psykers, but he is not the only person who possesses such talents. In fact, there are psychically able people in every human culture and on every world throughout the galaxy. In every generation yet more psykers are born.

Many of these people possess only minor, apparently harmless, talents such as preternatural luck with games of chance or the ability to see moments ahead in time. Such skills are, for the most part, benign but there are other, more dangerous, talents enjoyed by human psykers. The ability to move objects with the mind, to create fires, to call down lightning from the sky or to dominate other human minds are just a few of the many skills these people can use.

Psychic abilities come at a price. Some psykers are driven mad by precognitive dreams and visions. Others find their talents uncontrollable and wreak terrible damage on themselves and the people around them. Because of this, many psykers are treated as witches and executed or banished into exile.

However, there is an even greater danger to humanity than simply the talents and actions of individual psykers, although little is commonly understood of the true nature of the link between the warp and psychic talents.

Every psyker taps into the warp when they exercise their abilities. It is the source of the unnatural energy that powers their abilities. Unfortunately the warp is home to terrible creatures, unfathomable horrors who desire only to corrupt and destroy. Psykers accessing the warp through their talents inevitably attract the attention of these beasts. The greater the energy being channelled, the greater the attraction is.

Only the very strong willed are able to resist the attentions of the creatures of the warp, and even then only for a short time; only the Emperor himself appears immune. Eventually, the warp entities will be able to secure a foothold in true space, usually at the expense of the pysker's life. For a brief time the warp creature is able to survive in true space by possessing the pysker's body. Dreadful physical changes usually accompany this possession as the creature tries to mould the stolen flesh into something that parodies its form in the warp.

These vile monstrosities have only a short time before the body they possess is leeched of all of its life force. During this time, they will invariably embark on an orgy of destruction. Some creatures of the warp are more cunning and will inveigle themselves into human society, keeping secret their true nature for as long as possible. Usually they are seeking to nurture other psykers so that they can simply possess each in turn and maintain a presence in realspace.

The most powerful and dangerous of all of the denizens of the warp are the daemons of Chaos. Only a handful of people, if any, are aware of their existence. If the Emperor knows, he thinks it better to keep such dangerous knowledge to himself. He would understand that knowledge of such creatures would drive humanity to madness and anarchy.

The Chaos daemons are intelligent, cunning and malicious in the extreme. They are cruel reflections of the baser human emotions and so are expert at manipulating weak-minded psykers. They promise great power and riches, but typically any pact agreed with a daemon serves only them. Unlike the other denizens of the warp, the daemons have a greater purpose. Each is in thrall to a more powerful daemon and all daemons pay homage to one of the four Great Powers – the Chaos Gods Nurgle, Khorne, Tzeentch and Slaanesh.

Vendracon – *John Gravato*

The Children of Decay – *Adrian Smith*

Madail – *John Gravato*

The Astropaths

This special corps of interstellar communicators was created by the Emperor during the final months of the conquest of Earth. The Emperor had foreseen the need for these psykers as he contemplated the coming crusade to the stars.

For the most part the Emperor did not favour the use of psychic talents; even in the early days he was aware of the dangers they held for those using them and for humanity at large. However, he was able to identify those pyskers strong enough to withstand the temptations of the warp and so, with some prudence, certain psykers were employed in a variety of special roles.

An astropath is an astro-telepath, an individual capable of communicating with others of his kind over vast interstellar distances. This is an essential talent in a time when worlds are light years apart, and it is the only practical way for the Imperium to maintain any semblance of unity.

All astropaths undergo a special process that moulds their powers and at the same time strengthens them against psychic danger. This is called the soul-binding ritual and only the Emperor is able to perform it.

The soul-binding takes place in the Imperial Palace, where psykers are led before the Emperor one hundred at a time. Kneeling before the master of Mankind, they must endure terrible agony whilst he uses his power to reshape their minds – mingling an infinitesimal portion of his own power with theirs.

Unfortunately, the Emperor's mind is so powerful that not all of the candidates survive this ritual. Some are driven insane, and all have their personalities altered to some degree. The raw energy of the Emperor's will also has another effect; so powerful are the forces involved that many of the more delicate nerves can be damaged, especially the optic nerves. Consequently, all astropaths are blind, whilst many also lack a sense of smell, touch or hearing.

Astra Telepathica – *John Blanche*

Jubac Starsight – *Kari Christensen*

Kai Zulane – *Neil Roberts*

The Astronomican

Before expanding the Great Crusade to the stars beyond Sol, the Emperor ordered the construction of the Astronomican on Earth. Huge numbers of tech-priests were brought from Mars to oversee the project and great swathes of the Terran population were drafted to construct the towering machine-building.

At the time, the Astronomican was the single largest construct on Earth, but more amazing than this fact was that the entire device was merely a focus through which the Emperor could direct his fathomless psychic energies.

The psychic navigational beam from the Astronomican cuts through the warp, and those attuned to its unique frequencies and modulations, the Navigators, are able to use it as a point of reference when calculating journeys therein. Using this beacon they can plot a course that lasts days rather than weeks, or months rather than years.

The Emperor had realised a means by which interstellar travel was a practical proposition again.

The Astronomican shines through the warp, a beacon of energy that the Navigators can see and thence use as a guide as they chart their journeys across the galaxy. The beam is powered by the psychic energies of the Emperor himself, though few are aware of this. Despite this it is often referred to as his Divine Light or Light of the Emperor.

The Astronomican is not the sole means of navigating great distances through the warp. If he desires, the Emperor, with some effort, is able to project a signal into the Ether that Navigators or other attuned psykers can perceive.

In a similar way, the Emperor is able to shut down the Astronomican or interrupt the beam. Only a handful of individuals know that the great signal is powered by the Emperor's psychic powers. They live in fear that should he be disabled or killed, the galaxy would be plunged into a new Age of Strife.

The Navis Nobilite

The Navigators are an ancient strain of human. They have lived amongst humans since the days before even the Age of Strife. It is not known how the Navigators first came into existence, though some suspect the hand of the Emperor. Navigators are a special form of human variation or mutant. They must intermarry to breed true and each one is a member of a large interrelated family or House.

Navigators bear a special gene that allows them to see through the warp and hence guide a vessel as it attempts to plot a course in that otherworldly dimension. A human ship without a Navigator to guide it would be quickly lost in the maelstrom of currents, never to return. Even so, their natural ability only enables them to chart relatively short journeys through the warp with any degree of certainty.

However, Navigators are attuned to the special frequencies and modulations of the Astronomican. Navigators can perceive the beam across huge tracts of warpspace. This 'fixed point' allows them to calculate journeys in the warp with much greater accuracy and so enable them to guide vessels on much longer journeys than they would otherwise be able to.

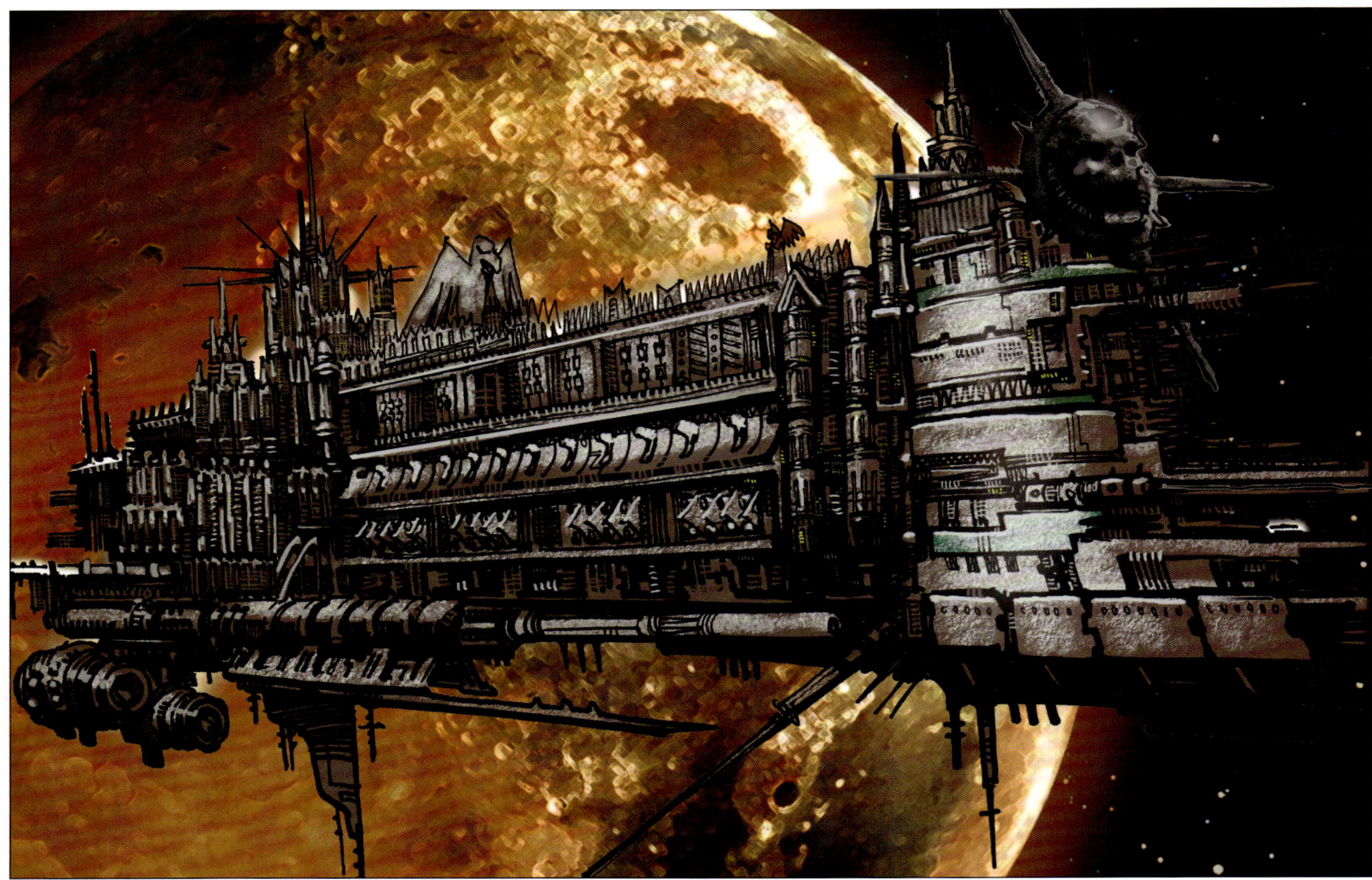

Reaper's Scythe – *Justin Norman*

Sanctioned Psykers

As the Great Crusade unfolded there were psykers, in addition to the astropaths and the Navigators, who were deemed strong enough to be allowed to operate freely within the Imperium. Great black ships had been ordered to visit each human world and return to earth with their cargo of psykers. Stringent testing ensured that the weak-willed or insane psykers could be isolated and dealt with. These were generally lobotomised and set to work as menials.

The more stable and strong-willed of the psykers were then apportioned to various Imperial organisations. The majority were sent to the Emperor's Palace to undergo the soul-binding ritual that would render them into astropaths. Others were enlisted by the Space Marine Legions to be trained in their new Librarius departments. Some psykers found themselves in the employ of other, more secret, Imperial organisations.

The Black Ships

The newly conquered worlds of humanity were told to expect the arrival of black ships to carry away their psykers. This was the most important commitment the Imperial Commanders had to the Imperial Tithe.

The Black Ships were operated by the Adeptus Astra Telepathica, the Imperial organisation that tested psykers. The vast majority of pyskers who were transported back to Terra were destined to undergo the soul-binding ritual. The lucky few that survived this would be enlisted in the corps of astropaths.

Amongst the crews of the Black Ships were the mysterious warrior-investigators known as the Sisters of Silence. The Sisters were recruited from the ranks of the Untouchables – rare human variants who are psychic blanks. The Untouchables are anathema to psykers, who find it difficult to be close to them. Their presence disrupts psychic abilities and they are apparently immune to telepathy and the like. The Sisters are able to identify hidden psykers and have the means to fight and contain them if necessary.

Cistar – *Andrea Uderzo*

Navigator – *Paul Dainton*

The Sisters of Silence

The Sisters of Silence were perhaps the most mysterious of all of the Emperor's servants. Each had sworn an oath of silence as a mark of fealty to the Emperor and to their mission. Although few in number, the Sisters commanded great respect within the Imperium and most servants of the Emperor regarded them with some awe. Few would willingly stand in their way or interfere with their activities.

The Sisters were warrior-investigators, tasked with the seeking and apprehension of untrained psykers. As such, they formed a department within the Astral Telepathy Division, the Imperial organisation whose responsibilities included the processing of all psychic humans. The Division operated the Black Ships, huge transport vessels that travelled to the myriad worlds of the Imperium to collect psykers and carry them back to Terra. It was on Terra that such humans were tested and their eventual fate decided. Many of these underwent the soul-binding ritual, and were then recruited into the ranks of the astropaths who comprised the majority of the Astral Telepathy Division. Each of the Black Ships had a small contingent of the Silent Sisterhood aboard.

The Silent Sisterhood was unusual within the Astral Telepathy Division in that its members were all non-psychic; in fact they are all Untouchables. These are strange and very rare variants of normal humans who are psychic blanks. Such individuals are bearers of the pariah gene, and are immune to psychic assault and telepathy. The mere presence of an Untouchable can disrupt psychic abilities. Psykers find Untouchables intolerable to be near and become visibly uncomfortable in their company; very close proximity or intimate contact can even cause great pain to them. This made the Sisters ideal for the role of identifying psykers secretly hiding within normal human populations, or discovering those innocently unaware of their own abilities.

The Sisters of Silence, although human, were well-trained warriors, which allied to their natural anti-psyker abilities made them dangerous opponents for any malcontent or rogue psykers they might encounter. They were equipped with a variety of weaponry and devices specifically designed to aid the nullification and capture of psykers. The Sisters were authorised to kill or destroy any psykers they deemed too dangerous to capture and send back to Terra for testing.

White Tigers Prosecutor Squad – *Dan Wheaton*

Null-Maiden – *John Blanche*

Winter Hawks Prosecutor Squad – *John Blanche*

Iron Lynx Prosecutor Squad – *Sam Wood*

Frost Lynx Seeker Squad – *David Hudnut*

Fire Hawks Prosecutor Squad – *Steve Belledin*

White Falcons Vigilator Squad – *John Blanche*

Ice Serpents Witchseeker Squad – *Chris Dien*

Nul-Maiden – *John Blanche*

Amendera Kendel – *Hugh Jamieson*

White Asps Support Squad – *Ralph Horsley*

Melaena Verdath – *Sam Wood*

Null-Maiden – *John Blanche*

Winter Crows Vigilator Squad – *Dan Wheaton*

Jenetia Krole – *Sam Wood*

Ice Leopards Witchseeker Squad – *John Blanche*

The Lady's Grace – *Chris Dien*

Raven's Claw Assault Squad – *Sam Wood*

The Mechanicum of Mars

For thousands of years, the planet of Mars has been ruled by the strange caste of tech-priests known as the Mechanicum or the Cult Mechanicus, worshippers of the mysterious Machine God. This religious sect rose to dominance on Mars during the early centuries of the Age of Strife. The entire planet became devoted to the study and manufacture of machines of every conceivable type and function.

When the warp storms flared and mankind began its dreadful period of isolation, the Mechanicum had been crippled, Mars suffering the same fate as the other worlds of humanity. The red planet was sundered from its colonies, its thrall Navigators no longer able to chart a safe course through the warp. That Mars did not devolve into anarchy and chaos is testament to the will of the tech-priests and their stoic determination to put faith in their Machine God.

During the Age of Strife, the Mechanicum were able to send ships to the other planets in the solar system. They concentrated their attentions on Earth, ancient seat of humanity's power. They knew the world harboured many secrets and that the warring barbarians of Terra would be unable to glean these and use them for themselves.

So it was that the tech-priests became bitter foes of the technologically suspicious Terran tribes. For centuries the Mechanicum sought to plunder the Earth of its machine secrets and steal what technologies they could.

They were also fixated with understanding what fate had befallen the galaxy. To this end they periodically dispatched great vessels into the warp in hope that some clues would be found. These were the Explorator Fleets of Mars. Over the centuries, thousands of such expeditions left Mars. Many founded new colonies that were to become the forge worlds, while others were simply lost for all time.

When the Emperor rose to power on Earth, the tech-priests of Mars recognised a kindred spirit. The Emperor was to them a man of science who valued the machine and technological advancement. As word filtered back to Mars, some tech-priests even began to equate the Emperor with their own Machine God in fulfilment of ancient prophecies.

The Emperor forged an alliance with the Mechanicum. In return for supplying materials for his armies and building a mighty warfleet for his crusade to the stars, the Emperor promised to protect the tech-priests and respect the sovereignty of their forge worlds. Furthermore, the Emperor gave to the service of the Mechanicum six of the Houses of the Navigators, to replace their long dead thrall Navigators, so that their ships might once again travel safely through the warp.

The Mechanicum appointed an ambassador to Terra – the Fabricator-General. The Emperor respectfully offered him a seat on the War Council.

Xi-Nu 73 – *Chris Dien*

Fabricator General Kelbor-Hal – *Des Hanley*

Alpha-Rho 25 – *John Gravato*

Sibilans – *Franz Vohwinkel*

Zeta-Phi 07 – *Kari Christensen*

Ambassador Melgator – *Kari Christensen*

Epsilon-Rho 32 – *Anne Stokes*

Dark Mechanicum – *John Blanche*

Alpha-Zeta 54 – *Chuck Lukacs*

Urtzi Malevolus – *Hugh Jamieson*

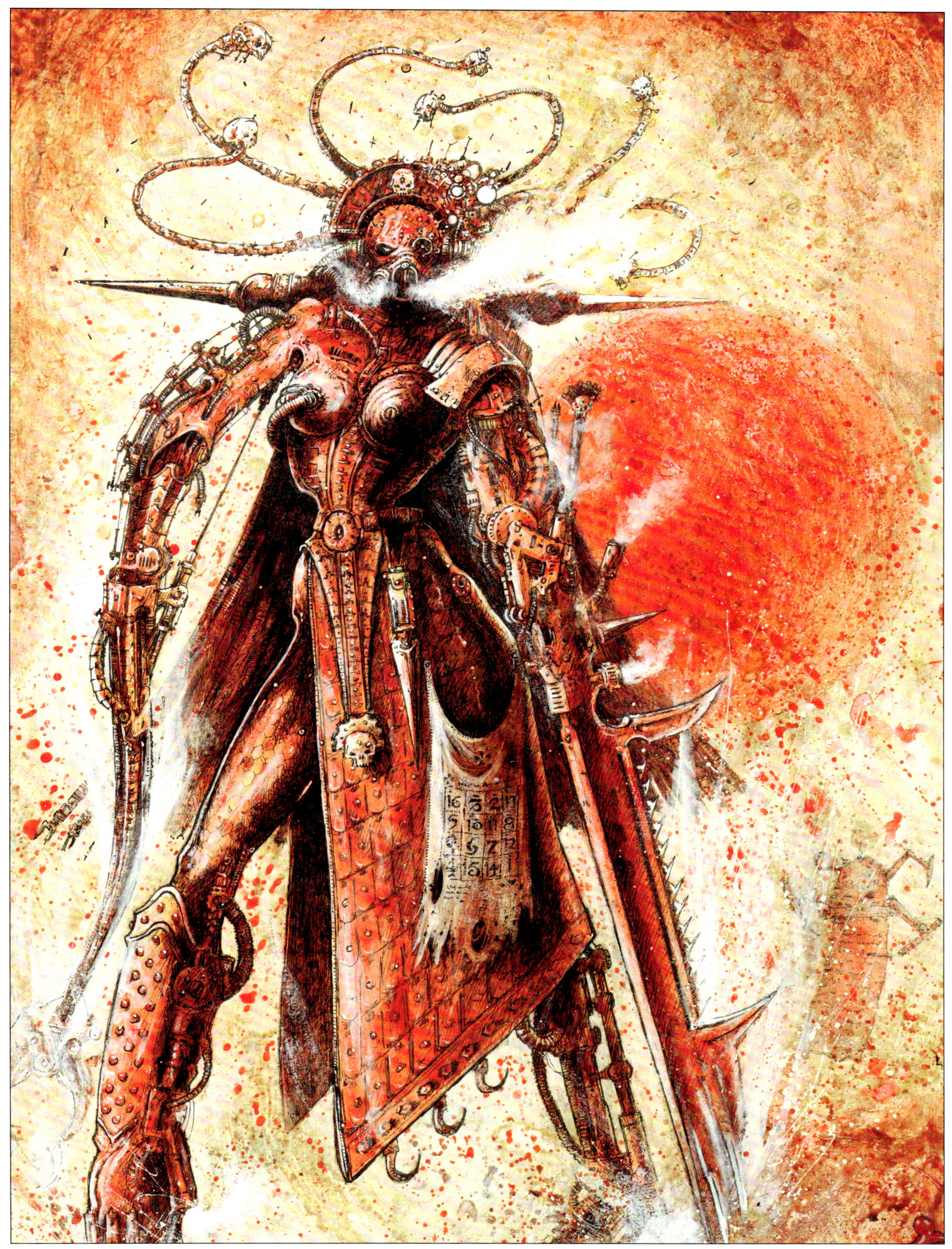

Koriel Zeth – *John Blanche*

Martian Emissary – *John Blanche*

Aratan – *Justin Norman*

Rhc-Mu 31 – *Paul Herbert*

The Emperor Honours Horus

After a series of glorious victories in the Great Crusade, the Emperor decided it was time for him to return to Earth and set in motion the next stage of his great plan to save humanity. He had every confidence that his sons, the primarchs, could complete the military campaigns. They had proved themselves time and again, and soon the galaxy would be utterly cleansed of the alien and other threats to the worlds of mankind.

Horus was his greatest champion, and the Emperor bestowed upon him the title of Warmaster, ceding to him control of all of the Imperium's military forces. The other primarchs were instructed to follow Horus and finish their mission. There was some disquiet that the Emperor had decided to no longer fight alongside them, but the Emperor was adamant. It was time, he said, for them to show him what great leaders they were, time for them to take the lead in the battle to save humanity!

The Emperor spoke to Horus:

'You are like a son to me, and together we have all but conquered the galaxy. Now the time has come for me to retire to Terra. My work as a soldier is done and now passes to you, for I have great tasks to perform in my earthly sanctorum. I name you Warmaster, and from this day forth all of my armies and generals shall take orders from you as if the words came from mine own mouth.

'But words of caution I have for you, for your brother primarchs are strong of will, of thought and of action. Do not seek to change them, but use their particular strengths well. You have much work to do, for there are still many worlds to liberate, many peoples to rescue. My trust is with you. Hail Horus! Hail the Warmaster!'

Upon declaring Horus the Warmaster and leader of all of his armies, the Emperor returned to Earth and his great Palace. The Emperor had much work to do, the exact nature of which he was unwilling to discuss with Horus or any of his generals. He drew to him certain advisors, chief among them Malcador and the Fabricator-General of Mars, and retired to the private vaults of his fortress.

Horus, meanwhile, set about his new duties. He immediately began to contact the other primarchs and make plans for the resolution of the Great Crusade. Many of them were dismayed that the Emperor would no longer be fighting at their side. Angron was particularly bitter, as he counted this as the second time the Emperor had failed him. Horus spoke to each primarch in turn. They felt that the Emperor had turned his back on them. Horus promised he would never let them down.

False Gods – *Phil Sibbering*

The Council of Terra

Upon his retreat to Earth, the Emperor called to his side Malcador and the Fabricator-General. He issued them with new commands. No longer were they to support the military campaigns; these were now safely in the hands of his primarchs and the new Warmaster, Horus. The Emperor needed time and all of his focus on his next great project.

To this end, the Emperor convened the first Council of Terra. Unlike the War Council, of which Horus was now leader, the Council of Terra would attend to the matters of state and the establishment and maintenance of Imperial Law across the myriad worlds of the Imperium. In particular, the Council of Terra was to administrate the Imperial Tithe. Under its auspices would fall all the civil government of the Imperium.

Malcador, the Emperor's most trusted advisor, was named as First Lord of the Council and would lead it in the Emperor's absence. The Fabricator-General, Chief Custodian Constantin Valdor and the leaders of the astropath and administrative divisions of the Imperium were also appointed to the Council.

Having established the new governing body of the Imperium, the Emperor took refuge in his vast laboratories and workshops beneath the Imperial Palace. He began work in earnest on his new project. This was the construction of great psychic-engines – only the Emperor knew the exact design and purpose of these strange machines; even his closest aides and those technicians who worked alongside him could only guess at their true function.

Whilst the Emperor was locked away in his subterranean factories, trouble was brewing. The primarchs were appalled at news of the formation of the Council of Terra. The Emperor's staunchest followers felt they had been let down by the Emperor. Why had they not been consulted and why did they not have seats on this ruling body? The less stable primarchs were outraged. Was this not a betrayal of all the wars they had fought and won in his name? Were their victories to count for nothing? It seemed that the Emperor was willing to turn his back on his generals, and give power to petty administrators and a sycophantic adept of Mars.

Hands of the Emperor – *Sam Wood*

Malcador the Regent

Malcador the Sigillite was concerned. For many months the Emperor had been locked away in his great dungeons, working on his secret project. Every day more requests came from him for men and materials. The mighty work on which the Emperor laboured night and day had been given the highest priority and Malcador had orders that none should disturb or impede this great endeavour. The vast resources of ancient Terra were increasingly directed towards supplying the Imperial vaults and the constant demands coming from within.

Malcador did not relish his job as regent, and every day seemed to bring forth new difficulties. The Space Marine primarchs openly resented his authority, constantly questioning his right to command them, and refused to maintain contact with him. The Mechanicum of Mars was restless, sending daily demands to be admitted to the Emperor's presence. Even the lowly clerks and administrators of Terra appeared to need to have orders repeated to them before carrying them out.

Despite all of these distractions, it had become clear to Malcador that a genuine crisis was building. Warp storms were hampering interstellar communications and the Astronomican was weakening. Entire regions of the Imperium were cut off from Terra. The Warmaster Horus had not been in direct contact with him for weeks, and Malcador had found it impossible to ascertain the whereabouts and wellbeing of most of the other Space Marine Legions. It felt to Malcador as if the Imperium was at its weakest point for many years, and would be easy prey for a determined enemy.

Many of the other primarchs were overdue in their reports to Terra. Jaghatai Khan and the White Scars had not been heard from since the appointment of Horus as Warmaster. Only garbled and incomplete messages had been received from Perturabo at Olympia.

Thankfully, there was a contingent of Space Marines still present in the Solar System – Word Bearers, though their primarch Lorgar was away on some mission with the rest of his Legion. Malcador was at least satisfied that ancient Terra was safe from any immediate threat.

Malcador resolved to deal with the difficulties of the Astronomican and made that his most urgent priority. If he could re-establish contact with Horus and the other primarchs, then surely they would rally to the Emperor's cause and the current crisis could be averted.

Benediction of the Emperor – *Carl Frank*

Jaghatai Khan – *John Blanche*

Horus the Doubter

Horus felt slighted when the Emperor retreated to Earth to meddle in his laboratories and dungeons. As worthy as the honour of being named Warmaster was, it was nothing compared to the sense of loss Horus felt as his spiritual father abandoned him. He had done his best since then to carry on the fight and lead the glorious Crusade. But many Space Marines had died and not once had the Emperor cared enough to honour them with his presence.

The other primarchs argued amongst themselves. They begrudged Horus his new rank and frequently questioned his decisions. Some simply ignored his commands or twisted his orders to their own purposes. He quickly learned to trust only a few of his brother-primarchs, those who would follow without question and those he could easily manipulate. Damn the Emperor for leaving him to sort out this mess!

As news filtered from Earth of the Emperor's latest pronouncements, Horus became ever more estranged from the man he saw as his father. More and more, he thought only of his mission to complete the conquest of the galaxy and bring even more glory to his Legions.

Horus's Pact – *Des Hanley*

Horus – *John Blanche*

Horus falls at Davin

The Warmaster joined his Legion, now named the Sons of Horus, on the moon of Davin. The Legion had some ties to the warrior-society of Davin, and it was at the request of the Davinite priests that the moon had been targeted. Cleansing the moon of its plague-worshipping cultists was a simple task for the Legion, but Horus was felled by an assassin's blade.

The wound festered and the medical experts of his Legion were unable to treat him. Horus was close to death. In desperation, Horus's Legion enlisted the help of the Davinites.

Horus was treated by a Davinite sect. He was carried into the Temple of the Serpent Lodge a dying man and emerged some days later apparently cured and bursting with energy. No one knows what rites were performed to save him.

So it was that the seed of heresy was planted in the heart of the Emperor's greatest champion and within some of the most powerful military forces in the galaxy.

The Davinite Lodges

The planet of Davin was once blessed with a progressive and civilised culture. Its isolation during the Age of Strife brought anarchy. The civilisation quickly descended into barbarism, the peoples of Davin becoming savage feral tribes.

Davin was now ruled by the warrior lodges. These semi-religious societies were focused around the veneration of various beasts. Each lodge was named after their beast: Lodge of the Bear, Lodge of the Hawk, Lodge of the Serpent, Lodge of the Crow and Lodge of the Hound, to name but a few. Dark priest-like monks led the lodges and performed the arcane rights of the sects.

To understand how such a planet could be tolerated by the more civilised cultures of the Imperium was to realise that Davin was but one of many hundreds of thousands of human worlds spread across the galaxy. And it would have remained completely unremarkable and unknown had not Horus the Warmaster been treated there.

Tsi Rekh – *Steve Belledin*

Priests of Thoros – *John Gravato*

Kenrich – *Kari Christensen*

Davinite Lodge Warrior – *John Blanche*

Davinite Lodge Priest – *John Blanche*

The Anathame

The anathames were extraordinary weapons, created by an alien race known as the kinebrach at the height of their interstellar culture. Appearing as simple blades, they were crafted using now-forbidden and mostly forgotten techniques and technologies – they were said to be the ultimate bane of an opponent, and once drawn in battle they became utterly inimical to the chosen target.

During the latter days of the Great Crusade the 63rd Expedition, led by none other than Horus himself, was engaged in diplomatic talks with a human civilisation known as 'the interex', negotiating their assimilation into the Imperium. At some point during the proceedings, one of these terrible weapons was stolen from the interex. The resulting war eventually brought about the complete and utter destruction of both the interex and the kinebrach.

Who stole the anathame is still officially a mystery, but it was rumoured that Erebus, the First Chaplain of the Word Bearers Legion who had accompanied the 63rd Expedition, had been responsible for the theft. Indeed, after Horus's rebellion began to gather pace, he made a gift of a cursed blade to the Emperor's Children, knowing that it would likely appeal to the primarch Fulgrim's vanity and love of exotic weaponry.

Furthermore, it was just such a blade that had wounded Horus on the moon of Davin. Whether this blade was indeed the same one is a matter of pure speculation, but it is unlikely that Erebus would have surrendered such a powerful weapon to Fulgrim without first sampling its power for himself.

Apothecary Fabius – *Sam Wood*

Fu grim, the Phoenician – *John Blanche*

Emperor's Lament – *John Gravato*

Chaos the Deceiver

Horus had listened to the Dark Gods of Chaos and made his pact with them. He would deliver to them the Emperor and they would give him the galaxy. It was a simple bargain and one that made sense to Horus. Humanity was under dire threat from the daemons of the warp, though few recognised the danger. If the Emperor knew, he seemed to ignore the threat.

The Dark Gods had whispered in his ear. 'We desire only the Emperor. His psychic might is destroying our realm. Even now he retires to his dungeon to work his selfish plot. He cares not for you or your warriors. He will put weak men above you. If the Emperor were to be sacrificed to us then we would have no interest in your worlds. You would be a just and rightful ruler of the galaxy. We give you the gift of mankind to do with as you will.'

Horus knew full well that the Emperor was the most powerful psyker that had ever lived, or would ever live. The Warmaster also knew that such powers were drawn from the warp. Wasn't it obvious that the gods of Chaos were right and that the Emperor was the problem, and had been the problem all along? Horus knew he must challenge the Emperor.

Horus the Betrayer

After his sojourn on Davin, the Warmaster was a changed man. Deep in the Temple of the Serpent, Chaos had whispered in his ear. Weakened by the physical trauma of his wounds, Horus's will was shattered and he listened to the seductive promises of the Dark Gods and made his evil pact with them.

Horus had been terribly wounded. As his body was healed, his mind was in turmoil. Why was the Emperor not with him in his hour of greatest need? Whilst his life was in the balance, why did the Emperor not rush to his side as he had done in the old days? Why did he ignore all they had achieved? Why did he favour the fops and clerks of Terra? Why should Horus now do as the Emperor bid? Was he not the one who had led the Space Marine Legions to countless victories? Did he not bear the scars of a thousand battles? Was the Emperor there to shed a tear as brave Space Marines died horrible deaths at the hands of their alien foes? No, it was Horus who had fought and bled and cried! Horus was the one who had planned the wars and the victories. It was Horus who had rightfully earned the loyalty of the Space Marines. Horus who should be acclaimed Lord of Mankind! The rightful Master of Humanity!

The Ruinous Powers had made their bargain clear to Horus. 'Deliver us the Emperor and we shall give you the galaxy!'

Horus Heresy – *Daarken*

Horus the Conspirator

The Warmaster drew to him those primarchs he could trust the most. He met with them each in turn, and corrupted them.

Angron of the World Eaters raged against the Emperor, his synaptic implants buzzing with fury. Twice he felt the Emperor had betrayed him. The other primarchs, those he saw as the Emperor's favourites, had treated him with contempt for the extremes he used to ensure his victories. He was a seething mass of resentment, and so was the easiest primarch for Horus to turn – he simply promised Angron blood!

Mortarion of the Death Guard was harder to persuade, but Horus was persistent and wore him down. A new age was dawning, he argued – an age undreamed of, with the primarchs at the head of it. They would rule with might and justice. Horus would need him, need his strength. The Emperor was weak and exhausted. It was the natural order of things that he be replaced.

Fulgrim of the Emperor's Children was closest to Horus. Throughout the Great Crusade they had fought side by side. This was the most bitter corruption: all that was good in Fulgrim – his honour, his quest for perfection, his love for the Emperor – was twisted by Horus into something dirty and cruel. Fulgrim was shattered, a broken man, all his dreams made dust. Horus promised to restore his honour and make his dreams live again.

The Warmaster had corrupted his three closest comrades, persuading them to fight alongside him in the coming struggle against the Emperor who had betrayed them. What hand the Dark Gods of Chaos had in their corruption is unknown, but they had chosen their own path and it led inexorably towards a doom they could not possibly have foreseen.

Angron, Mortarion and Fulgrim returned to their Legions and began to spread their heresy. Slowly, they secretly sowed corruption through the ranks using the warrior lodges recently adopted from the Sons of Horus. Most of their Space Marines were easy enough to turn – their loyalty lay with their primarch, their father and mentor. They would fight and die for him.

However, some amongst their Legions would not be so easily swayed. These were the warriors for whom the Emperor was like a god, many of them men of Earth, the original recruits into the ranks of the Legions. Their loyalty to the Emperor pre-dated that to their primarch. Careful not to reveal their hand, the primarchs noted which of their men they could not trust. These Space Marines were earmarked for a dark fate.

Butcher's Nails – *Neil Roberts*

Horus Plans Ahead

Having corrupted those closest to him, the Warmaster now turned his attentions to the other primarchs and their Legions.

He ordered the primarchs Lion El'Jonson, Sanguinius and the redoubtable Roboute Guilliman to muster their Legions in preparation for a series of campaigns in the far-flung reaches of the galaxy. Perceiving no obvious reason to doubt the Warmaster's motives, the three primarchs set about planning their missions and transporting their Legions. So it was that three of the most staunchly loyal Legions, the Dark Angels, the Blood Angels and the Ultramarines, were sent by Horus to regions far from Earth and from the Isstvan System.

The Warmaster sought to minimise the threat to his plans from the other Space Marine Legions. He was sure of the loyalty of his own Legion, the Sons of Horus, and he had the Death Guard, World Eaters and Emperor's Children being attended to by Angron, Mortarion and Fulgrim. They assured him of their loyalty.

The Word Bearers, Alpha Legion, Raven Guard, Salamanders and Iron Hands were actively involved in various campaigns across the Imperium; their time would come. The White Scars and the Night Lords were unaccounted for, and the Imperial Fists were too close to the Emperor for Horus to chance contacting them without raising suspicion.

This left Magnus the Red's Thousand Sons, the Iron Warriors of Perturabo and Leman Russ's Space Wolves, all of whom were currently headquartered on or near their respective home worlds.

Horus Rising – *Neil Roberts*

XI
XI

The Heresy Spreads

Horus the Warmaster, having secured the loyalty of four Legions of Space Marines, now hoped to draw more forces into his web of deceit. He contacted Perturabo of the Iron Warriors Legion. Perturabo had a fearsome reputation for war and destruction, but was a petty, jealous primarch. The warrior lodges within his Legion had already started to agitate for Horus. Horus informed the primarch of rebellion fomenting on the Iron Warriors home world of Olympia. Perturabo was determined to take decisive action and win the favour of the Warmaster. He began the Siege of Olympia.

Horus despatched agents to other Legions and began the process of winning to his side various Imperial commanders and forge masters. The latter held positions of authority on the forge worlds of the Mechanicum. They also controlled the fearsome Titan Legions of the Collegia Titanica. With these powerful machines on his side, Horus considered that he might even be able to force the Emperor to submit without more bloodshed.

Triumph – *Neil Roberts*

Forrix – *Alex Boyd*

Gignere, Reaver Titan – *Wayne England*

Deathshroud – *Adrian Smith*

Kullar-Hal – *David Hudnut*

Serghar Targost – *Ralph Horsley*

Odovocar – *Karl Richardson*

Khârn – *Wayne England*

Dark Mechanicum Tech-priest – *Daarken*

Isstvan III

Galaxy in Flames – *Neil Roberts*

Isstvan Rendezvous

Horus arranged to meet with the primarchs Angron of the World Eaters, Mortarion of the Death Guard and Fulgrim of the Emperor's Children at the Isstvan System. The third world of the system was in revolt and the Warmaster had declared his intention to quell the rebellion and bring the instigators to justice.

A massive war fleet gathered above the planet of Isstvan III as elements of four Space Marine Legions began to arrive. Fulgrim was delayed but some of his Emperor's Children did make the rendezvous. Horus's task force therefore consisted of the majority of his own Legion, the Sons of Horus, plus significant portions of the Death Guard, World Eaters and Emperor's Children Legions. With three primarchs in attendance this constituted one of the largest concentrations of military force seen since the battle for the Pargor Hith System during the Great Crusade.

They met on Horus's flagship, the battle-barge *Vengeful Spirit*, to discuss the coming storm. Angron and Mortarion reported on the status of their respective Legions. They assured Horus that the majority of their Space Marines had been inducted into the warrior lodges and could now be trusted to follow him when he declared himself to be the rightful Emperor.

However, both of the primarchs had identified elements of their Legions whose loyalty to the Emperor was unshakeable. These loyal Space Marines would pose a great threat to Horus's conspiracy if they were not dealt with. Lord Commander Eidolon, speaking in Fulgrim's absence, confirmed that the same was true of sections of the Emperor's Children. Horus revealed to his co-conspirators his shocking plan to rid their Legions of these dissident factions.

Angron, Primarch of the World Eaters – *Wayne England*

Katheron – *Steve Belledin*

Chaggrat – *Dan Wheaton*

Caphen – *Steve Belledin*

Rorrorg – *Paul Carrick*

Chondon – *Des Hanley*

Mycaelis – *Al Eremin*

The Death of a World

The planet of Isstvan III was in revolt and had declared its independence from the Imperium. The Imperial commander, Vardus Praal, was suspected of secretly being a mutant, possibly a dangerous psyker. Horus had orders to quell the rebellion and bring Praal to Earth for judgement. This provided Horus with the perfect opportunity to rid himself of those Space Marines whose loyalties he was not sure of. Horus, Angron, Mortarion and Eidolon met in council and decided which of their formations they could trust and which they could not. Orders were passed to the officers of the World Eaters, Death Guard and Emperor's Children Legions and the assault of Isstvan III began. Those sections of the Legions whose loyalty to Horus could not be guaranteed by their leaders were commanded to prepare for an assault on the planet beneath.

The first wave of attacks on the rebel planet by the Space Marines of the three Legions was devastating. Within hours the rebels were in utter disarray. Tens of thousands of the planetary defence forces had been crushed in a series of hammer-blow assaults. The Space Marines were jubilant; the Emperor's law would be quickly reinstated and the miscreant rebels brought to justice.

Just as victory seemed assured, disaster struck the Space Marine forces on the surface. All communications with the orbiting fleet ceased and the encircling battleships began to bombard the planet. Deadly virus bombs rained down – they were devised to cleanse planets of all life, and so it was on Isstvan III. The six billion inhabitants of the planet had no chance of survival.

Isstvan III had become a dead planet.

Horus the Warmaster had at last declared his hand and openly defied the Emperor. Ordered to quell a rebellion on Isstvan III and reinstate law and order, he had instead ordered an orbital bombardment that had utterly annihilated the population. He had also planned that the virus bombs would destroy the host of Space Marines he could not trust to fight for him in the coming struggle with the Emperor.

However, the Warmaster's plans were upset. Some loyalist Space Marines remained onboard the orbiting ships. Among them was Captain Garro of the Death Guard, a Terran, one of the original recruits to the XIV Legion. As soon as the bombardment began, Garro instinctively withdrew from the conflict. Captain Tarvitz of the Emperor's Children had a similar reaction. The loyalists were immediately attacked and slaughtered by their traitorous brethren. A few escaped aboard the commandeered frigate *Eisenstein*, led by Garro, whilst Tarvitz seized a Thunderhawk and made for the planet below.

On the planet's surface had been over one hundred companies of Space Marines drawn from the Sons of Horus, Emperor's Children, Death Guard and World Eaters Legions. Of these, fully two-thirds miraculously survived the bombardment, thanks to the warning they received.

Purity of Will – *Eric Ren*

Keilerol – *Ralph Horsley*

Kollanus – *Kenson Low*

Dawn's Fire – *Al Eremin*

Darkhe – *Ralph Horsley*

Gladiator Drop Pod Group 27 – *Anne Stokes*

Krast – *John Gravato*

Betrayal

It was immediately apparent to the orbiting Horus and his co-conspirators that the virus bombs had failed to destroy the loyalist Space Marines on Isstvan III. As the firestorm abated, communications channels crackled into life. Frantic signals blared out from vox-units and comms-relays. Never in the history of the Legions had there been such a terrible act of betrayal. The Space Marines on Isstvan III were incensed beyond reason.

That they had been betrayed by their own primarchs simply added to their fury. They demanded blood!

Whilst Horus was trying to work out what to do next, Angron, headstrong as ever, took it upon himself to launch a new attack on the planet. The World Eaters primarch made planetfall at the head of fifty companies of Space Marines. Horus was furious but had little option but to back up Angron's rash move. The Sons of Horus, and remaining Emperor's Children and Death Guard units, were ordered to their gunships and drop pods.

The conflict on Isstvan III was the first battle in the history of the Imperium when Space Marines of the same Legion fought on opposite sides. Former comrades and brothers-in-arms became bitter foes. Betrayal and treachery abounded. On the devastated planet, it was kill or be killed. No quarter was asked and none offered.

On one side stood Horus the Warmaster, self-declared True Master of Humanity. With him were the corrupted primarchs: Angron of the World Eaters and Mortarion of the Death Guard. The best part of their three Legions and a host from the Emperor's Children Legion were at their command. Against them stood the remnants of the Isstvan III first wave, Space Marines still loyal to the Emperor who had been most sorely betrayed. Chief among the loyalists was Captain Tarvitz of the Emperor's Children. He was determined to take his vengeance on the traitors.

Angron, Lord of the Red Sands – *Sam Lamont*

Kaesoron – *Franz Vohwinkel*

Bakhart – *Dan Scott*

Charosion – *Chris Trevas*

War on Isstvan III

On the devastated planet of Isstvan III warriors of the Death Guard, World Eaters and Emperor's Children Legions, Space Marines still loyal to the Emperor, found themselves betrayed by the basest act of treachery. After quelling a revolt on the planet's surface, they had been first subjected to a nightmare orbital barrage and had then been attacked by Space Marines of their own Legions, traitors declaring for Horus and claiming him as the True Emperor!

As the battle between the Space Marines raged across the ruined landscape of Isstvan III, more evidence of Horus's perfidy was revealed as the loyalists encountered strange newcomers. Amongst these were black-robed cyborgs using macabre weapons and sporting fell runes on their clothing. It was clear to some that Horus had won to his side servants of the Mechanicum of Mars. The implications of this were clear to the loyal Space Marines. If Horus had control of the Mechanicum, then he would be able to call upon the services of the mighty Collegia Titanica and their gargantuan Titan war machines. Furthermore, if Mars were allied with the Warmaster, it would provide him with the perfect launching point for an attack on Terra and the Imperial Palace itself.

As the war continued, the Warmaster also committed some of his Imperial Army regiments to the fray. These units were indentured warriors recruited through the Imperial Tithe and had sworn allegiance to their Space Marine overlords. Unaware of the broader implications of Horus's treachery, the Imperial Army simply followed orders and did as commanded by their superiors. Amongst Horus's troops were also bands of ferocious cultists from the planet Davin. These barbarians openly chanted the names of their dark gods and displayed the foul runes of Chaos. At the fore were sinister sorcerers – the dark priests of Davin.

Mordant – *David Hudnut*

Skane – *Al Eremin*

Rylanor – *Des Hanley*

Phordal – *Mark Gibbons*

Eitholchin – *David Hudnut*

Strike and Fade – *Andrew Hepworth*

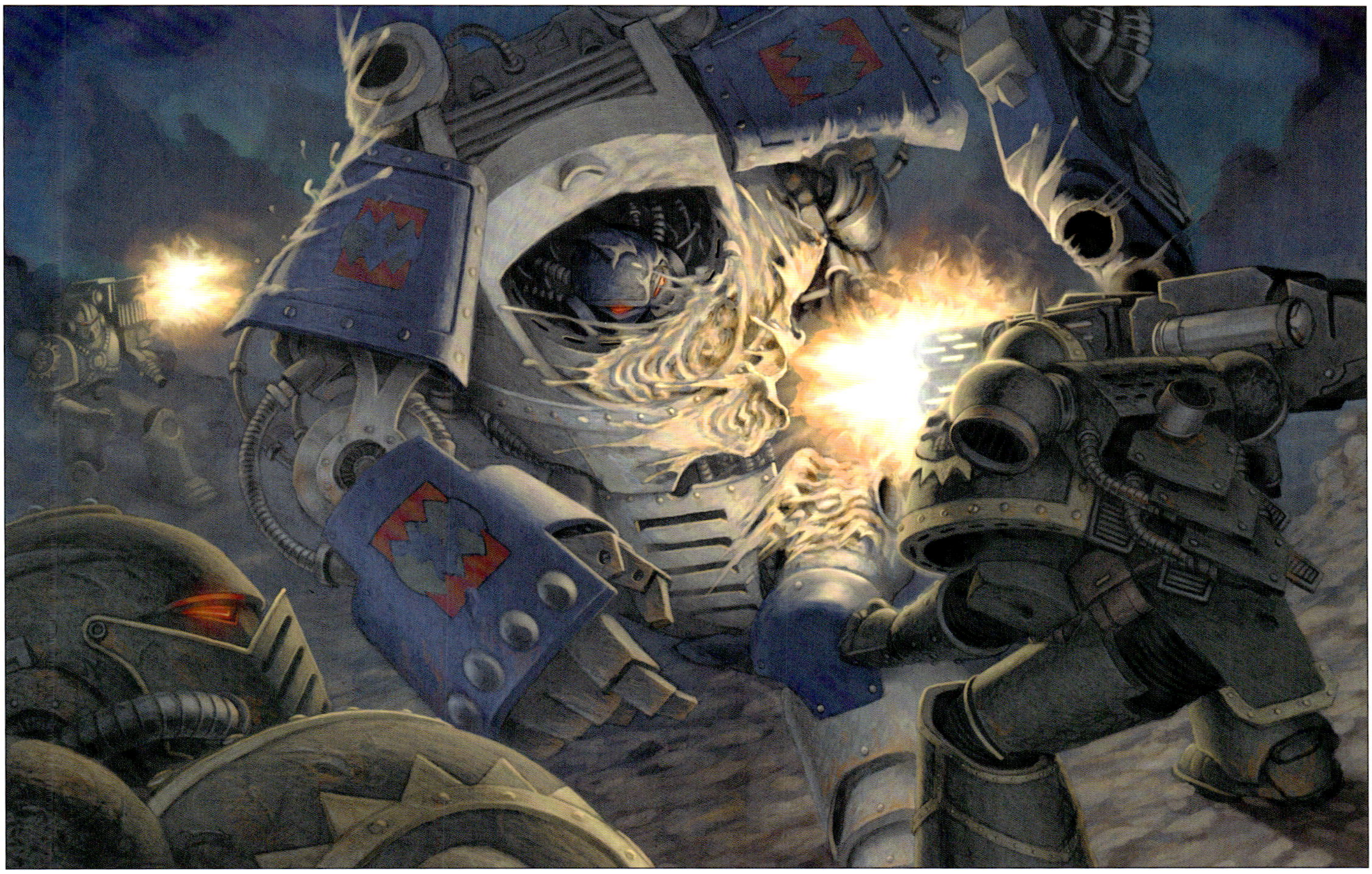

Karhkul – *Eric Polak*

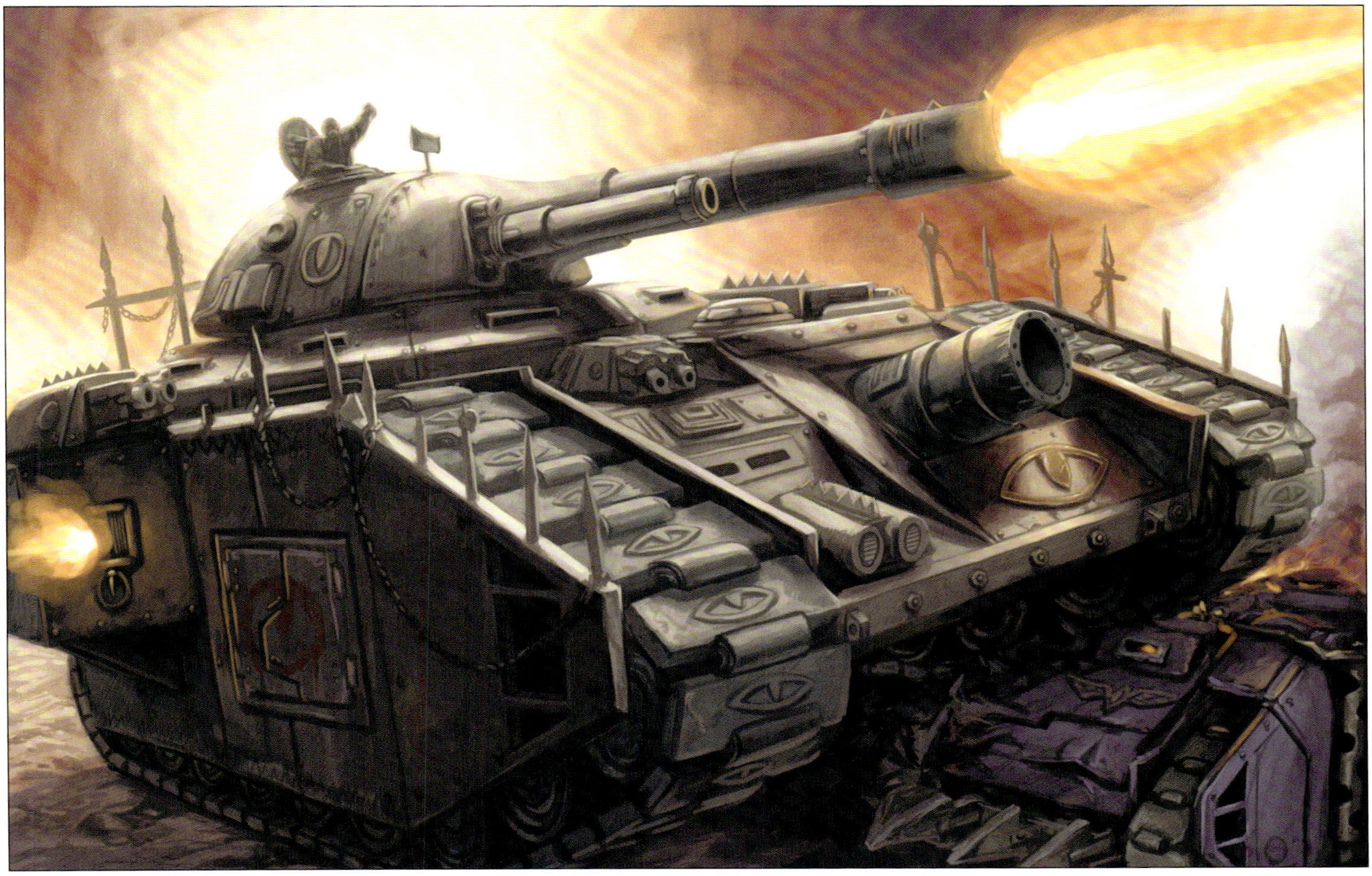

Khatek – *Dan Scott*

Flight of the Eisenstein

As the traitorous forces of Horus launched their orbital barrage on the loyal Space Marines on Isstvan III, Captain Garro of the Death Guard seized the frigate *Eisenstein*. Garro was a staunch loyalist, a Terran who had fought countless battles alongside the Emperor during the Great Crusade. The unfolding events at Isstvan III were hard for him to fathom. His instinct led him to abandon his post, and with seventy fellow loyalists he was determined to flee the Isstvan System and make for Earth.

Garro's lightly armed cruiser was no match for the powerful battleships of Horus's blockading fleet, and it took many hits as it sped past their massive gun batteries. The crippled ship limped away from Isstvan III. It was severely damaged, all the astropaths aboard had perished in the fire-fight and its lone Navigator was mortally wounded. The ship was incapable of interstellar communication and had little chance of successfully traversing the immaterium.

All Garro could hope for was that the *Eisenstein* could escape from Isstvan III and somehow find a way to get to Earth to warn the Emperor of Horus's treachery. There was no way that the damaged vessel could outrun the pursuing traitors in realspace; Garro would have to risk the warp. He gave the command and, with a huge lurch, the ship made the jump into that dark and terrible place. The warp was restless. Great storms were brewing in the aether. The Navigator was unable to chart a safe course, and knew that if they stayed in the warp they could be lost for all time.

Garro ordered the vessel to jump back into realpace. The loyal Space Marine had no idea where or when the emergency warp-jump had taken them. As the ship exited the warp, the Navigator collapsed, finally succumbing to his wounds. The warp engines were dangerously unstable and could have exploded at any time, destroying the ship or, worse still, casting it back into the warp to be lost for all time.

The *Eisenstein* was damaged beyond repair, its superstructure dangerously close to collapse, and they had been cast adrift in an unknown region of space. They had escaped, but for Garro's loyal comrades, it seemed that all hope had now abandoned them and there was naught they could do but pray for a miracle. Garro had other ideas, and ordered the warp engines to be set for self-destruct and then ejected from the listing ship. He reasoned that the exploding engines would act as a beacon in the warp, attracting any nearby ships. Hopefully they would be friendly!

It was then that fate intervened in the form of Rogal Dorn, primarch of the Imperial Fists Legion, who came upon the broken ship. Dorn and his fleet had been becalmed nearby by the growing storms of the immaterium. The exploding warp engines of the *Eisenstein* had flared in the warp and the Imperial Fists Navigators had been able to pinpoint their position.

Garro presented himself to Dorn and told him of the events at Isstvan III. The primarch was predictably dismayed; he and his Legion were staunch loyalists. Dorn had held Horus in high esteem. He admired him greatly and had never thought to question his motives. This cowardly act of betrayal could have no justification. Dorn made two resolutions. The first was to order the greater portion of his fleet to Isstvan III to break the siege and relieve the loyalists fighting there, and the second was to personally escort Garro to the Emperor. Despite the increasing turbulence of the warp, the Imperial Fists fleet embarked to Isstvan III and Rogal Dorn made his way to Earth with Captain Garro and his loyal crew.

Nathaniel Garro – *John Gravato*

The Flight of the Eisenstein – *Neil Roberts*

Quemondil – *Ed Cox*

Joradan – *Hugh Jamieson*

Kargul – *Wayne England*

Mahrke – *James Ryman*

On the Surface

Captain Saul Tarvitz, last loyal officer of the Emperor's Children Legion, surveyed the grim tableau before him. He stood amidst the ruins of a once magnificent city. Its name had died with those who had built and lived within its fabulous palaces and marbled halls. Now it was little more than a heap of rubble. Here and there, skeletal remnants of the city's largest buildings stood proud of the surrounding devastation. Tarvitz had climbed one such outcrop to attempt an overview of the area and assess the tactical situation.

From his vantage point, Tarvitz could see only death and destruction. There was barely anything left of the city that could be called architecture – as far as he could see, there was only ruin. Death littered the rubble; every kind of corpse it was possible to imagine lay there on the cracked and broken stones. Old, rotted corpses that had not even had the courtesy of a burial ritual lay next to the fresh corpses of recently felled Space Marines and traitor soldiers. It was a grim sight.

Tarvitz drew breath as he stared out across the ruin, his brow knotted in concentration as he strained to see or hear any enemy activity. There was none. He was suspicious nonetheless. For the last few months he had never known the enemy to relent in their attacks. The fighting had been constant, the death continual. He led a small band of no more than a hundred Space Marines – the last loyal survivors of the Death Guard, World Eaters and Emperor's Children Legions, warriors whose loyalty to the Emperor had made them deadly adversaries to the traitors of Horus. Space Marines who had been most foully betrayed by their former comrades.

They had been sent to the surface of Isstvan III to quell a revolt amongst the populace. It had been an attack in force – thousands of Space Marines landing in drop pods and gunships – and it had overwhelmed the rebels with minimal effort. An easy enough task for warriors as skilful and powerful as the Space Marines. For a brief moment, the victors celebrated their triumph. Then came the act that defined all that followed. Instead of laurels for their victory, the orbiting fleet sent death down onto the loyal Space Marines. Thousands upon thousands of virus bombs were launched at the planet. The planet's population of six billion people were virtually annihilated in that one action. Only a last second warning and their superhuman resilience had saved the Space Marines on the surface from sharing their fate.

After the orbital strike came the assault by the traitors. As the smoke and fire of the virus bombs dispersed, the loyalists saw the drop pods falling to the planet's surface. As these landed they disgorged their deadly cargo of raging World Eaters Space Marines led by the fearsome primarch Angron. The loyal Space Marines were dismayed by the appearance of Angron's warriors, who attacked without pause, paying no heed to any past allegiance or kinship. In their wake came the other traitors: the Emperor's Children, the Death Guard and the Sons of Horus. Although deeply shocked by this turn of events, the loyalists gathered their forces and fought back against the treacherous onslaught.

For long months, the war on Isstvan III had raged between the betrayed loyalist Space Marines and Horus's traitors. At the beginning, the two sides were evenly matched, but as time passed the traitors' strength had grown and that of the loyalists had waned. Horus had sent new troops to the planet: more Space Marines, tithed Imperial Army regiments and war machines of the Mechanicum, including mighty Titans. Increasingly, the loyalists found themselves outnumbered and outgunned and had been forced to retreat into smaller, isolated groups.

Reduced to hit-and-run counterattacks and small-scale skirmishes, the lack of loyalist

Karst – *Wayne England*

warriors had prevented any major efforts to strike back at the traitors who were content to isolate the loyalists and overwhelm their pockets of resistance one by one. As time wore on, the loyalists were reduced to a fraction of their original fighting strength.

The loyalists had decided to make their last stand in the heart of the ruined city. Here the traitor hordes would not be able to make their advantage in numbers tell. The loyalists had dug in and they commanded strong defensive positions around what had been the city's central administrative sector. Even so, the fighting over the last weeks had been fierce and the loyalist force had suffered many casualties. Now Tarvitz – the most senior of the surviving loyalists – had but a hundred Space Marines at his command, barely a company. It seemed as if these men would soon be overwhelmed and annihilated.

Then things had changed. At first it was the withdrawal of the traitor Space Marine troops. Without warning they had quit the battle, leaving behind the indentured troops of the Imperial Army and the Titans of the Mechanicum to continue the fighting. The defenders were puzzled by this move because the opposing Space Marines had been the most serious threat to them, despite the power of the Titans and the huge numbers of traitor Imperial soldiers.

The defending loyalists then fought with renewed vigour, perhaps sensing an opportunity to break out of their self-imposed blockade. But their numbers were too small and their ranks too thinly spread for this to tell. The mood of the loyalists had darkened as they began to realise that not only were they most likely to die, but they would also be denied the chance to wreak vengeance on those who had so vilely betrayed them – their former brothers-in-arms, brothers-in-spirit, brothers-in-blood, the traitor Space Marines who followed Horus.

And then the attacking traitor army had suddenly retreated. One moment it was pressing forward, almost suicidal in its assaults against the dug-in loyalists, and then it was gone. From his lofty viewpoint, Tarvitz had watched the enemy streaming away in all directions. The retreat was orderly, but hasty, and before long the traitors had disappeared from view.

An eerie calm settled over Isstvan III and this worried Tarvitz even more than the relentless attacks by the traitors had done. He was deeply suspicious of the traitors' retreat. Horus must have some new evil to unleash upon us, he thought. His mind ran through a host of imagined scenarios, desperately trying to work out which it was that he and his men should prepare for. He cast his thoughts back to the beginning and suddenly realised what was about to befall them. As he began to warn his troops, the first missiles of the orbital bombardment tore down through the clouds above to strike the ruined city. Within seconds, the entire region had become a churning, roiling miasma of explosions, heat and fire. It would be a miracle if any of the loyalists could survive this onslaught.

Saul Tarvitz – *David Gallagher*

Galaxy in Flames – *Neil Roberts*

Sorruk – *James Brady*

Saeverin – *Ben Peck*

Valoc – Paul Herbert

Typhon – *Eric Polak*

Battle's Glory – *Steve Belledin*

Tantaeron – *David Hudnut*

Morturg – *Chris Trevas*

Horus meets Fulgrim at Isstvan

Horus the Warmaster stood on the bridge of the *Vengeful Spirit*, his great battle-barge and command centre. The planet of Isstvan III loomed large in the viewport, flashes of light dancing across its blackened atmosphere, the only sign to Horus that a violent battle was taking place on the planet below.

Fulgrim, primarch of the Emperor's Children, entered the vaulted chamber. Horus turned to face the fabulously armoured warrior and fixed him with a steely glare. The Warmaster's visage was grim, his mood black. Fulgrim was clearly unsettled.

'My lord, I have returned to you. How goes the battle?'

'Time for that later. Where have you been? Why has it taken so long for you to return? Your mission was a simple one. I was expecting you to be here days ago. Are the Iron Hands with us? Give me your report.'

'There were some difficulties. Things did not go as we had planned. Manus was intractable, irrational. The situation became… messy. Suffice to say, the mission failed. He will not join with us. He is a powerful and determined warrior. I was fortunate to escape unharmed.'

'Escape? You dolt! Is Ferrus Manus still alive?'

'Yes, but his fleet is crippled and his Legion far from Earth. He cannot be a threat to us.'

'That remains to be seen. I was a fool to give you this task. I had thought that your past friendship with Manus would aid you in turning him to our cause. It has only stopped you from disposing of him. Instead of an ally you have delivered to me a most dangerous enemy. You must hope this error can be corrected, Fulgrim, or my wrath will be terrible indeed!'

'Sire, when next Manus and I meet, only one of us shall survive to tell of it. This I promise to you!'

Drask – *Eric Polak*

Guorzlat – *Paul Herbert*

Agnomen – *Eric Ren*

Eudicius – *Torstein Nordstrand*

A Disturbance in the Warp

Horus had powerful allies. As he launched his attack on the planet of Isstvan III, the daemons of the warp stirred. The Warmaster had desired them to remain hidden. He did not want his pact with them to be known by the Emperor and his sycophants, least of all the other primarchs. This could upset his plans. He instead made them aid him in more subtle ways.

The Ruinous Powers were restless. They could sense weakness in the enemy; the Emperor was distracted, his voice rarely touching their realm. Now was the time to strike him down, they argued. If they were given the chance to confront him then Horus could win his throne easily. But Horus resisted their calls. Better, he thought, to bide his time and strike when ready, at the hour of his own choosing.

But the daemons would not be still. Like beasts in a cage, they paced back and forth across the weirdness of the warp. As their agitation grew, the warp began to boil and wrought storms.

In the wake of their distress, the energy weave of the warp was wracked with shocks and maelstroms. Great storms appeared in the aether. This served Horus well, for he knew that the warp storms would disrupt his enemy's communications. The Emperor's astropaths would be muted, his Navigators blinded and his great fleets crippled.

Orbital Bombardment – *Jon Hodgson*

Ligh: Hammer – *Eric Ren*

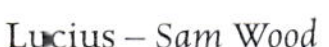

Lucius – *Sam Wood*

Ignatius Grulgor – *David Gallagher*

Charmosian – *Mark Gibbons*

Aboard the Vengeful Spirit

Maloghurst the Twisted, Horus's equerry, had an audience with the Warmaster. They met in Horus's private chambers aboard the *Vengeful Spirit*. The Warmaster voiced his concerns:

'The battle on Isstvan III was unforeseen and is causing us unnecessary delay. We are in great danger of losing the advantage of surprise over the Emperor and his sycophants. Despite the best efforts of our allies in the warp, heralds of warning are even now making their way to Terra. We may only have days left to us before the Emperor realises he has been betrayed. If we cannot finish this, and soon, he will strike back.'

'We fear that the Emperor already knows. This much we have gleaned from our daemonic allies,' Maloghurst replied.

Horus then addressed a group of his most senior warriors.

'If the Emperor makes a move against us, he will rely upon those primarchs and Legions who he trusts. Foremost amongst those are the deadly triumvirate of Guilliman, Sanguinius and El'Jonson. These three will be dealt with, and will present no particular threat to us for a time. Russ is headstrong and undisciplined – he will keep his Legion occupied in a fruitless battle against the Thousand Sons for some while. Dorn is a different proposition. We must avoid confronting him if at all possible. The Khan is out of our reach, but I fear him not and believe he will ultimately side with us.

'Of the rest, it is clear now who is with us and who will remain loyal to the Emperor. This knowledge is ours alone; the Emperor's ignorance of these loyalties will be his undoing. No more efforts are to be made to convert the loyalists. I will not have another Ferrus Manus debacle. Is that clear?'

The assembled primarchs, chieftains and dark priests nodded their assent.

Subversive Tactics – *Dan Wheaton*

Vengeful Spirit – *Justin Norman*

Khaggort – *John Wigley*

Ezekyle Abaddon – *Paul Dainton*

Prospero

A Thousand Sons – *Neil Roberts*

The Red Sorcerers of Prospero

Magnus the Red was an imposing figure: a red cyclops-giant. He was a very powerful psyker, probably the most powerful psyker of all the primarchs. Furthermore, he had been raised on Prospero – this unusual human world was a paradise planet that embraced the psychic mutations that had engulfed its population. Instead of becoming outcasts, the psykers of Prospero became its leaders. Magnus had risen to the position of the planet's pre-eminent sorcerer and leader of the ruling council.

Upon meeting Magnus, the Emperor had cautioned him about the dangers of sorcery and the nature of the warp. The Emperor realised that Magnus was very powerful. Possibly feeling that it was more dangerous for the young primarch to remain ignorant of the secrets of the warp than it was for him to know them, the Emperor showed him the truth.

Magnus feigned shock and horror at what the Emperor revealed to him. He immediately agreed to renounce sorcery and to re-educate the people of Prospero. But Magnus secretly dismissed the Emperor's warnings. He had already peered into the warp with his one great eye and was obsessed with the power and beauty it promised him.

The Thousand Sons

Magnus had been united with his Thousand Sons, the Space Marine Legion who bore his genes. The Legion adopted Prospero as its new home world and many of Magnus's followers on the planet were recruited into their ranks.

Despite the Emperor's warning, the primarch was obsessed with the warp and the study of sorcery. The Legion of the Thousand Sons had been plagued with psychic mutancy in the years leading to their unification with Magnus. When they did meet, Magnus was able to offer a solution to them. He secretly taught them the ways of the sorcerers of Prospero, to embrace their psychic talents as a gift rather than suffer them as a curse. The Thousand Sons had become a secret cabal of warlocks.

The Thousand Sons fought bravely during the Great Crusade and few could doubt their achievements. However, some of the other primarchs could never bring themselves to fully trust Magnus and his Thousand Sons. Leman Russ regarded Magnus as sly and devious, Mortarion openly accused the cyclops of dabbling in sorcery and Corax twice refused to field his Raven Guard Legion alongside the Thousand Sons.

Phosis T'kar – *Michael Phillippi*

Rehahti – *Michael Phillippi*

Catacombs of Tizca – *Rick Sardinha*

Space Marine Librarians

Magnus the Red, primarch of the Thousand Sons Legion, was instrumental in the development of the Space Marine Librarians. Some of the primarchs had long wanted to exploit the powers of psychically talented Space Marines. In some Legions, psychic mutation was relatively common and it was felt that there must be ways for such individuals to continue to be of use to their Legion without presenting any danger.

Magnus and a number of other primarchs created a program of training and development for psykers that supplemented the traditional process of creating a Space Marine. The Emperor sanctioned these first experiments with psychic Space Marines as a means of controlling the spontaneous outbreaks of psychic mutation within the ranks of certain Legions. Then the Emperor had been asked to approve the recruitment of psykers into some of the other Legions. The Librarians had been loyal and effective warriors, and the Emperor appeared to accept their presence on the field of battle.

The Librarians had become a powerful addition to the ranks of the Space Marine Legions.

The Librarian Crisis

As the Great Crusade progressed, most of the Space Marine Legions had established Librarius departments. The Librarians proved themselves as worthy as any other Space Marines in battle after battle.

However, the primarchs argued amongst themselves and with the Emperor about the Librarians. Some desired to extend their Librarius departments and recruit even more pyskers whilst other primarchs were vehemently against the entire notion of the Librarians. Leman Russ argued that they were simply warlocks by any other name. Mortarion accused Magnus the Red of sorcery.

The Emperor was planning to retreat to Earth and continue his great work in the seclusion of his Palace vaults. Perhaps he was concerned about the Librarians and the dangers they would present when he was no longer fighting alongside them. Certainly he was dismayed at the accusation against Magnus. Before he departed for Earth, he summoned the War Council to session on the planet of Nikaea.

Hathor Maat – *Carl Frank*

Prospero – *John Blanche*

The Council of Nikaea

On the planet of Nikaea, the Emperor had summoned the War Council to resolve the Librarian crisis and for Magnus to face charges of sorcery. The Emperor was enthroned on a high dais and looked down upon the primarchs and other dignitaries assembled in the ancient amphitheatre.

Each in turn made their representation to the Emperor. Some primarchs spoke against Magnus, others spoke in his defence. Mortarion repeated his charge that Magnus was employing sorcery. Magnus told of the great deeds achieved by the Librarians and pointed at the astropaths around them as evidence of the Imperium's absolute reliance on psykers. He refuted the charge of sorcery. 'If I am guilty of anything, it is the simple pursuit of knowledge,' he said.

The Emperor made his ruling. Beyond the exceptions of the Navigators and astropaths, he was adamant that the Legions not employ psykers. Even the hint of sorcery had become dangerous and unacceptable. He commanded that the primarchs close their Librarius departments forthwith and ordered that the primarchs themselves not indulge their undoubted psychic talents. The Emperor said it was not clear whether Magnus had been using sorcery, but that he should immediately cease employing psychic powers.

The Council of Nikaea had been the Trial of Magnus the Red. He was accused of sorcery and of introducing sorcerous practices to the Space Marine Legions through the institution of the Librarius.

The wrath of the Emperor was barely contained as he pronounced judgement on Magnus. Although there was no substantive evidence that Magnus has been communing with the Dark Powers of the warp, the Emperor was enraged. He had trusted Magnus to do as he had asked him years before when they had first met. Then the Emperor had shared with Magnus secrets of the warp to which only they were privy. Now Magnus appeared to have ignored the Emperor's warnings and was at the very least dabbling in the black arts of sorcery.

Magnus was ordered to return to Prospero and reorganise his Legion, to disband the Legion's Librarius and to re-deploy the Librarians to the battle companies. The Emperor censured his use of psychics and dismissed Magnus with a final threat. 'If you treat with the warp, Magnus, I shall visit destruction upon you, and your Legion's name will be struck from the Imperial records for all time.'

The Emperor's Light – *Dan Wheaton*

Ahzek Ahriman – *Alex Boyd*

The Chaplain Edict

After the Council of Nikaea, the Space Marine Legions had been instructed to abolish their Librarius divisions. The Emperor decreed that henceforth no Legion was to employ psykers in battle, nor were they to continue their studies into the mysteries of psychic talents. Those Legions who had Librarians – psychically empowered Space Marines – were instructed to reassign them to standard fighting units and to forbid the use of their abilities.

First Lord of Terra, Malcador the Sigillite, leader of the Council of Terra, was not satisfied that all of the Legions would follow the Emperor's edict. He knew that many of the primarchs placed great value on their Librarians and the powers they could unleash on the battlefield. For some of the Legions, the deployment of psykers had become central to their strategies and tactics.

He resolved to find a way to ensure these Legions obeyed the Emperor and observed the psyker ban. His thoughts turned to Lorgar and the Word Bearers Legion.

Whilst the Emperor worked his secret labours in the Palace Vaults, Malcador the Sigillite issued a new edict through the Council of Terra in the name of the Emperor. This was the Order of Observance, more commonly known as the Chaplain Edict, and its inspiration was the Word Bearers Legion.

The Word Bearers primarch, Lorgar, had been raised on the cult world of Colchis. In time, Lorgar had become its martial and spiritual leader. His first meeting with the Emperor was believed to be a fulfilment of an ancient prophecy, an event that reinforced the religious fervour of the people of Colchis, and Lorgar himself. On becoming primarch, Lorgar had introduced officer-clerics to his Legion. These warrior-priests were named Chaplains, and their role was to minister to the needs of the Space Marines and ensure that their faith in the Emperor was strong.

Inspired by this, Malcador ordered the other Space Marine primarchs to appoint Chaplains who would ensure the spiritual wellbeing of their Legion and enforce the psyker ban. These officers were to be picked from those Space Marines who were the most steadfast in their duties, and who had demonstrated the strongest loyalty to their primarch and to the Emperor.

Most of the primarchs loyally followed the edict and began to appoint officers to the rank and duties of Chaplain. Some did not. Lorgar was quietly amused by the irony of the new edict – his Legion had already secretly fallen to Chaos.

Given the vagaries of communication across the vastness of the galaxy, it would not have

Berus – *Paul Carrick*

seemed unusual or suspicious to Malcador that not all of the primarchs had voiced their consent to the edict immediately. It was also certain that some of the primarchs behaved duplicitously, and while they assured him they were doing as the Emperor had ordered, they were not. In time, their dishonesty became clear.

Xavier – *James Ryman*

Magnus Retreats to Prospero

Magnus had retreated to his home world – the paradise planet of Prospero. He was bitterly disappointed at the outcome of the Council of Nikaea. The Emperor had made his ruling, and through it his feelings, clear. Magnus was to stop all sorcery and psychic activity on pain of death. Furthermore, the development of Space Marine Librarians was halted and the Librarius departments ordered to be disbanded.

Magnus raged against the Emperor and his ruling. He had no intention of giving up the power and the glory the warp had offered to him. He would continue to study the warp and work his spells. He met with his senior Librarians and they agreed to continue their sorcery in secret.

None can say when Magnus was tainted by the warp, but his actions suggest that his corruption was well progressed by the time of the Council of Nikaea. It is probable that his senior officers and Librarians were also corrupt at this point. Magnus had no problems persuading his Legion to collude with his plan to secretly continue their study of the warp.

Uthizzar – *Sam Wood*

Silver Spires – *Jen Page*

Magnus the Red – *John Blanche*

Magnus, the Crimson King – *John Blanche*

Magnus's Precognition

Magnus had put his faith in sorcery and the dark powers of the warp. The Emperor had censured him for such activity and warned him that he would have no hesitation in destroying Magnus were he to disobey his commands.

The Warmaster Horus was being treated on the feral planet of Davin. Unbeknownst to anyone else, the Warmaster was being seduced by the Ruinous Powers and would soon challenge the Emperor. Except that Magnus knew. Peering into the warp with his one good eye, the Red Sorcerer had seen the Warmaster make his pact with Chaos and he saw much more besides. Much of what Magnus saw was madness and turmoil, but he also saw events that could only be the future. His dream foretold of the epic events that were yet to unfold, of Horus's betrayal, of the primarchs who would die, of those who would betray the Emperor and of those who would defend him. Of his own fate, the dream was silent.

The vision disturbed Magnus and he gathered about him his secret cabal of Thousand Sons sorcerers to discuss its meaning and implications. After some deliberation, they resolved to contact the Emperor and warn him of Horus's betrayal. They decided against the use of their astropaths to send the message to the Emperor – they desired a quicker, surer method of communication: they would send the warning by daemonic spell!

Magnus's Warning

Magnus the Red, primarch of the Thousand Sons Legion and secretly a sorcerer in commune with the dark powers of the warp, had a terrible vision. The vision revealed to Magnus the betrayal of Horus and the coming civil war. Magnus and his sorcerous cabal had decided to contact the Emperor and warn him of Horus's heresy by use of a powerful spell.

No one is sure why Magnus took the decision to warn the Emperor in the fashion he chose. It was certain that the Emperor would recognise the taint of Chaos in his message and would have no option but to prosecute him. The Legion would be expunged and Magnus and the other sorcerers put to death. Perhaps Magnus thought that the Emperor would be distracted by the betrayal of Horus. Maybe Magnus wanted to set the Emperor and Horus at each others' throats. Perhaps he hoped the Emperor would destroy Horus and that he, Magnus, could claim leadership of the Heresy. Or perhaps he had other motives that can only be guessed at.

In any case, the cabal of the Thousand Sons joined with Magnus to cast a mighty spell. This potent conjuration flew across time and space. Breaching the protective wards and hexes around the Imperial palace the spell lanced into the brain of the Emperor, instantly filling him with the knowledge of Magnus's dark vision and details of Horus's impending betrayal.

The XV Legion – *Neil Roberts*

The Emperor Reacts to the Warning of Magnus

The psychic defences of the Emperor's Palace on Terra had been breached by a daemonic conjuration of unprecedented power. Magnus the Red and his cabal of secret sorcerers had cast a spell to warn the Emperor of the impending betrayal of the Warmaster Horus, a betrayal the primarch had foreseen in a dark precognitive vision.

No one knows what reaction Magnus expected to receive to his warning. If he thought that the Emperor would be pleased with him, he sorely misjudged him. The Emperor flew into a terrible rage, appearing to ignore the content of Magnus's message. He was consumed with anger that Magnus should so flagrantly have disobeyed his orders to renounce sorcery and psychic teachings.

The Emperor called to his side the primarch Leman Russ of the Space Wolves. Russ and Magnus were old rivals and there was some bitterness between them. The Emperor commanded Russ to move on Prospero and prosecute the rebel primarch. His orders were clear: Magnus and his Thousand Sons were consorting with the warp, in direct contradiction of personal instruction from the Emperor. Magnus was to be brought back to Terra to face judgement!

Garan – *Paul Jeacock*

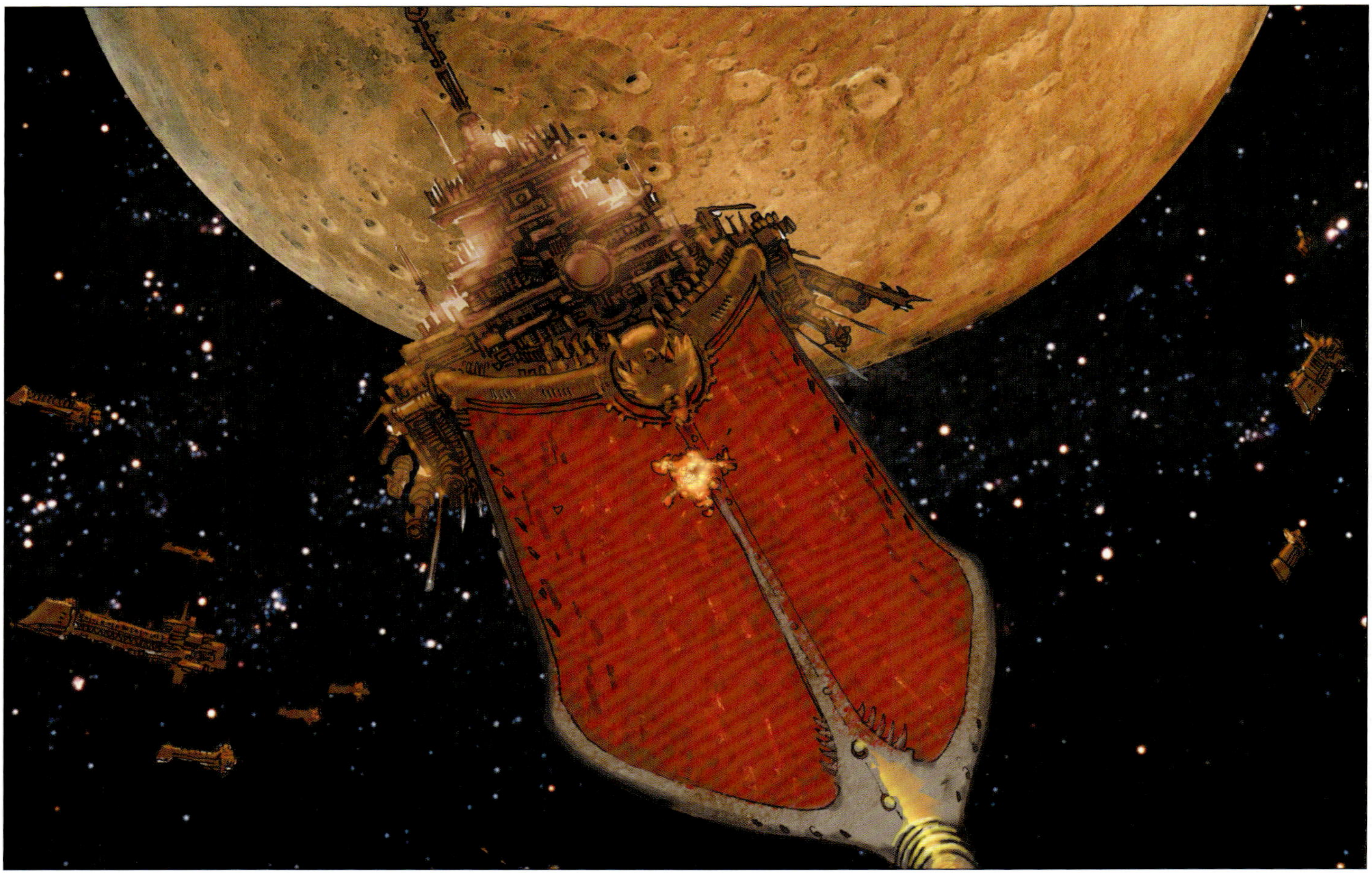

Ragnarok – *Justin Norman*

Leman Russ – *John Blanche*

Cleanse and Burn – *Wayne England*

Space Wolves

The Space Wolves Legion was known across the galaxy for its martial exploits. Of all of the Space Marines, the Space Wolves were most like their primarch in character. Uncouth, undisciplined and barbaric by comparison to the other Legions, they were nonetheless a powerful force of arms, admired by their allies, feared by their foes.

Leman Russ was never one for following rules; as long as his Space Marines were prepared to fight and die for him, he was satisfied. He knew his troops had superb battlefield instincts and he trusted them to achieve their objectives without being burdened with a host of what he regarded as petty regulations. Because of this, the organisation and structure of the Space Wolves was quite different from that of the other Legions.

The Space Wolves Legion was organised into thirteen Great Companies, each one a sizeable army numbering many thousands of warriors. The Great Companies were more akin to barbarian warbands than to formal military organisations, each led by a mighty Wolf Lord.

Bjorn – *Adrian Smith*

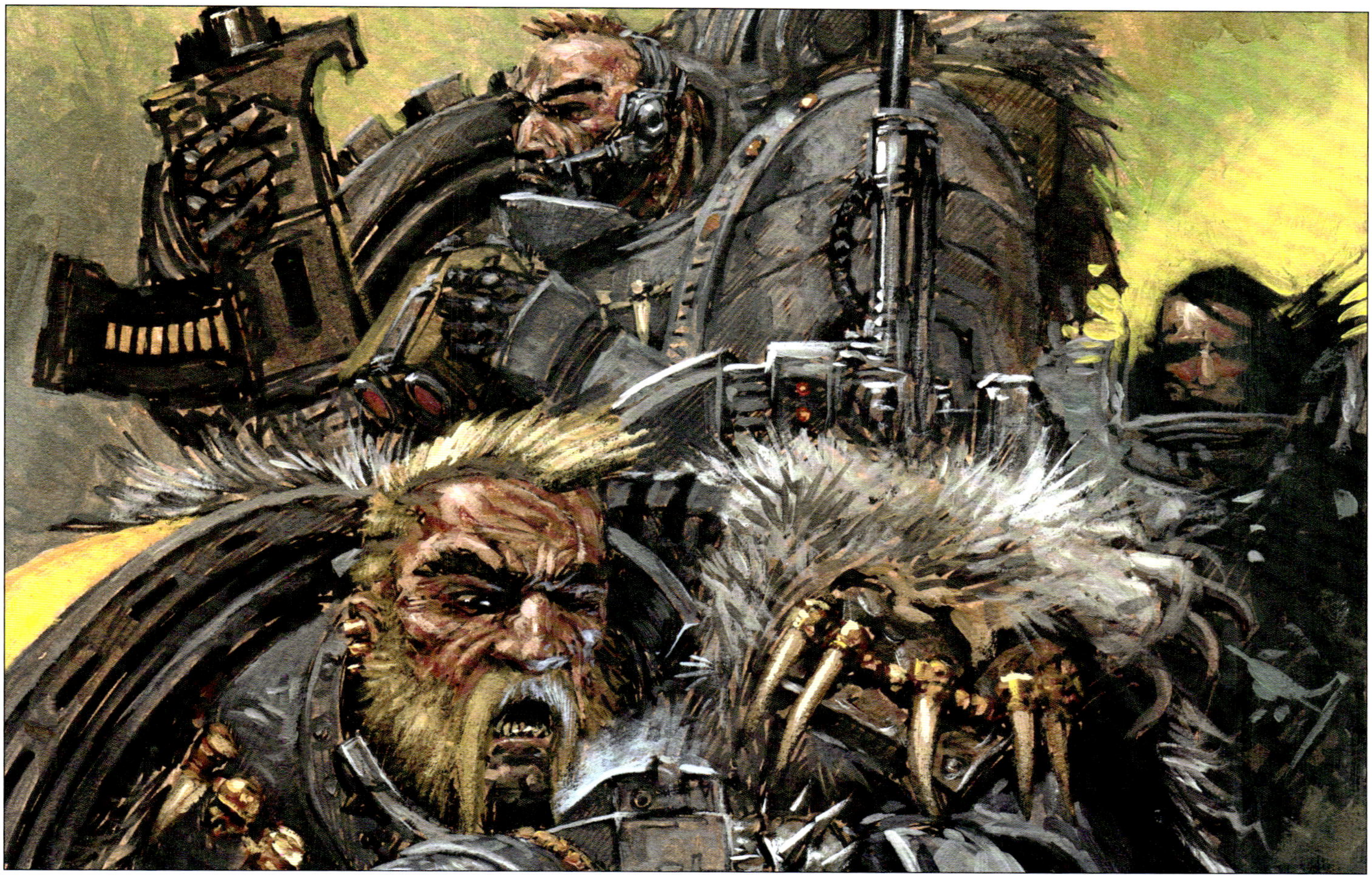

Sigfas[illegible]i – *Adrian Smith*

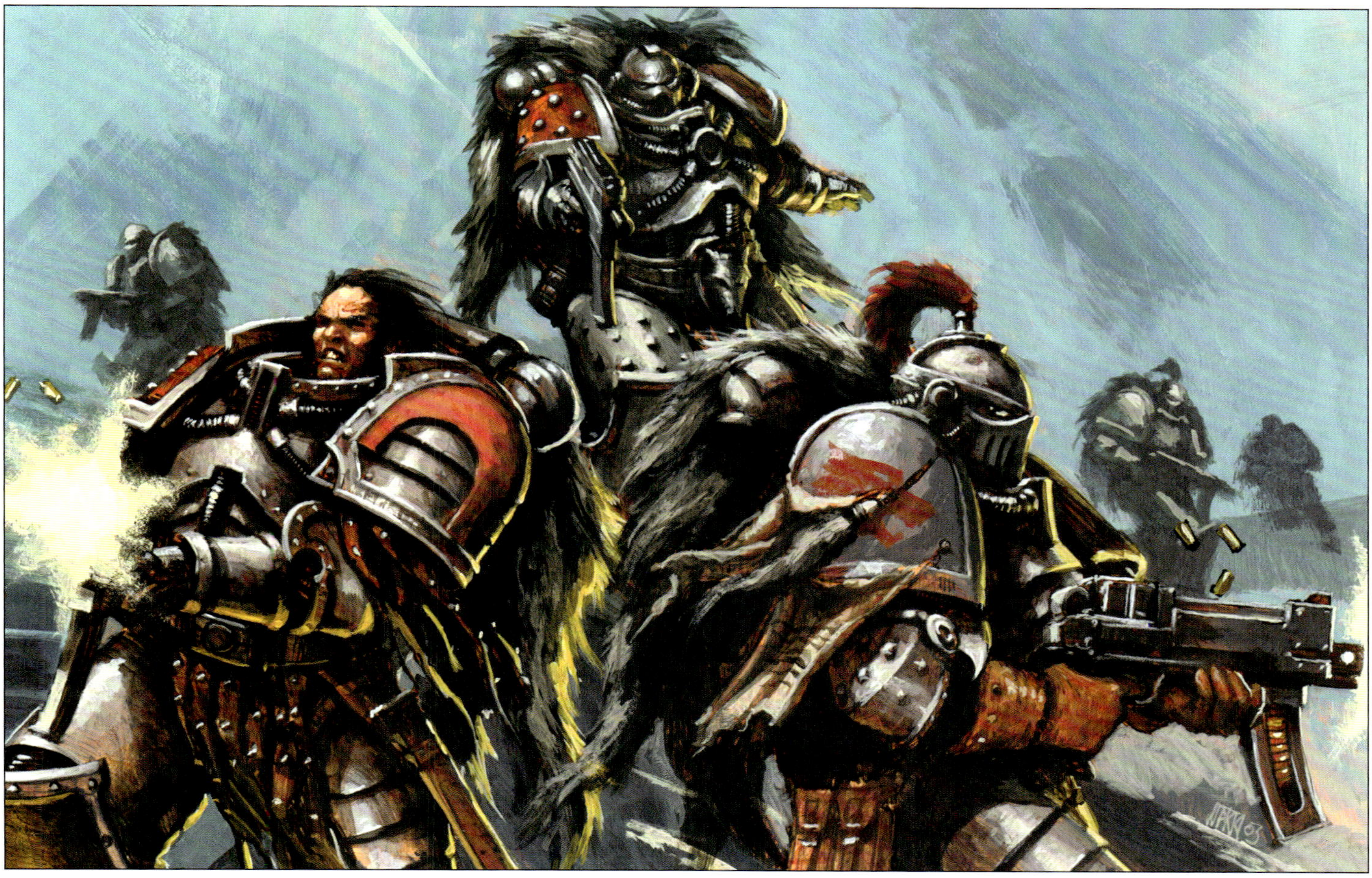

Kol[illegible]yr – *Karl Kopinski*

Curse of the Wulfen

The Space Wolves Legion was a close-knit brotherhood and there was a great deal of respect and comradeship between the Space Marines from Terra and the warriors of Fenris. Although the latter troops were organised into their own distinct squads, known as Fenris Bloods and Fenris Hunters, they also led some of the squads of Terran Space Wolves (the Hunter, Claw and Long Fang squads). The officer corps and the elite Wolf Guard were drawn from the ranks of both Terrans and Fenrisians.

Both Terran and Fenrisian Space Wolves could succumb to the curse of the Wulfen. This condition was usually diagnosed during the process of surgically and psychologically modifying a normal man to become a Space Marine, but it could also strike later in a Space Wolf's life. The curse was akin to lycanthropy – the smitten warrior would become savage and beastlike in behaviour, unable to quell the rage inside. The Wulfen were remarkably hirsute, even by Space Wolves standards, and their canine teeth grew into large dagger-like fangs. All of the Wulfen were assigned to the 13th Great Company and fought together in feral groups known as Wulfen Packs.

Space Wolves Recon Squad – *Eric Polak*

Leiknir – *Adrian Smith*

Tammikk – *Adrian Smith*

Olfun – *Adrian Smith*

The Razing of Prospero

The Space Wolves opened the Battle of Prospero with an orbital barrage. The beautiful planet was quickly reduced to rubble, the manicured gardens and glass temples shattered beyond recognition. At a signal from Russ, the Space Wolves launched the first of their assaults.

The Thousand Sons had revealed themselves to be a coven of witches, and the Emperor authorised Leman Russ to exact summary justice on them for their heresy. The Space Wolves were aided by a detachment of the Emperor's own bodyguard, the Legio Custodes, and by the Silent Sisterhood. The latter were Untouchables, carriers of the pariah gene, psychic blanks who were immune to psychic assault and anathema to the sorcerers of Prospero.

The Space Marines and Custodian Guard had the task of defeating Magnus's Legion on the field of battle and arresting the malcontent primarch. The Sisters of Silence had to apprehend and detain any and all surviving psykers for transportation back to Earth. There they would be judged, with due sentence served upon them.

Hundreds of battles raged across the planet as the Space Wolves and Custodian Guard launched attack after attack against the defending Thousand Sons. The once magnificent paradise world of Prospero was reduced to smouldering rubble by the ferocity of Leman Russ's warriors. To their credit, the Thousand Sons reacted quickly to the surprise assault, and their defence was well-organised and determined. They countered the loyalist firepower with deadly psychic spells, unleashing the dark fury of the warp upon their loyalist aggressors. Victory was no easy task for either side to achieve.

Prospero Burns – *Neil Roberts*

Sobek – *Chris Trevas*

Amsu – *Neil Hodgson*

Pa-Siamun – *Chris Trevas*

Apophis – *Des Hanley*

Silver Osprey Vigilator Squad – *Sam Wood*

Ornulfr – *Adrian Smith*

Thorbrand – *Paul Dainton*

Mjcllnir – *Franz Vohwinkel*

The Varangi – *Adrian Smith*

Jorlund – *Carl Frank*

Dómárr Gonnarrsson – *Adrian Smith*

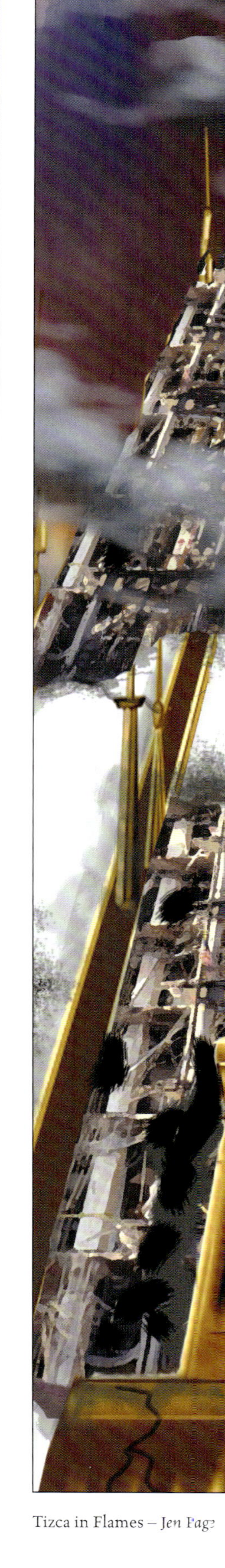

Tizca in Flames – *Jen Page*

Leman Russ, the Wolf King – *John Blanche*

Seek and Destroy – *Ralph Horsley*

Prahopte – *Dan Wheaton*

Jortan – *John Wigley*

Myskia – *Adrian Smith*

Jafari – *Neil Hodgson*

Tolbek – *Chris Trevas*

Amur is – *Karl Kopinski*

Seraphis – *Wayne England*

Aesir – *Franz Vohwinkel*

Khalid – *Ralph Horsley*

Karsso Tolk – *Torstein Nordstrand*

T'kar's Cabal – *Michael Phillippi*

Besenmut – *Torstein Nordstrand*

Nebmaetre – *Justin Norman*

Ahriman's Bodyguard – *Alex Boyd*

Qaa – *John Gravato*

Isstvan V

Raven's Flight – *Neil Roberts*

Horus at Isstvan V

After the dreadful battle for Isstvan III, the Warmaster Horus established a new headquarters on the fifth planet of the Isstvan System. He had a plan to destroy the last remaining loyal Legions still in his way, a plan that was to be fulfilled on this barren, lifeless orb. This would remove the final obstacle standing between him and the Imperial Throne of Terra and dominion over all the worlds of the Imperium. He was sure he would soon be crowned Emperor.

Horus had conceived of the plan even before the events on Isstvan III had started. He knew full well that the Emperor would seek to crush any rebellion long before it could threaten Terra itself. The attack on the third planet of the Isstvan System had been intended to goad the Emperor into attacking him. Horus had prepared for this. It was why he had instructed certain primarchs to keep their alignment secret. Whatever forces the Emperor could send against him would include among their number many who had committed themselves to the Warmaster.

This duplicity would give the rebels an unbeatable advantage in the ensuing battle. The Warmaster reasoned that any troops loyal to the Emperor would be physically and spiritually broken by the sudden emergence of so many enemies.

The Trap is Set

The warp storms raging across the immaterium were the consequence of a massive upsurge in daemonic activity within the Realm of Chaos. The daemons of Chaos wanted to break out of their domain and invade that of mankind. In their frustration and anger, they churned the currents of the warp.

Horus used this to his advantage. The storms disrupted both travel and communication through the warp for any who could not influence or control the daemons. Whilst the warp storms raged, the loyal astropaths and Navigators of the Imperium could not easily carry out their duties. This interference had crippled the loyalist efforts to understand what was happening across the galaxy, let alone do anything about it. It had enabled Horus to isolate the most powerful and loyal Legions in remote corners of the Imperium and it had allowed him to operate without hindrance in the Isstvan System.

Now Horus wanted the daemons of Chaos to relent, to quieten their rage and let some regions of tranquility settle over the warp. This was because he now desired the Emperor to attack him so that his trap could be sprung. The Warmaster drew to his side the corrupt dark priests of Davin and explained his intentions. The powers of Chaos were sure to cooperate, they assured him.

Horus Gathers his Lieutenants

Horus called together his most trusted lieutenants for a final briefing on the battle that was to come.

'As I speak to you, the false Emperor has dispatched his forces to attack us. We face the most awesome concentration of military might the galaxy has ever seen. Fully seven Space Marine Legions are heading towards us from Terra. The Emperor and his weakling supporters believe they will triumph over us, that his army will crush us and that we shall be destroyed or cowed into meek surrender. He is wrong!

'This is not the time nor place of our defeat, it is instead our time and place of victory. I, Horus, greatest of the primarchs, have outwitted him. I have orchestrated the whole affair. It is I who persuaded the powers of the warp to allow the Emperor's task force to navigate its way to Isstvan. And it is I who planned the composition of his army. More than half of the Legions he sends to confront us are in fact our staunchest allies.

'The Emperor's loyalists are heading to their doom!'

'All hail the Warmaster! Horus! Horus!' cried the assembled warriors.

Fulgerion – *Steve Belledin*

Halden-Tai – *Michael Phillippi*

Wreath – *Steve Belledin*

Dasturkh – *James Brady*

Justicar's Sword – *Dan Scott*

Wronde – *Carl Frank*

Gragin – *Justin Norman*

Darkhogat – *David Millgate*

The Iron Column – *Franz Vohwinkel*

Fleiste – *Des Hanley*

Lachost – *Wayne England*

Asceton – *Franz Vohwinkel*

Gurtur-Fol – *Kenson Low*

Abakhol – *Sam Wood*

Geldurk – *Paul Herbert*

The Legions Muster at the Isstvan System

Rogal Dorn, acting on the Emperor's behalf, had ordered seven Space Marine Legions to the Isstvan System. Their mission was to attack the arch-traitor Horus and destroy his rebellion against the Imperium. The task force had been placed under the command of Ferrus Manus, primarch of the Iron Hands Legion.

Ferrus had sped to the Isstvan System in his fastest ships with his Legion's veteran companies. He was desperate to fight the traitors. Months previously, he had been confronted by Fulgrim, primarch of the Emperor's Children Legion. The two primarchs had been close friends, and Ferrus was dismayed and angered by Fulgrim's attempt to get him to betray his oath of loyalty to the Emperor and side with Horus. A bloody fight had ensued as the two argued. Enraged by Fulgrim's treachery, Ferrus had ordered his Space Marines to detain the errant primarch and his bodyguard. The Emperor's Children fought back and both sides suffered severe casualties before the traitor was able to escape.

In the long weeks since the confrontation, Ferrus had been unable to contact the Emperor with the hideous revelation of the betrayal of Horus and Fulgrim as he and his Legion were becalmed by warp storms. When he was finally able to communicate with Terra, he learned the full extent of the betrayal. This served only to fan the flames of Ferrus's anger. On receiving the orders to attack Horus from Rogal Dorn, he immediately set course for Isstvan.

Ferrus Manus impatiently paced back and forth across the bridge of his sleek command ship. He had arrived at the Isstvan System with ten companies of his finest veterans. The rest of the Iron Hands were following in the Legion's slower vessels. Ferrus did not expect them to arrive in time to participate in the initial assault. This did not concern him overly, as he was assured of the services of the full complement of five other Legions and a huge contingent of the Word Bearers. The Salamanders and Raven Guard Legions had already reached the rendezvous point in their large warfleets and their primarchs, Vulkan and Corax respectively, were waiting for the order to move on the fifth planet.

Ferrus pressed his chief astropath for news on the whereabouts of the rest of his command. The waiting was interminable; he was desperate to move quickly. Not only was the fate of the Imperium in his hands, but he also had a personal score to settle with the vile Fulgrim.

Finally, he got the news he wanted to hear. The remaining four fleets were only hours away and would break their warp-jump close to the fifth planet. Ferrus let out a cry of relief. At last he could seek his revenge on Fulgrim and crush the rebellion.

Vaddon – *Kenson Low*

Konenos – *Neil Roberts*

Bargotal – *Franz Vohwinkel*

Malbon – *Franz Vohwinkel*

Fortronus – *James Ryman*

Cohors Nasicae – *Sam Wood*

Wrathe – *Sam Wood*

Ferrus Orders the Attack

Ferrus spoke with Vulkan and Corax.

'Loyal primarchs, the hour of our destiny has arrived. Our comrades are but a short time away. The Legions of Perturabo, Night Haunter and Alpharius, and the warriors of Lorgar, will be with us soon; they are mere hours behind us.

'I have decided that the honour of drawing first blood in this battle falls to us. Your Legions and my stalwart veterans will lead the assault. Our astropaths and diviners have identified the enemy's position and deduced the optimal attack pattern and landing zones. We go for full planetary assault configuration. Logic-engines should be transmitting the dropsite details to you as I speak. My veteran companies will take the vanguard. Corax, your Legion is to secure the right flank and centre. Vulkan, you have the left wing. As soon as we land, we make for the target points identified on the tactical hologrids marked as references Gamma twelve to twenty-four and Theta seven, eight and nine.

'I have instructed the others to make planetfall as soon as they break warp. They are to secure the dropsite and reinforce our assault. Hologrids Omega and Righteous contain details of their deployments.

'The traitors are not expecting this attack and we have the advantage of surprise. The Emperor damn us if we waste it!'

Ferrus Manus, the Gorgon – *John Blanche*

Cortan – *Torstein Nordstrand*

Galbovax – *Chris Dien*

The Loyalist Assault of Isstvan V

Ferrus Manus launched his attack against the traitorous forces of Horus the Warmaster headquartered on the planet of Isstvan V. Ferrus had with him his entire brigade of Iron Hands veterans, and the Salamanders and Raven Guard Space Marine Legions of Vulkan and Corax.

The forces of Horus were encamped along the northern edge of one of the planet's largest deserts, the Urgall Depression. This landscape was a featureless plain of black sands and scattered scrub, rising gently to low hills upon which the traitors were deployed.

As the command to attack was broadcast from Ferrus's flagship, the sky above the Urgall blackened as ten thousand drop pods rained down onto the planet from the loyalist fleet in orbit. Huge explosions ripped through the traitor lines as the orbiting fleet unleashed a torrent of fire from its massive guns, bomb bays and missile launchers. As each drop pod landed, it disgorged its cargo of Space Marines, who immediately began assaulting the traitors. Following in the wake of the drop pods, hundreds of drop-ships and landers carrying heavier equipment and large war machines began their urgent descent to the planet's surface. Within minutes, the entire loyalist force under Ferrus had made planetfall. Then the battle began in earnest.

Harmokan – *Torstein Nordstrand*

Arendi – *John Gravato*

Avernii – *Andrea Uderzo*

Arkan – *John Gravato*

Rad-Urzon – *Torstein Nordstrand*

Blade of Fury – *Franz Vohwinkel*

Tyche – *Ralph Horsley*

Rethaerin – *James Brady*

Planetfall

Ferrus Manus and his personal retinue were amongst the first of the loyalist forces to make planetfall. His drop pod crashed down into the heart of the traitor encampment. The defenders fought back, but the ferocity of the loyalist assault threatened to sweep them from the hilltops they occupied. Ferrus and his veterans quickly established a position, as did the Legions of Corax and Vulkan. The plan was to strike hard and fast, to overwhelm the traitors and drive them from the hills. Within an hour or two, the remaining four Legions of the task force made planetfall to the rear to reinforce the assault and mop up any lingering resistance.

The fighting was bloody as Space Marine fought Space Marine. Despite their differing loyalties, the two sides were well matched. The loyalists, though outnumbered by Horus's forces, had the advantage of surprise and initiative. For a while, it seemed that Ferrus's plan would work, as his troops began to make inroads into the enemy lines. The traitors were being slowly but surely driven from their defensive positions as the loyalists consolidated their advance with a series of hit-and-run attacks right across the battlezone.

The carnage was terrible, on a scale never seen before, but the forces of Ferrus Manus were winning. The Emperor's loyal warriors took heart when the first landing craft of the follow-up Legions broke through the cloud cover and appeared above the Urgall Dropsite.

Trador – *Franz Vohwinkel*

Halmech – *Torstein Nordstrand*

Firestorm – *Al Eremin*

Telcantor – *Torstein Nordstrand*

Thellion – *John Gravato*

Grogor – *Steve Boulter*

Rongar – *Carl Frank*

Gauste – *Franz Vohwinkel*

Horus Orders his Mock Retreat

The battle for Isstvan V raged across the low hills along the northern edge of the Urgall Depression. The attacking loyalist Legions under the command of Ferrus Manus had seemingly surprised the forces of the arch-traitor Horus and his fellow conspirators, and were now fighting against the very heart of their entrenched positions. Many thousands of Space Marines had been killed and still the battle went on. Both sides were suffering tremendous casualties; the carnage was appalling. Horus smiled. If he cared about the losses his own Legions were taking, he showed no sign of it; his devious plan was about to come to fruition.

'At the first sign from our secret allies, you are all to draw back your troops,' he commanded his fellow traitor primarchs. 'It must appear as if we are cowed by the appearance of fresh enemies. This will convince the Iron Hands primarch to overstretch his forces. The fool Manus does not realise that we will soon have him caught in a deadly vice from which there will be no escape for him or his Emperor-loving followers.

'Once our allies have secured the dropsite for us, we can counter his puny assault with our full strength. Mark my words well, Angron, Mortarion and Fulgrim, your Legions will sate themselves fully before this day is done. Our victory here will pave the way to the Throne of Terra and then the galaxy!'

Agapito – *John Cadice*

Imaldhorn – *Justin Norman*

Corvus Corax – *John Blanche*

The Fury of Ferrus

Ferrus Manus fought with righteous anger. He was surrounded by his most experienced warriors, hand-picked veterans of the Iron Hands Legion. Against them were arrayed the traitors of Fulgrim's Emperor's Children Legion. No quarter was asked or given as the opposing Space Marines fought to the death. Blood and gore drenched the combatants as bolter shells blasted through the ceramite casings of power armour, and chainswords severed arms, legs and heads. The loyalist Iron Hands, bolstered by the presence of their primarch, were slowly winning the fight.

Ferrus was determined to win. He had been frustrated beyond measure by the events that had led him to this place. His previous encounter with Fulgrim and the traitor's attempt to turn him, the months he and his Legion had been stranded on the far side of the Imperium, unable to contact or be contacted by the Emperor, the passion with which the traitor Space Marines had fought back against his attack; all had conspired to fill him with rage and set his heart upon a quest for vengeance. The object of his most fervent ire was Fulgrim. The primarch of the Emperor's Children Legion had once been his greatest ally and friend. Ferrus was appalled that Fulgrim, of all those he knew, was the one who had tried to turn him traitor. Fulgrim must pay for his treachery, thought Ferrus.

The battle for the dropsite raged on. Ferrus of the Iron Hands had led three Legions of Space Marines in an audacious assault against the traitor Legions of Horus on the fifth planet of the Isstvan System. Thousands of Space Marines had died in the bloody battle that ensued; thousands more were dying still as the fighting continued.

The loyalists had driven a wedge deep into the enemy position. At the fore was the awesome figure of Ferrus, cleaving, hacking, shooting the traitors before him, all the while barking out orders to his troops. For Ferrus this was not only a battle, this was vengeance, revenge for perfidy most foul. This was his time to punish the miscreant followers of Horus and especially to mete out justice to the despicable Fulgrim. Ferrus looked for a sign that he could set aside his duty of command and seek a duel with Fulgrim. He yearned to confront the viperous primarch and settle once and for all the enmity that they now had between them.

Ferrus did not have to wait long for his sign. In the distance behind them, the loyalists could see the first landing craft of the Night Lords Legion breaking through the cloud cover above the dropsite of the Urgall Depression. Four more loyal Legions were about to enter the battle, they thought. Within minutes, craft from the other Legions had been identified. The Iron Warriors, the Alpha Legion and the Word Bearers had joined the Night Lords. The dropsite has been secured, thought Ferrus. Now, at last, I can exact my revenge upon Fulgrim.

As the drop-ships and landing craft of the Night Lords, Iron Warriors, Alpha Legion and Word Bearers set down on the planet's surface, the traitor forces seemed to lose heart for the fight. They began to pull back from their emplacements and bunkers. The traitor primarchs Angron, Fulgrim and Mortarion could clearly be seen ordering their troops to abandon the hills. For Ferrus and his fellow loyalists, Corax and Vulkan, this was a clear sign that they were winning and that the end was near.

Ferrus voxed a message to his compatriots.

'The enemy is beaten. Look how they run from us. Now we push on! Let none escape our vengeance!'

Corax and Vulkan were hesitant. Their Legions had fought tenaciously and well.

Comech – *Andrea Uderzo*

But their casualties were not light. Both primarchs thought it better to consolidate their current positions and let the other unblooded Legions continue the fight whilst they regrouped.

'Lord Manus, let our fine allies earn some honours in this battle. We have fared well, but are nonetheless bloodied and battered. None could say we have not acquitted ourselves with glory this day. Let us take a moment to catch our breath and bind our wounds before we once again dive headlong into such a terrible battle.'

But Ferrus was not to be dissuaded from his fury. He gathered about him his Iron Hands warriors and thrust deep into the mass of enemies before him, his eyes fixed only upon the gloriously garbed figure of Fulgrim. Let the others rest and lick their wounds, he thought, I will not let any other have the satisfaction of settling affairs with that fiend.

Horus's Pride – *David Millgate*

Gabriel Santar – *John Gravato*

Honorius – *David Millgate*

Racharus – *Chris Dien*

Promodon – *Justin Norman*

Kon-Drayur – *Franz Vohwinkel*

Ferrus Confronts Fulgrim

Amidst the carnage of the Urgall Hills, two great primarchs faced each other: the gore-splattered Ferrus Manus of the Iron Hands Legion and the fantastically bedecked lord of the Emperor's Children, Fulgrim.

'At last we meet again, foulheart. Long months have I waited for this. You, who I once called friend, have betrayed our Emperor and you have betrayed me. This is the moment of reckoning. I will deal bloody vengeance upon your head, Fulgrim, even as your traitorous cohorts are put to the sword by the Emperor's loyal sons.'

'You are a fool, Ferrus. I came to you because of our friendship, not despite it. The universe is changing, the old order upset and a new dawn approaching. I offered you the chance to be part of the new order and you threw it back at me. I cannot give you a second opportunity to join us. The Emperor is a spent force. Even now he distracts himself on some trivia while his kingdom is in flames. Horus is his rightful heir. It is the Emperor who has betrayed us all.'

'I expected no less from you than these treasonous lies. How can you not see the truth? Horus is mad. Mad for power. Look at the death all around us. This cannot be justified. I am the Emperor's loyal servant, and through me his will and his vengeance will be done. You shall all hang from the Gate of Traitors for your acts of sedition!'

'No, Ferrus, it is you who is undone. Look you now to the north. See there the strength we have to counter your piffling attack. And look you now to the south. The Legions you see there are not loyal to the Emperor, they are all of them to Horus sworn!'

'You have stumbled into a trap, my old friend,' said Fulgrim spitefully. 'The allies you expected to be at your back are instead sworn against you. Instead of glorious victory, you have earned only dismal defeat and certain death. I give you one last chance to throw down your arms. Submit to me here. For the sake of friendship past I shall plead your case with Horus, though he commands your death.'

Ferrus was stunned by the revelation that the four Legions supposedly supporting his attack against the traitors were themselves aligned with the heretic Horus. With mounting horror, he realised that there could be no escape for him or for the other loyalists.

'You have long since lost the right to call me friend, viper! I shall not submit to you or any of your kith. Death holds no fear for me, only dishonour! The Emperor's loyal warriors will not surrender, now or ever. You will have to kill every one of us to claim victory.'

'Then so be it. I am sorry it has come to this.'

At this, the two primarchs leapt at each other. This was a fight from which only one of them would walk away.

Fulgrim and Ferrus – *Neil Roberts*

Hammer of Justice – *Dan Wheaton*

Brantar – *Chris Dien*

Pa-Gurbod – *Ed Cox*

Cyriarus – *James Ryman*

Drader or – *Tiernen Trevallion*

Grav-Attack – *Eric Ren*

The Dropsite Massacre

The veteran companies of the Iron Hands Legion fought gallantly beside their mighty primarch, Ferrus Manus, but they were hopelessly outnumbered by the sudden appearance of the full strength of Horus's traitor Legions. In moments, the Iron Hands were swamped by foes too numerous to count. World Eaters, Death Guard, Emperor's Children and Sons of Horus Space Marines poured over the Urgall Hills. The loyal Space Marines struggled to maintain any semblance of order and cohesion as they desperately tried to hold off the onslaught. At the very heart of their resistance, Ferrus Manus was locked in bitter hand-to-hand combat with the traitor primarch Fulgrim. Whatever the odds, the stout-hearted Iron Hands would not desert their beloved primarch.

Meanwhile, the Salamanders and Raven Guard Legions were falling back to the dropsite to regroup and rendezvous with the four Legions – the Word Bearers, Iron Warriors, Alpha Legion and Night Lords – that had landed there. Vulkan and Corax, the Legions' respective primarchs, were still unaware that their erstwhile allies were in fact sworn to Horus. This soon became apparent to them as the four new Legions began firing on them. The loyal Legions were caught between two traitor armies as the Iron Hands veterans failed to hold off the counterattack launched by Horus from the northern hills.

The Salamanders and Raven Guard were massively outnumbered. Lesser troops would simply have given up in the face of such overwhelming opposition, but the warriors of Vulkan and Corax were Space Marines, and so they fought. Even so, it was a massacre!

Frontal Assault – *James Brady*

Ares's Fury – *Dan Wheaton*

Van Kordal – *Ed Cox*

Vulkan Lives – *Neil Roberts*

Decimius – *James Brady*

Tourbadon – *Ed Cox*

The Iron Hands Betrayed – *Neil Roberts*

Fulgrim and the Warmaster

The Warmaster met with Fulgrim.

'You requested a private audience with me, Fulgrim. What have you to report?'

'My esteemed lord and master of Isstvan, I have brought you a trophy.'

At this, the primarch held up the severed head of Ferrus Manus. He casually tossed the grisly object at the feet of Horus.

'So you have fulfilled your oath to me. Good. But I fail to see why this presentation required so private a meeting. All of my captains should share in this triumph.'

'With the greatest respect, mighty Horus, I am afraid that Fulgrim did not entirely fulfil his oath to you. He did strike down his old friend and comrade, but he could not find the strength within himself to complete the task. I did it for him!'

'You… You are not Fulgrim? Who are you? Are you some kind of spy or assassin? Should I call my guard, or do you think you can best me? Do not think me weak like Ferrus… I can break you like a straw!'

'Perhaps this is true, but I have no desire to test either you or myself in such a wasteful and fruitless trial of combat. Nor do you have need to call your guardsmen. I am here to pledge myself to your cause. Who am I? It should be clear to one so powerful as you that I am a creature of the warp – a humble servant of the great power that is Slaanesh. I have claimed this mortal shell as my own – and I must say how pleasing it is to me. The sensations are quite unique, though; I shall no doubt have to make some adjustments to it in time.'

'What has happened to Fulgrim?' Horus asked of the daemon now inhabiting the body of his primarch underling.

'Fear not; he is safe, quite safe. He and I have a long history and I wouldn't wish him any lasting ill. You see, I have been his conscience for many years – quietly talking to him through the long nights: advising him, comforting him, cajoling him, pleading with him, steering his course of actions. I was the voice that persuaded him to take your side in this conflict of mortals – yes, you have me to thank for his dutiful obedience. But at the end he was weak, too weak to deal the deathblow to his old friend. In his pain he cried out to me for help. I could not but help him; after all we have been so close for so long, he is like a brother to me. Of course I could not help him as a voice, so we made a little pact. I would have his body, do that which he could not, and he would have eternal peace. A shame, but there you have it.'

'Is he dead? Answer me, damn you! Answer me!'

'No, he is not dead. He is here inside me, utterly aware of all that transpires. His cries of anguish are a great comfort to me. He and I have much to talk about. He is not really happy, I suppose, but I am unwilling to let him fade away. I enjoy our discussions too much. I don't suppose I will ever tire of them.'

Horus was appalled at this. But he said nothing. The daemon-Fulgrim had pledged its allegiance to him and it was patently a powerful entity. Best to keep it as an ally, he thought; and he certainly could not do without the Emperor's Children Legion at this juncture. However, Horus resolved to destroy the daemon and rescue Fulgrim from his torment when the time was apt. Horus and the daemon-Fulgrim agreed to keep its true nature to themselves. The daemon had no particular desire to reveal itself, and Horus was convinced that such a revelation would create many problems for him at this time.

Chemoscion – *Thomas Manning*

Fulgrim – *Sam Wood*

Vengeance – *John Gravato*

Antonin – *James Ryman*

Horus's Heresy

In the wake of the Dropsite Massacre, Horus convened a summit of his most senior officers to outline his plans for the forthcoming war. With him were the primarchs Mortarion, Fulgrim, Angron, Lorgar, Night Haunter, Perturabo and Alpharius; as well as the rebellious Fabricator-General Kelbor-Hal and various high-ranking Sons of Horus officers.

'We have achieved much, but there is still more for us to do. Our victory here will count for little if we do not press onwards. Now is the time for us to take the war to the Emperor himself. We are to make preparations for an invasion of Terra and an assault upon the Imperial Palace. This will be no easy task.'

The assembled warriors cheered as one. 'Aye! Victory for Horus! Death to the Emperor! Death to the Emperor!'

Horus outlined his plans. 'Night Haunter is to take his Legion to the planet of Tsagualsa within the Eastern Fringes. From this base he is to strike at the Imperial strongholds of Heroldar and Thramas. These two systems present a clear danger to our operation. If not dealt with they could provide the enemy with an opportunity to outflank us. Thramas, in particular, needs to be neutralised as the system contains a number of forge worlds which remain loyal to the Emperor. I have also received reports that the Dark Angels have been sighted in the sector. If these reports are true, you will have more than enough to worry about, Curze.'

Night Haunter winced at Horus's use of his near-forgotten former name, but nodded his understanding of the duty he had been given.

Horus addressed the traitor primarch Alpharius of the Alpha Legion.

'Alpharius. You have a vital duty to perform for me. Despite our glorious victory on the plains of Isstvan V, our enemy can yet call upon the services of a number of powerful Legions. I am sure that Lorgar's Word Bearers can keep Guilliman and his Ultramarines busy at Ultramar for some time to come, but I am concerned about those Legions rather closer to Terra. The White Scars have been operating in the Chondax System, close to Prospero where we know the Space Wolves have been active.

'The White Scars are almost at full strength and so represent a danger to us. We do not know what condition the Space Wolves are in after their attack on Prospero, but we must assume that they also could present a very real threat. Certainly, the two Legions together would be a grim alliance indeed.

'You must seek out and engage the White Scars Legion of Jaghatai Khan and the Space Wolves Legion of Leman Russ, and prevent them from joining forces.'

Horus turned his attention to the primarch Perturabo of the Iron Warriors.

'Master of Olympia, there is a large force of Imperial Fists making headway for the Isstvan System. Rogal Dorn despatched these troops to reinforce the Imperials on the third planet. Our allies within the warp have been able to delay their transit for many months – long enough that they can never complete their original mission, nor have they been able to participate in the battle here on Isstvan V. Now they must be dealt with. We cannot allow such a strong complement of Space Marines to infiltrate our space. They could seriously disrupt preparations for the attack on Terra.

'You must take your Legion to the Phall System where Dorn's loyalists are regrouping and smash them! Do not seek to fight a protracted battle against them. Cripple their fleet and eliminate their ability to manoeuvre! In the aftermath of our victory there, I will have need of your special skills – once we take Terra, the Palace fortifications will need to be repaired and bolstered lest any remaining Imperials try to win back what they will surely soon lose.'

The Bastion Wall – *John Gravato*

Ambush – *Neil Roberts*

Outflank – *Chris Trevas*

'The die is cast and I am set upon a course from which there is no turning. This is a frightful gamble that could result in my utter oblivion, or in the most fantastic triumph. But the Gods are with me, and I am sure that at my journey's end I will have usurped the throne of Terra and, for the sake of the human race, deposed the Emperor and taken his place as the one true Lord of the Galaxy.

'Some call me "traitor" and "heretic", but it is my destiny to rule the stars in the name of humanity. Am I not the greatest of the primarchs? The Emperor's first and most favoured son? Am I not therefore his chosen one? It is my right to rule, by natural law of succession, and by right of arms earned on a thousand battlefields. The mighty hosts of the Imperium call to me for leadership. The other primarchs and their Legions look to me for guidance. Only the Emperor stands between me and the throne of Terra. The time has come for me to seize that throne, and seize it I shall, for it is not my fate only that hangs in the balance.

'The lords of the warp have shown me a glimpse of the future fate of the Imperium if the Emperor is left to tinker with forces he cannot master. This future is a rotten place. Death and dishonour are the only medals the warriors of mankind can win in that dark time. It is a galaxy without hope for the sons of man. Foul aliens hold dominion over our worlds. The power of our glorious armies lay shattered by their numberless hordes, our peoples merely livestock decimated to sate their vile hungers. In this dark future, the ragged human masses do not have the strength to challenge their overlords, to fight against the terrors the universe has yet to unleash upon them. They meekly cower in their primitive hovels and pray to an uncaring god, a carrion lord, a master of despair. He will be an Emperor who does not hear their cries, who does not feel their pain, who does not sense their fears.

'Yes, the Emperor of Mankind will forsake his people. He will turn his back to them to win his place amongst the Gods. The Emperor cares only for himself. He is obsessed with his own power and glory. He has deceived his sons and followers. We have no place in his grand scheme. He has been biding his time, waiting for the opportunity to spurn us and ascend to godhood. Whilst we have fought war after war for him, he has been secretly building his power in the warp. The creatures of the warp are innocent pawns in his deadly game. They have assured me they have no interest in our affairs. They do not oppose him for nought. To them he is a hurricane, a whirlwind, a cosmic storm of destruction that threatens to rip them asunder. He has wounded them and they fight back as a wounded lion cornered in a cave. The great powers of the warp seek only respite from the Emperor's predations, and they have bargained with me to achieve that goal. I shall give them his head, and in return I will receive the galaxy to do with as I will.

'I am the saviour of the future. I am the one who will bring lasting glory to mankind. Only I can offer genuine hope to the masses of a future free from pain and servitude, free from death and dishonour.

'I am Horus. I am the Warmaster. I am the future Master of Mankind.'

Horus's Anger – *David Hudnut*

The Silent War

Legion of One – *Neil Roberts*

Malcador and Captain Garro

Malcador the Sigillite looked up at the two towering figures standing before him. They were the primarch Rogal Dorn of the Imperial Fists Legion, who Malcador knew well, and a Space Marine, wearing the heraldry of the Death Guard, who was unfamiliar to the Regent.

'These are dark days, Primarch Dorn. The Emperor will be pleased to learn his most loyal champion has returned to the Imperial Palace.'

'Thank you, Sigillite. My journey here has been fraught with peril. I am sure the Emperor will be unhappy with the news I carry with me. Let me introduce Garro, captain of the Death Guard Legion. We must speak with the Emperor on matters most grave.'

'The Emperor is… unavailable, he will not see you at this time. He has appointed me Regent in his stead. You must tell me everything.'

So Captain Garro told of the events at Isstvan III, and the treachery of Horus was revealed in all of its horror to Malcador.

Oath of Moment– *Neil Roberts*

The Sigil of Malcador – *John Gravato*

The Sigillite – *Neil Roberts*

Malcador meets with Rogal Dorn

Malcador the Sigillite and Rogal Dorn, Primarch of the Imperial Fists, met in council in the Imperial Palace on Terra.

'Primarch Dorn, you and I have known each other for many years. For longer than a normal man might count two lifetimes, we have been comrades and friends. We have faced many dangers in that time and have overcome them, but I fear we have now come to the end of the road. The treacherous Horus has broken his oath of loyalty to the Emperor, and in doing so has become the arch-enemy of the Imperium. We know he has the major part of four Space Marine Legions at his command, and if what Garro has told us is true, his heresy has embraced the Mechanicum of Mars, and who knows how many Imperial Commanders now side with him. We have had no news of Leman Russ's mission to Prospero, nor of Roboute's return to Ultramar. The fate of the Blood Angels is unknown and we cannot communicate with Lion El'Jonson of the Dark Angels. Your own Imperial Fists Legion has gone to confront the villain, but we have heard nothing and must assume the worst.

'We cannot easily penetrate the warp storms raging throughout the immaterium. We are virtually blind. Our forces are scattered across the galaxy and we receive daily reports of alien attacks and revolutions on worlds the length and breadth of the Imperium. For reasons I cannot divulge, the Emperor is locked away in his palace vault. I am not a warrior, I do not know what to do for the best. Of all of the primarchs, I value your opinion the most. Tell me what I should do.'

Malcador's Despair

Malcador was deeply saddened. That any Space Marine could betray his oath of loyalty to the Emperor was almost inconceivable to him. That four primarchs could do such a thing threatened to unhinge his mind and send him into madness. Of course, he knew that the primarchs were not perfect beings, that they argued with each other, that they were jealous of each other's triumphs, that they vied for power and prestige and that they even occasionally came to blows, but he never imagined that they would ever be anything other than absolutely loyal to the Emperor.

He never imagined that any of them could commit the heresy that Horus now seemed determined to carry out.

Malcador felt out of his depth. His life had been utterly devoted to the Emperor's service since their fateful meeting long years previously at the Sigillite Fortress, but he had never been a warrior or a general. His skills lay in administration and lawmaking, and although he shared a mysterious psychic bond with his master that no other could understand or rival, he was denied access to the Master of Mankind. Now his most fervent desire was that the Emperor would leave his secret work in the Palace vaults and take back command of the Imperium. But he knew this would not happen, and his heart sank.

'Fear not Sigillite. As long as I draw breath, this evil shall not conquer us. I, Rogal Dorn, Primarch of the Imperial Fists, most loyal champion of the Emperor, will not waver in the duty that now falls to me. I will not shirk from this fight. The traitor Horus and his misguided followers will rue the day they crossed swords with me.'

Rogal Dorn, the Emperor's Champion

Rogal Dorn had returned to Terra with the loyal Death Guard Captain Garro carrying dire news of Horus's traitorous actions at Isstvan III. Upon arrival, he had discovered that the Emperor was locked away in the Palace vaults working on some secret project and had appointed Malcador the Sigillite as Regent in his stead. The Regent had begged Dorn to take command of the still-loyal Legions and deal with Horus. Dorn accepted the duty and immediately began to organise the Imperial forces of Terra in preparation for the coming war.

Dorn's first task was to try and ascertain where each of the Space Marine Legions were situated. This was almost an impossible task as the continuing warp storms disrupted both travel and communications through the warp. Some astro-telepathy had been possible and some ships had been able to travel to the Solar System from outlying stars, but without the Emperor's mighty psychic powers to call upon, such endeavours were at best unreliable and threatened any who attempted them with mortal peril. Many sectors of the Imperium could not be contacted by Terra and the whereabouts of the majority of the Space Marine Legions could not be ascertained.

The primarch pressed Malcador for a solution to the warp storms.

'Malcador,' Rogal Dorn said, 'we must find a way to defeat these warp storms if we are to have any chance of success. If I can make contact with the other primarchs and combine all of our forces, we can crush Horus's rebellion with ease. He has only four Legions with him and we know that many of those Space Marines have fought against him. Even if we discount the Space Wolves of Russ and the Thousand Sons of Prospero we can match him with the strength of a dozen loyal Legions. But I need to talk to the primarchs. Is there a way to penetrate the storms?'

'Even as I speak, the Astronomican signal is being reinforced, Lord Dorn. Hundreds of new psykers are being attached to the machinery of the great beacon each day, but the death toll is horrendous. The harder we push them, the quicker they burn out and die. I'm not entirely sure how long we will be able to sustain the beacon at the increased level. We are making some progress, but time is against us and I have reason to suspect that matters are far worse than we could have possibly imagined.'

'Tell me more, Malcador.'

'These warp storms are not mere random energy fluctuations, they are being orchestrated by malign intelligence. I fear that Horus has struck some kind of alliance with the denizens of the warp. In fact, it is clear to me that he has made a pact with the Dark Gods themselves – he has cast his lot with evil and has become a Champion of Chaos!'

The Imperial Fists primarch, Rogal Dorn, was undeterred by Malcador's revelation about Horus and his alliance with the Ruinous Powers of the warp. It simply strengthened his resolve to fight and to win. That Horus had been corrupted by Chaos made sense of his betrayal and that of the other traitor primarchs. Mayhap Horus and the others had been possessed by daemons, he thought. Although the idea that a foul creature of the warp could best a primarch was anathema to Rogal Dorn, it was far more palatable than the thought that they might willingly have taken up arms against their fellow Space Marines and the Emperor.

It also made sense of the events on Prospero and the Emperor's prosecution of the Thousand Sons. If Magnus the Red and his Legion had been engaged in sorcerous practices, it was likely they could have been more easily possessed by daemons, he thought. Perhaps it started there, and it was through Magnus that the Warmaster had become corrupted and possessed, he reasoned. No matter, there will be time enough in the future to analyse the history of the infection. For the time being, the most important thing to do was to prepare a defence and plan for the fight against the Warmaster.

Again the primarch pressed Malcador for a way to defeat the warp storms and to contact the rest of the primarchs.

It was a mighty gamble. Each day hundreds of psykers died as their life energies were exhausted by the effort required to power the Astronomican's signal. Without constant recruitment of new psykers from the worlds of the Imperium, there would soon be no more psykers available for testing and harnessing to the great machine. If the beacon failed, then all communication and travel through the warp would become impossible.

But slowly and surely, the gamble began to pay off. With each passing day, the Astropathic Corps was able to process more and more signals from the distant star systems of the Imperium. Across the vastness of space, human worlds were able to communicate with each other, and with Terra. At long last, the first messages from some of the Space Marine Legions were interpreted and transmitted to the logic-engines of Malcador and Dorn's command centre.

Dorn and the Sigillite surveyed the reports in front of them. Every missive told the same tale. Across the Imperium war was raging. On countless worlds traitorous rebels were revolting against their loyal leaders and huge numbers of Imperial Commanders had declared for Horus and were denouncing the rule of the Emperor. Many of these traitor commanders were launching attacks against neighbouring loyal planets. The Mechanicum was split between loyalists and traitors, and even on Mars fighting had broken out between the two factions. The loyal tech-priests of Mars were calling on Terra for help to suppress the rebellion there. Even more disturbing were the reports of alien attacks against human worlds. As humanity was ripping itself apart, the alien races were rising up to feed on the carcass.

Malcador wept as he read one disastrous report after another. He could not take in the details of the reports, but the enormity of the threat to the Imperium was clear to him. If this rebellion could not be stopped then everything that the human race had worked to achieve over the last three centuries would be destroyed. Humanity would either perish by its own hand or would be devoured by a tide of alien insurgents, unable to mount anything more than a token resistance against the ghoulish hordes.

Dorn was more stoic. He fixated on the reports from the primarchs. Many of the Legions had still to be contacted, but those who had been able to send messages were eager to fight against the rebels. Dorn was quietly pleased by this. It seemed that the heresy of Horus had not infected any Legions other than those with the Warmaster in the Isstvan System.

After a time, Rogal Dorn took stock of the situation. After making contact with many of his fellow primarchs on various missions across the Imperium, a plan began to formulate in his mind as to the best course of action to take next. Of course, he still had major concerns about some issues that he could not resolve. The Ultramarines could not be contacted and he had severe regrets about not being able to call upon the skills of Roboute Guilliman – in his opinion the best strategist of all of the primarchs. The Dark Angels were also a problem. It transpired that Horus had previously ordered their primarch, Lion El'Jonson, on a mission but Dorn did not know what this was or where the Lion had gone. A contingent of the Dark Angels Legion had been left on station at their home world of Caliban, and this world was now reporting that it was in the midst of a civil uprising. Of the fate of the Space Wolves and the Thousand Sons, Dorn simply had no information, and it appeared that Sanguinius and most of the Blood Angels had simply vanished from the face of the galaxy.

Further difficulties bothered the golden primarch. The Emperor was still closeted in

Rogal Dorn – *John Blanche*

his Palace vaults and would not – or could not – grant him an audience. Dorn struggled to understand what could possibly be more important to the Emperor at this time than the danger facing the Imperium. Malcador the Sigillite had counselled him to have faith in the Emperor and trust that he had not abandoned them. Unfortunately, the Emperor had also taken the Custodian Guard into the vaults and their might was denied to Dorn. Whatever operation he was to command would have to do without the Emperor's elite bodyguard.

Finally, the revolt on Mars was growing and the loyal tech-priests there were desperate for help from Terra. The loyalists had revealed to Malcador's astropaths that the Space Marine armour manufacturing facilities on Mars were being specifically targeted by the traitors.

The primarch of the Imperial Fists convened a meeting of the most senior officers and staff present on Terra. Among the various dignitaries and soldiers were Malcador the Sigillite, Imperial Regent, and Captain Sor Talgron of the Word Bearers Legion.

'We have little time for formalities, so let's get straight to it,' Dorn said. 'Our first duty is to send a task force to Mars to protect the Imperial munitions and materiel facilities. Mars is too close to Earth to allow the rebels to establish a base there. Furthermore, the Martian factories contain massive stocks of Space Marine armour of a new design. These improved suits cannot be allowed to fall into the hands of the traitors. My four companies of Imperial Fists veterans will lead this task force. The balance of the brigade will be drawn from the sundry regiments of Imperial Army and auxiliary units we have stationed on Terra and the moons of Saturn and Jupiter. The task force have their orders and are making headway to Mars as we speak. The new armour suits are to be evacuated and distributed to loyal Legions as a top priority.'

Sor Talgron interrupted the primarch: 'My lord, would it not be more advisable to send all of the available Space Marines to Mars? I have forty companies of Word Bearers eager to fight at my command.'

'No. I have a far greater honour for your troops, lord commander. We must stop this heresy at its source. Your Word Bearers, in concert with as many other Legions as we can muster, are to be ordered to the Isstvan System to confront the traitor himself. You are going to find and destroy Horus and his fellow renegades!

'In addition to the Word Bearers contingent, I have been able to contact six loyal primarchs within striking distance of the traitors. Thus, the following Legions have been ordered to rendezvous at the Isstvan System: the Iron Warriors, the Night Lords, the Iron Hands, the Salamanders, the Raven Guard and the Alpha Legion. Together with the Word Bearers, these Legions will launch a pre-emptive strike against the traitor and his cowardly minions. Ferrus Manus of the Iron Hands will command the assault. It seems that we will be able to re-supply all of our attacking forces with the improved suits of power armour from the stocks we have on Terra and those we will repatriate from Mars. Our loyal forces outnumber the traitors, will be better equipped than them, and we fight for a just cause.

'The White Scars Legion of Jaghatai Khan is too distant from Isstvan to participate in the attack and so I have ordered him to Terra forthwith. As and when I can contact the remaining primarchs, I will have a better understanding of their status and potential course of action.

'Intelligence we have gathered indicates that Horus has established his headquarters on the barren planet designated as Isstvan V. Mark the name well, my friends – future generations will honour it as the place where the Emperor's vengeance was done on those who would betray him.'

Malcador's Chosen – *Dave Millgate*

Alpha-Theta 11 – *Wayne England*

Malcador's Doubts

The Imperial Regent Malcador met with Rogal Dorn in secret.

'Friend Dorn, I have some doubts about the way events have transpired. I feel I must voice these concerns to you. It may have some bearing on what you are intending to do. My primary concerns are the warp storms and the fact that we have been able to overcome them these past days.'

'Surely this can only be a good thing, Sigillite. After all, the cost of reinforcing the Astronomican signal has been the blood of many innocents. You cannot now tell me that their sacrifice was in vain.'

'That remains to be seen. I fear the worst. Despite all of the efforts to boost the power of the Great Beacon, and the huge toll of lives this has entailed, we should not have been able to repair our communications so quickly. Some external force has acted upon the warp, aiding our efforts to navigate through it and to send messages across the void of space.'

'I do not see why you think this a threat. Perhaps this is the secret work the Emperor is doing. Who else has the power to do such a thing? Have faith, Malcador. Look upon this turn of events as a blessing. Trust in the might of the Master of Mankind!'

'I truly hope you are correct, primarch, but my doubts remain. If it is the enemy who is manipulating the currents of the immaterium, it would bode ill for the mission your Legions are about to embark upon. They could be heading into a carefully planned trap.'

War in the Shadows

From the moment that Horus's treachery became known to him, Malcador began his covert war of information and propaganda against the traitors. The Sigillite maintained a wide network of sleeper agents and spies across the galaxy, and it was now that he started to activate them. As reports started to flow to Malcador from the myriad worlds of the Imperium, huge sections of the Imperial Palace were repurposed to house the staff needed to organise them. Yet despite the incredible volume of information collected and codified by his agents, it was still maddeningly unclear to Malcador what was happening.

Disturbances in the warp were making it increasingly hard to communicate with the outlying systems – in some cases, contact had become impossible. The Sigillite redoubled his efforts to pursue this Silent War against Horus. For millions of people on Terra and throughout the Solar System, this battle of intelligence-gathering was the first hint of the coming war that came to be known later as the Horus Heresy.

Malcador's secretive espionage and the vast resources he devoted to it eventually brought him into conflict with Rogal Dorn. The Imperial Fists primarch was staunchly military in his reaction to the unfolding events, and all of his solutions were solidly pragmatic. He had no stomach or patience for the kind of activity that the Sigillite was engaged in – Dorn's energies were focused on preparing Terra's military defences for the attack that he was sure Horus would launch against the Imperial throne-world.

So did the two great champions of the Imperium find themselves at odds with each other, and inadvertently began to divide their efforts and the resources of Terra. It is true that they were both working towards the same goal, but they frequently worked at cross-purposes. Dorn would seek to strengthen the armour and weapons of the Imperium, blockading Mars and fortifying Terra, while Malcador would send emissaries to steal back secrets, assassinate traitor leaders or recover lost artefacts. Communication between Malcador and Dorn became less frequent as they threw themselves into their respective tasks. Without regular contact, with decreasing coordination of their efforts and with resources becoming more scarce by the day, it was inevitable that mistakes and misunderstandings would occur. Key resources would be redeployed without warning, important materials would mysteriously go missing or be reallocated to a different department. The situation became so confused and damaging that enemy subterfuge was presumed to be the cause of much that was going wrong.

Nemesis – *Neil Roberts*

Burden of Duty – *Neil Roberts*

Knights Errant

Some of Malcador's most powerful agents in his Silent War against the traitors were the elite group of Space Marines who were known as the Knights Errant. These warriors were mostly recruited in secret from within the ranks of the loyal Legions to serve the Sigillite directly. The specific criteria by which a Space Marine was marked for service as a Knight Errant were known only to Malcador, as indeed were their duties and the missions with which they were tasked.

Upon returning to Terra to warn of the betrayal of Horus, Nathaniel Garro of the Death Guard Legion was kept in isolation and subjected to many tests and trials. Eventually he was judged worthy by Malcador and was inducted into the ranks of the Knights Errant – indeed he was appointed as the *Agentia Primus*.

Thereafter, Garro travelled with the authority of the Sigillite. His mission was to scour the galaxy in search of certain Space Marines named by Malcador's plans, and to covertly recruit them into the secretive organisation.

Garro was not alone. Many others were called upon by Malcador to serve in this way, among them men such as Iacton Qruze, Tylos Rubio and Macer Varren. There are no records of exactly how many Space Marines were recruited to serve in the Knights Errant, and for all those known it seems that countless more were lost either by chance or by the hazards of the galactic war.

A high proportion of the Space Marines recruited to the Knights Errant were former Librarians in their parent Legions, or at least had a propensity for latent psychic talent. This became particularly important to the Sigillite as the war progressed and he was made aware of the influence of Chaos: individuals possessing psychic powers, with appropriate training and preparation, were a powerful weapon in the fight against the daemonic forces of the warp.

So it was that the Knights Errant did invaluable duty in Malcador's covert war. It was from their ranks that Malcador also selected the eight champions whom he would later present to the Emperor as part of his continuing preparations for the defence of the Imperium.

A Dark Mechanicum

Horus had been busy in the months leading up to the incident on Isstvan III. He had despatched agents to dozens of forge worlds to secretly agitate on his behalf. The forge worlds were sovereign to the Mechanicum of Mars, the ancient order of tech-priests, with whom the Emperor had struck an alliance at the start of the Great Crusade.

Forge masters, senior adepts of the Martian priesthood, ruled the worlds of the Mechanicum. Horus's agents used subtlety and deceit to convince them to side with the Warmaster in the coming struggle against the Emperor. Within the Mechanicum, a schism had developed. Some tech-priests regarded the Emperor as the living manifestation of their Machine God. Others thought this a blasphemy, and that the Machine God was still entombed beneath the red sands of Mars. The agents of Chaos suggested that it was the Emperor himself who had presented himself as their god in order to strike a bargain with the Mechanicum that served him and him alone.

Horus's deceitful spies spoke to the forge masters of the Emperor's hidden plans to turn on the Mechanicum, steal their secrets, enslave the tech-priests and seize their machines. For many of the forge masters, this was a prospect they could not bear to countenance, and they assented to support Horus. When the time came, these forge worlds would declare for Horus, and the Emperor's fate would be sealed.

Having won the tech-priests to Horus's side, his agents then began to entice the forge masters with the promise of power such as only the dark forces of Chaos could offer. The silver tongues of the Warmaster's agents were subtle about this: a hint here, a gentle suggestion there. Slowly but surely, one by one, the forge masters fell under the spell of Chaos. It was the rise of the Dark Mechanicum!

Soulforge – *Neil Roberts*

The Fall of Mars

Rogal Dorn had ordered his four companies of Imperial Fists veterans to Mars to aid the loyalist faction of the Mechanicum and secure the munitions factories from falling into the hands of the traitors. The Imperial Fists led a large force drawn from various Imperial Army garrisons scattered across the Solar System. First Captain Sigismund was in command, with fellow captain Camba-Diaz as his second.

The initial phase of the action had gone well for the loyalists and they successfully secured a swathe of territory across the northern hemisphere of the planet. Within this arc of loyalist control lay the important munitions factories of Mondus Gamma and Mondus Occullum. Within these two vast industrial complexes, the Mechanicum fabricated the weaponry and power armour for the Space Marines.

It was a temporary victory. The loyalist Mechanicum faction was much smaller than had been guessed at by those on Terra. The loyalist forces on Mars found themselves to be massively outnumbered. In addition to the greater portion of tech-priests, the traitors could also call upon the services of seven Titan Legions. Within hours of securing the munitions factories, the loyalists were being pressed back. It was clear that they could not win this battle.

Camba-Diaz ordered an emergency evacuation. Barely a thousand loyal warriors were able to escape from the planet's surface before the factories fell into the hands of the traitors. The desperate rearguard action of the loyalists and the sacrifice of many thousands of lives at least secured the shipment off-world of many tens of thousands of newly fabricated Space Marine armour suits.

Mechanicum – *Neil Roberts*

Rogal Dorn Assumes Command

The primarch of the Imperial Fists Legion had been charged with commanding the defence of Terra. Dorn and his confidants feared the worst regarding the fate of the seven Legions they had sent against the Warmaster. These fears were more than realised when the first communiqué from Isstvan V finally reached Terra and told of what had happened there.

It reported the betrayal of the Iron Warriors, Alpha Legion, Word Bearers and Night Lords Legions. It also told of the death of Ferrus Manus, struck down and beheaded by the treacherous Fulgrim.

In the wake of the Dropsite Massacre on Isstvan V, as the full horror of what had transpired there became clear to him, Rogal Dorn realised he had to do everything he possibly could to bolster the Earth's defences. The traitors had won control of Mars, from where the enemy forces could easily strike at the very heart of the Imperium. Worse still, the battle to try and wrest control of Mars from the rebels had all but exhausted Dorn's available Space Marine units. Ancient Terra, capital world of the Imperium and seat of the Emperor's Palace, was dangerously exposed.

Dorn had no choice but to assume that the Legions not involved in the massacre at Isstvan V remained loyal to the Emperor. Of these, the White Scars of Jaghatai Khan were the closest Legion and had already been ordered to return to Terra prior to the launch of the ill-fated Isstvan mission. The Imperial Fists primarch sent Jaghatai an urgent message impressing upon him the need to not let anything prevent him from getting his Legion to Earth. Similar communications were despatched to Leman Russ, Sanguinius, Roboute Guilliman and Lion El'Jonson, ordering them to move to Terra with some urgency. There was no way Dorn could know if any of them received these orders.

Dorn also continually tried to recall the rest of his own Legion, which had been attempting to reinforce the loyalists on Isstvan III. He had no knowledge of their progress or current status. The primarch pleaded with Malcador to do everything he could to make contact with his warriors.

The Astronomican Crisis

The Astronomican had been constructed to focus the Emperor's fathomless psychic powers into a psychic navigational beam that lanced through the otherworldly dimension known as the warp. This beacon was the only thing that enabled long-range warp-jumps to be made. Without the Astronomican, it would be impossible for the Imperium to function. Mankind would be plunged into a new Age of Strife, the human worlds cast adrift in space at the mercy of predatory aliens and other dangerous entities.

And the Astronomican was failing!

Malcador the Sigillite requested an audience with the Emperor. In the dark bowels of the Palace vaults they met.

'Why do you disturb my labours, Sigillite? Outside of these dungeons I have given you powers of regent. I trust your judgement in all things. I do not have time for any more disturbances. What peril is there that you cannot deal with yourself?'

'Forgive me, my lord, but the Astronomican is failing. Is it your desire that now we should let its light be extinguished? Are your plans so far progressed that I need not worry about so calamitous an event as this?'

'No, you are right to worry. It is too soon, far too soon. The light must be kept burning until I complete the project. Damn Magnus the Red! Since his untimely interference, my psychic might is needed to stave off a grave threat to my work here. Even my vast power is not great enough to deal with this issue and fuel the Astronomican's beacon.'

'My lord, it has been many months since any have undergone the soul-binding ritual. As we speak, there are thousands of psykers in holding cells awaiting an audience with you. Could we not utilise their talents in service of the great beacon?'

'This could only be a temporary solution. Their powers are insignificant measured against my own. I would still need to provide the correct modulations and frequencies for the beam and the effort of powering the beacon would quickly strip their life essence from them. You would have to recruit many tens of thousands to this sacrificial duty. Still, it would provide me with some respite and allow me to complete the task at hand.'

'Great Emperor, the lives of even a million innocents are but a small price to pay for the safe future your project promises Mankind.'

'This is a dreadful sacrifice for us to make, but so be it! I command you to make this terrible thing happen, Malcador.'

Malcador worked quickly to adapt the workings of the Astronomican so that the collective power of thousands of human psykers could be utilised in place of the Emperor's matchless might.

Thousands of psykers were taken from their holding cells where they had been awaiting the testing of the soul-binding ritual. Each psyker was wired into the huge construct that is the Astronomican, and its arcane technology amplified and focused their weird powers into the resonating harmonics of the mighty beacon. It was a death sentence; all were fated to give their lives to the vast machine. The lucky ones died quickly, within a few hours of being attached to the Astronomican. The less fortunate suffered a lingering death lasting many months.

The Sigillite was hopeful that the newly reinforced energy of the beacon would cut through the rising storms within the warp, so that he could re-establish contact with the primarchs and confirm their loyalty to the Emperor, and also secure travel and communication across the Imperium.

The Outcast Dead – *Neil Roberts*

Signus Prime

Fear to Tread – *Neil Roberts*

Daemons of Chaos

The ruinous powers of Chaos were frothing at the bit. They wanted to join Horus's campaign, destroy the Emperor and gain unfettered access to the material world. For too long they had been restricted to only temporary sojourns in the realm of Mankind, unable to claim a more permanent foothold.

The Eye of Terror offered them a tantalising glimpse of what could be. This strange region is a giant gateway between the dimensions, a place where the warp and the material world intermingle. The worlds within the Eye are fabulous monuments to the glory of Chaos; ever-changing, violent and strange. But the daemons of Chaos cannot freely travel beyond the Eye's confines.

Similar portals are scattered across the galaxy, but none so big or so permanent as the great Eye of Terror. The majority of these holes in space have only a fleeting existence before they collapse back into the warp, taking great chunks of the material world with them. In this fashion, many worlds have been sucked into the warp.

Outside the Eye of Terror, the daemons of Chaos have to resort to possession to enter the material world, or rely on powerful psychic conjurations. One method by which a Chaos daemon can sustain a presence in the material world is to possess a psyker. Every time a psyker utilises his talents, a tiny portal is opened to the warp. This offers a chance for the creatures of the aether to enter the material world through the psyker's brain. Those of strong will and training are able to resist such predations. The weak-willed and untrained are easy prey. Possession eventually destroys the host, leaving only a withered, hideously disfigured husk, and the daemon is wrenched back into the immaterium.

The other way in which Chaos daemons can exist in the material world is through summoning. A powerful psyker with the correct knowledge and suitable safeguards in place can open a portal between the realms, allowing a daemon to enter the material world. Such summonings are fraught with danger, the conjurer at grave risk of being possessed. A large, powerful group of psykers can cooperate to open a gateway large enough for many daemons to traverse the dimensions. As long as the summoning spell is maintained, the daemons can survive in the material world indefinitely.

Yria the Seducer – *John Gravato*

Delial – *Dan Wheaton*

Fell Reavers – *Karl Richardson*

Harriers of Signus – *John Gravato*

Seducers – *Chris Dien*

Kyriss the Perverse – *Adrian Smith*

Ravagers of Signus – *John Gravato*

Sanguinius Betrayed

Horus the Warmaster, commander of all the Emperor's armies, ordered the primarch Sanguinius to the Signus Cluster – a tri-star system of the Ultima Segmentum near to the galactic rim. His Legion, the Blood Angels, were to cleanse the worlds and moons of Signus of alien invaders and release the humans thereon from their xeno-overlords.

Sanguinius had no reason to doubt Horus. In fact, he greatly admired the Warmaster and had fought many campaigns at his side. Their relationship was so close that it had even incited jealousy amongst their brother primarchs on occasion. Sanguinius was relishing the opportunity to once again prove the value of their bond.

The Blood Angels duly set course for Signus, unaware that they were heading into the most foul of traps. Unbeknownst to Sanguinius, the Signus System had been infested by Chaos. Kyriss the Perverse, Greater Daemon of Slaanesh, and his daemonic host now ruled Signus.

Ferveus – *Kenson Low*

Clonatus – *Jon Hodgson*

Madidus – *Michael Phillippi*

Hermia – *Justin Norman*

Signus Daemonicus

For untold generations, the Signus Cluster had been a centre for human civilisation. Great cities littered the worlds of the system and huge industrial complexes burrowed into the surfaces of their moons.

But amongst the uncounted millions on Signus lurked sinister cultists of Chaos. Agents sent to the world by Horus from Davin and other cult worlds infested the rabble, and in their numbers hid the witch-cabals that had summoned the daemons to Signus. When they received a signal from Horus, they rose up in violent insurrection and seized power. Chaos daemons stalked the hives and established foul palaces across the entire system. The human population was enslaved, reduced to fodder for the minions of Chaos. Powerful summoning spells by the witch-cabals allowed the daemons free reign over Signus. In addition to this, thousands of psykers had been possessed.

Signus had become a realm of Chaos and a domain of daemons. Kyriss the Perverse, Greater Daemon of Slaanesh, ruled the Signus System. All were in thrall to this mighty daemon and his teeming hordes.

The daemons were aided by the machinations of Chaos cultists. These bands of madmen opened their worlds to the creatures of the warp, conjuring powerful summoning spells and offering themselves up for possession. The rest of the human population of Signus had been annihilated or enslaved, their fate to be consumed by the horrors from the warp.

The entire system became a charnel house, a place of evil and a home for daemons. Horus set his trap and into it rode the Blood Angels, the unwitting Sanguinius at the fore. There was never so base a betrayal as this – Sanguinius looked to Horus as a brother, and he never would have believed that he could be sacrificed to the foul denizens of the warp.

The Blood Angels fleet was assaulted as it entered Signus. Malevolent energies surged across the void, attacking the minds of the psychically-sensitive crews. Navigators and astropaths were crippled or killed in the initial onslaught, their brains fried by the dark malice of Chaos. The iron will and training of the Space Marines protected them from this attack, although some did succumb to madness.

Panic spread through the Blood Angels fleet as the non-Space Marine crews and auxiliaries faced the fury of Chaos for the first time in their lives. Kyriss sent an image of himself to Sanguinius, declaring ownership of Signus in the name of Slaanesh and challenging the primarch to take it back from him.

As the ships' klaxons blared out their warnings, Sanguinius and his Space Marines took control of the situation. They quickly erected psychic baffles and restrained deranged crewmen. Unbowed, Sanguinius and his senior officers planned their counterattack. Despite the fact that they had never before fought against such a foe, the Blood Angels were sure that they would prevail.

'This foul creature will know what it is to face my wrath. I shall strike him down, I shall be an Angel of Vengeance!'

Furies – *Wayne England*

Sanguinius, the Angel – *John Blanche*

Blood Feud – *Jon Hodgson*

Hengist – *Mark Poole*

Traitor's Gambit – *Chris Trevas*

Ka'bandha – *Dan Wheaton*

Cathedral of the Mark – *Neil Roberts*

The Blooding of Signus

In a few short months, the daemon host of Kyriss of Slaanesh and his deluded cultist allies undid hundreds of years of civilisation. Entire planets were ravaged: the verdant plains of Scoltrum burned to a cinder, the towering mega-hives of Holst razed, the ocean world of Ta-Loc boiled and the planets of Kol, Phorus and Signus Tertiary were utterly destroyed. Millions died as the daemons ran riot across the system, millions more were corralled into vast prison camps to await their doom. Foul runes of Chaos marked the capital hives of Signus Prime as each greater daemon staked a claim in the name of their patron god.

Despite the crippling assault he had endured, the primarch and his loyal troops counterattacked, launching a series of attacks across the planet of Signus Prime. On the Plains of the Damned, the ferocious Space Marines confronted vast hordes of deranged human cultists and packs of monstrous daemons.

Sanguinius had sworn to personally confront and vanquish the perverted Kyriss and led his elite companies to besiege the Cathedral of the Mark – the daemon's defiled palace.

The planet of Signus Prime was awash with blood. The blood of loyal Space Marines, cut down in their thousands by the foul hordes of Kyriss, mixed with the blood of multitudes of slain cultists, traitorous allies of the daemonic rulers of Signus, and the sickening remnants of banished daemons. The Plains of the Damned burned as the Blood Angels forced their way into the very heart of the daemon's realm. Amongst the serried ranks of the cultists stalked packs of Chaos daemons, howling in triumph as they fell upon isolated bands of Space Marines to rend them limb from limb, then screeching in fear as they in turn were torn apart by the ferocity of the Blood Angels' counter-charge.

Sanguinius ordered his Legion to strike for the Cathedral of the Mark, where he could confront and destroy Kyriss of Slaanesh, and thence reclaim the planet in the name of the Emperor. Space Marines, Chaos daemons and insane human cultists were locked in bloody conflict. On the battlefield of Signus, Sanguinius faced Ka'bandha, Greater Daemon of Khorne. The mighty Bloodthirster stood before the besmirched and defiled Cathedral of the Mark.

'Why do you fight us, so-called angel? You may be able to best me, but you cannot hope to defeat Chaos. My Lord Khorne is powerful beyond any means you can measure. Your Emperor is weak and foolish; even now he hides from us. Is he afraid to fight?'

'Begone, daemon! I would deal only with your master, Kyriss. Be gone, or I shall cut you down.'

'Kyriss is no master of mine, little angel. I answer only to Khorne. Blood for the Blood God! You have no idea how powerful we are. Our faithful ally Horus set this trap for you and even now is preparing to attack Terra with his Legions. You are a creature of blood as much as I am. Join with me, join with Khorne! You can be his most exalted champion. Together we can defeat the pervert Kyriss and rule these worlds in the name of the Blood God!'

'Horus is your ally? But he is the Warmaster, and my friend. This cannot be true. I will not believe your lies, daemon. There is nothing you can say that would entice me to cast aside my oath of loyalty to the Emperor. I will destroy you and all of your foul kin!'

Enraged by the daemon's taunts and fearing his claims to be true, the angelic primarch launched himself at the towering monster before him. At his side were the elite of his Legion, companies of veterans, Dreadnoughts and Terminator squads. The daemon was surrounded by a massive horde of bloodletters, hounds and furies. The two forces engaged.

The fight was fierce and bloody, the carnage appalling. Hellblades sliced through power armour and bone, daemon fangs pierced Space Marine flesh, arcing plasma fire boiled daemon blood, power swords split daemon skulls. The bloodthirster staggered back under a rain of blows from Sanguinius's great sword. He swung his huge axe back and forth to deflect the primarch's attacks. The clash of sword against axe rang across the battlefield, a death knell for the fallen.

Sanguinius seized the initiative, his frenzy taking the Bloodthirster by surprise; his sword stabbed into the daemon's chest, ripping open a gaping wound. The massive creature roared in pain and anger and lashed his whip at the primarch's legs. Sanguinius was momentarily unbalanced as his legs were crushed in the whip's coils. The daemon smashed him to the ground with the flat of his axe. The winged hero was stunned, helpless before the daemon's wrath. As his vision cleared, he looked up at the mighty monster towering over him.

'Come at me again, daemon! Feel the lick of my sword a second time if you dare!'

Ka'bandha looked down on the wounded primarch. 'I let you live this time, manling. Your legs will heal, but this wound will always fester.'

At this, the beast let out a mighty bellow and flashed across the battlefield, cutting a huge swathe through the ranks of the Blood Angels with his great axe. Five hundred Space Marines died a horrible death as their bodies were torn apart. The psychic backlash of so many of his sons dying so suddenly blasted Sanguinius into unconsciousness. The Blood Angels were leaderless, their fate to be decided…

Angels and Daemons – *Neil Roberts*

Gida'ljal – *Michael Phillippi*

Horsa – *Dave Millgate*

Vinaeum – *Dan Scott*

Barabas – Al *Eremin*

Leonatus – *Justin Norman*

Crimson Spectre – *Rick Sardinha*

Amicus – *Ed Cox*

Cloten – *Eric Ren*

Raldoron – *Ed Cox*

Vallerus – *John Gravato*

Saevin – *Wayne England*

The Angel Sanguinius

Signus Prime was a charnel house. The occupying daemonic horde had enslaved or murdered the indigenous population and had made no effort to clear away the millions of corpses that littered the streets of its once-thriving cities and townships. Added to this unspeakable carnage were the broken bodies of thousands of dead Space Marines – Blood Angels who had been drawn into a trap of Horus's devising.

Even worse for the Blood Angels was the fall of Sanguinius, their angelic primarch. The winged primarch had fought a bloody aerial duel with a mighty daemonic lord of Khorne as his warriors battled a daemon army on the field below. Sanguinius had dealt the creature a terrible wound and in response the greater daemon had crushed his legs, cast him to the ground and with a howl had slaughtered nearly five companies of the Blood Angels as it fled the scene. The trauma of this act of malevolence had stunned the primarch into unconsciousness.

An army of ordinary men faced with such events would have surely been swiftly defeated. However, Space Marines are by no means normal men and the Blood Angels did not falter. Rather, they redoubled their efforts to banish the daemon horde. Filled with vengeful fury, the Legion fought as it had never fought before. The Blood Angels went berserk, and in their mania they smashed the daemons asunder.

The Blood Angels Legion had all but annihilated the daemonic horde of Signus Prime. In a berserk fury, unmindful of any personal injury, the Space Marines had swept across the planet destroying any daemon, mutant or cultist they could find. The brutal violence of the daemon Ka'bandha had unleashed something dark within the psyche of the Space Marines, a thirst for blood that would not be slaked until every taint of Chaos had been erased from the planet. The Blood Angels were unstoppable, the hordes of Chaos could not resist them and they crumbled before them.

As the planet was cleansed, the rage of the Blood Angels subsided. Their fury ebbed and they slowly began to realise that they had won a great victory. The daemonic horde and its cultist allies had been utterly destroyed – those daemons they had not killed had fled back into the immaterium. Even the mighty Kyriss of Slaanesh, self-proclaimed master of Signus, had been banished.

The Blood Angels freed Signus from its thrall – but they had little stomach for celebrating. The cost of victory was far higher than any could have wished. Hundreds upon hundreds of Blood Angels had been killed in the fighting, their primarch lay broken upon the ground and the berserker rage they experienced had left a brooding shadow on their souls.

The Angel Sanguinius was a primarch, and as such he had powers and abilities beyond even those of his Space Marine warriors. Created ages ago in the furnace of the Emperor's laboratories, and forged through myriad trials of battle, he and his fellow primarchs bestrode the galaxy like gods. Even as Sanguinius regained consciousness, his crushed legs were beginning to heal. The pain was excruciating, but was as nothing compared to the searing anguish he felt as he remembered the heinous slaughter of his troops at the hands of the fell daemon Ka'bandha.

Within a few days the Angel was able to walk, though not without discomfort. The physical pain was nothing to him, but the agony in his heart would not abate. As his legs grew stronger and the pain from them slowly subsided, he noticed a change in his Blood Angels. When he had first woken from his comatose state a dark mood was upon the Legion. The Space Marines were sullen

Orexis – *Carl Frank*

and despairing. Now, despite the trauma they had only recently suffered, they had regained their composure and optimism. Sanguinius thought that his Blood Angels must be affecting this brighter mood to help him, since his own thoughts were dark and torrid, his mood grim. Whatever befell him in the future, he vowed to himself that he would have his vengeance on the daemon Ka'bandha.

The Blood Angels fully understood the gravity of the situation facing the Imperium. This was a war that would decide the fate of the galaxy. That the fighting would be hard and that yet more of the Legion's precious blood would be spilled was also clear. But Sanguinius and his warriors wanted to be rid of Signus – the place held only dark memories for them and they yearned for vengeance against those who had set the trap into which they had fallen.

Sanguinius immediately gave orders to his commanders to prepare for the evacuation of Signus. The last of the Blood Angels' corpses had been stowed aboard the fleet – they would receive honourable burial on the slopes of Mount Seraph on Baal Secundus. Sanguinius ordered that nothing of the Legion remain on Signus, or any of the other planets and moons of the system. There would be no memorial, no mausoleum, no gravestone and no inscription there to tell of what had happened to the Legion. The scarce few surviving indigenous people of the system were arranged passage to nearby human systems. Warning beacons were stationed at the warp-jump points to ward off any future unwary visitors from setting foot on any of the planets or moons. Signus would be left dark, lifeless and rotting.

And so Sanguinius and the Blood Angels returned to the light of the Imperium.

Sanguinius Triumphant – *David Hudnut*

Calth

Know No Fear – *Neil Roberts*

The Secret Treachery of Lorgar

Long before the events on Isstvan III and the heresy of Magnus the Red, Lorgar had secretly committed himself and his Space Marines to the service of the Ruinous Powers. Lorgar was a puritanical, religious zealot. It is said that he experienced visions in which he foresaw the coming of the Emperor. The ancient scriptures of Colchis foretold the coming of a messiah, and Lorgar was convinced that this was indeed the Emperor. A series of bitter religious wars ensued as Lorgar fought to impose his doctrine on the planet. When the Emperor did come to Colchis, the entire world was in thrall to Lorgar and his Cult of the Emperor.

Lorgar praised the Emperor and the people of Colchis rejoiced. The Emperor was dismayed. He had long rejected claims to his own divinity. He wished only to unite Lorgar with the Word Bearers Legion, and for Lorgar to join him in his Great Crusade.

Lorgar assumed the role of primarch but continued his worship of the Emperor, schooling his new charges in this faith. He set about his new duties with relish. He created Chaplains who were schooled in the doctrines of Colchis and the Cult of the Emperor. The Word Bearers, for a time, were the Emperor's most strident supporters and Lorgar his most zealous believer.

However, as time went on, the Emperor grew increasingly frustrated with Lorgar's persistent claims of his divinity and the Word Bearers' desire to leave no stone unturned in their quest to promulgate the Cult of the Emperor. In his zeal, Lorgar perpetrated terrible acts in the name of the Emperor. Entire worlds were punished for not demonstrating sufficient piety.

As the Great Crusade progressed, the relationship between the Emperor and Lorgar soured. Lorgar was determined to promote the Emperor's supposed divinity and had taken to sermonising on every human world he conquered or visited. Much valuable time was lost as Lorgar ordered the construction of cathedrals to the Emperor on each of the worlds he had conquered. It appeared to the Emperor that Lorgar was more concerned with preaching than with pursuing the military objectives with which he had been tasked.

The Emperor was also dismayed that Lorgar was becoming ever more merciless with those who refused to accept the Emperor as a god. He was brutal and oppressive in pursuit of righteousness. Religious pogroms characterised the Word Bearers' endeavours on the worlds they conquered. Many innocents died at the hands of Lorgar's Legion for refusing to accept the divinity of the Emperor, and those who were not considered devout enough were killed.

The Emperor reproached Lorgar and informed him that his mission was not for faith, but for battle. Whilst Lorgar was occupying his time with useless displays of piety, human worlds across the galaxy were suffering under the yoke of alien oppression. This was not what the Emperor desired. He did not intend his Great Crusade to be perverted in this way. The Emperor's mission was to *save* humanity, not to enslave it! The Emperor ordered Lorgar to cease his religious activities and renounce his belief that the Emperor was divine.

'You take my name in vain, Lorgar. I demand loyalty from you, not worship. My mission – *our* mission – is to lead humanity out of the Dark Age of Strife and into a new dawn. There are horrors enough in the galaxy, dark forces that seek to pervert our actions and hamper our cause, without us adding to the grief of mankind. Your zeal does me great harm. I am no god and have no desire for the multitudes to see me as one. Humanity must put aside superstition and fear. I put my faith in science and logic, as should you!

'Look to Roboute Guilliman of the Ultramarines. He has faith in excess. He has faith that our mission is holy, not I. His example is the one I would command you to follow!'

Lorgar appeared contrite and retreated to his command ship. For a month, he did nothing. His Legion sat idle, waiting for their orders. Just when it seemed that the Emperor would have to speak with him again, Lorgar sprang into action. The Word Bearers began a campaign that was remarkable for its speed and destructiveness. It appeared that Lorgar had taken the Emperor's words to heart and was now doing what he had been ordered to do.

The Word Bearers pursued their new objectives with an energy and vitality that surprised and delighted the Emperor. It appeared that Lorgar had learned his lesson well.

The truth was sadly different. The Emperor's words had shocked Lorgar so deeply that he had retreated to his private chambers to try to resolve the deep conflicts within him. At first, he would admit no one to his presence, in the hope that contemplative solitude would bring him the answers he so desperately needed. When this failed, he turned to his most devout followers. Kor Phaeron of Colchis had been the first to cast

The First Heretic – *Neil Roberts*

Aurelian – *Neil Roberts*

doubt on the Emperor and his motives. If the Emperor would not accept their worship, there were others who would, he argued. It was First Chaplain Erebus who first uttered the names of the Ruinous Powers. Were these not the true Gods of Colchis, to whom they had sworn fealty before the false-god Emperor had tricked Lorgar with a false vision? Lorgar had found his answer. The Emperor had deliberately misled him into thinking he was a god, subverting his worship away from those who rightly deserved it! Lorgar committed himself to the Dark Gods; he became a servant of Chaos.

As time passed, Lorgar and his lieutenants perverted the ministries of the Chaplains, who became his Dark Apostles, and the corruption of the Word Bearers had begun.

Fearing the wrath of the Emperor, Lorgar determined to keep his newfound allegiance to Chaos a secret. His single Legion was no match for the combined strength of all of the others. Kor Phaeron was impatient. He had utter conviction in the strength and righteousness of the Ruinous Powers. He wanted to throw off the cloak of deceit and bring the glory of Chaos to the Imperium. The other primarchs would soon see the error of their ways and join with the Word Bearers if they declared themselves, he argued.

Erebus was more circumspect. He counselled Lorgar to work in shadow and build his power base in secret, to bide his time until the right moment arrived to strike back at the Emperor. 'There are worlds aplenty whereon the seed of truth has been planted, worlds much like our own Colchis. Let us send envoys to these worlds, win them secretly to our cause. Further, we should nurture close bonds with the other Legions. We may have allies amongst them we cannot guess at, as yet.'

Lorgar knew he did not command the respect of the other primarchs. For the most part, they had shunned him and had been unwilling to listen to his theories of the Emperor's divinity. In his heart, he knew they would not follow him. They would follow the accursed Guilliman, the angelic Sanguinius or Rogal Dorn of the Imperial Fists and, of course, they would follow Horus, the First Primarch. The thought struck Lorgar that if Horus could be won to their faith, there was no limit to what they could achieve.

In the stygian depths of the Temple of the Serpent Lodge, the Dark Apostle Erebus met with the recovering Warmaster Horus:

'My Lord Lorgar, Primarch of the Word Bearers, greets you and swears fealty to you as Warmaster and Prophet of Truth. The false-Emperor is weak. His time is over, his mission spent. Now we look to the strong to lead us onwards. We look to you, mighty Horus. Hail the Warmaster!'

Through long hours the two conferred. Horus told of his pact with Chaos and of his new mission to free the galaxy from the Emperor's shackles. Erebus explained that Lorgar was eager to take action. He wanted to openly oppose the Emperor. Horus cautioned him to be patient. He had yet to formulate his strategy and there was much work to be done. He told Erebus to return to his master with instructions that the Word Bearers were to maintain their veil of secrecy. In the fullness of time, they would get their desire and the Word Bearers would stand proudly at his side in the coming war against the Emperor.

Lorgar Strikes for Horus

After the atrocities of Isstvan, Warmaster Horus sent word to Lorgar of the Word Bearers. Now was the time to strike, he told the Chaos-worshipping primarch. Horus was aware of the bitter hatred that Lorgar had for Roboute Guilliman of the Ultramarines. He told Lorgar of the orders he had given to Guilliman. Lorgar quickly agreed to launch a surprise attack on the Ultramarines Legion while they were gathered at Ultramar. The loyalist Legion would be caught completely unawares and the Word Bearers primarch was sure he would be able to annihilate them.

Lorgar and Horus agreed that the Word Bearers were to continue to keep their alignment a secret from the Emperor. To this end, Lorgar ordered his Legion to Ultramar. The powers of the warp gave them sure and speedy passage across the restless immaterium.

Command of the Calth assault forces was given to Kor Phaeron, one of Lorgar's greatest champions, and a warrior who bore a deep hatred for the Ultramarines. Supporting him was Erebus, the former Chaplain and now the Chief Dark Apostle of the Word Bearers.

Kor Phaeron, the Dark Cardinal – *John Gravato*

Erebus – *Franz Vohwinkel*

Ingenuus – *Michael Phillippi*

Berranus – *Chris Trevas*

Mlatus – *Justin Norman*

Trajan – *Wayne England*

The Ultramarines Muster at Ultramar

The Ultramarines Legion, under the command of their primarch, Roboute Guilliman, had been ordered by Horus to go to the Veridian System, far to the galactic south-east. Horus claimed that the worlds of Veridian, including Calth itself, were under threat of an ork invasion force from the Ghaslakh Empire.

Roboute and a sizeable portion of his Legion had been stationed near the moons of Saturn. He immediately set course for Ultramar, a region of space ruled by the Ultramarines. Here he was able to rendezvous with more elements of the Ultramarines Legion and take on supplies. Roboute commanded his Legion to assemble at Calth.

As his fleets began to arrive, it was clear that something was wrong. None of his allied astropaths were able to pass messages through the warp. Something was blocking their astro-telepathy and dreadful storms were hampering the navigation of his ships. The Ultramarines Legion was cut off from the rest of the Imperium. It was then that the perfidious forces of the Word Bearers Legion struck!

Marius Gage – *Steve Belledin*

Lycius Mysander – *Sam Wood*

The Battle of Calth

The Word Bearers launched their surprise attack against the Ultramarines. Lorgar personally commanded his fleet of warships elsewhere, whilst his most trusted lieutenants were tasked with making the first strike against the planet of Calth.

From the battle-barge *Infidus Imperator*, Lorgar's greatest champion, Kor Phaeron, launched a full-scale invasion of the Calth System. Supporting him was the arch-fiend Erebus, foremost Dark Apostle of the Word Bearers.

Calth's sister planets were being destroyed by Lorgar's ships, massive geo-nuclear strikes ripping them apart. Calth's sun was being bombarded with radiation and chemical warheads that were boiling away its surface and threatening to send it supernova. The Ultramarines fleet was scattered by a succession of hammer blow assaults from the warships of the Word Bearers.

The Legion of the Word Bearers descended onto Calth, Dark Apostles at the fore, bolters singing, accompanied by hordes of frenzied cultists. The battle for Calth had begun.

Voidlock – *Neil Roberts*

Arius – *John Gravato*

Justarius – *Ralph Horsley*

Calth 3rd Infantry – *Eric Polak*

Quor Vondar – *Jim Pavelec*

Brotherhood of the Knife – *Paul Herbert*

Quo: Gallek – *Michael Phillippi*

Gal Vorbak – *Franz Vohwinkel*

Macragge's Honour – *Neil Roberts*

Telcior – *Kenson Low*

Sinon – *Al Eremin*

The Sentinels of Calth – *Franz Vohwinkel*

Ichi-on – *John Gravato*

Ruinstorm

Lorgar's treachery knew no bounds and, in his thirst for vengeance against the Emperor and his loyal followers, was near limitless in its intensity and its ingenuity. The vile primarch and his Legion had forbidden knowledge of the warp – no doubt bartered from its foul denizens with blood and souls – and knew dreadful ways to manipulate it to do their bidding. Inspired by the warp storms that had crippled the worlds of mankind in ages past, and kept Terra completely isolated from the rest of the galaxy during the Age of Strife, he hatched a devious plot to once again plunge humanity into an abyss of terror. The Word Bearers would create a new tempest in the warp, one that they alone could control, one which would be used to further the strategies of the traitors and which would utterly defeat any loyalist attempt to navigate or communicate through that weird dimension.

All that was needed to launch this monstrous and dangerous plan was sufficient sacrifice and terror in the real world. The numerous atrocities committed in the Isstvan System reverberated through the immaterium, stirring the daemonic energies and threatening to ignite the mystic conflagration, but it was not enough. More blood and suffering was needed, and the Word Bearers' invasion of Calth would provide the first step along the path.

Whilst Kor Phaeron launched his military attack on Calth and wrought his devastation upon the XIII Legion fleet, the Dark Apostle Erebus embarked on a series of unspeakable rituals on the planet's surface. As the blood of the defenders flowed and their pain and terror rose amidst the violence and atrocities perpetrated by the traitors, Erebus and his chosen followers despoiled the air with foul hymns and sacrilegious chants. Thousands upon thousands of daemons were summoned to the planet through great rips in space. As they appeared, they immediately joined in the slaughter, accelerating the carnage and increasing the intensity of the chants. The ritual tore at the veil between realities – insane energies lashed to and fro, sweeping vast numbers of bodies, dead and living, into the warp even as mewling hordes of daemons stampeded over each other to gain egress to the material plane. The violence of the ritual was beyond measure and Lorgar's plot was sealed: the Ruinstorm had been ignited.

The storm split the Imperium asunder, plunging the worlds of mankind into a new age of darkness and isolation. All interstellar travel by loyalists was crippled and astro-telepathy was effectively blinded as communication between the stars became

Honour to the Dead – *Neil Roberts*

near-impossible. The storm gave Lorgar almost complete control of all navigation through the warp. To his fellow traitors he gave 'secret paths' through the aether, secure routes that not only made travel predictable and safe but also massively shortened journey times and reduced the time dilation effects of warp-travel. The worlds of the Imperium were at the mercy of the predatory traitors – countless systems were completely cut off by the warp storms. Unable to call for help or receive any relief, and equally incapable of fleeing to safety, they could only await their inevitable fate. Many systems succumbed to surprise assaults by traitor fleets simply appearing without warning.

Loyalist fleets trying to navigate the hellish tides found themselves thrown horribly off course, left stranded in the vast emptiness of the interstellar void or cast to the furthermost reaches of the galaxy. Many simply disappeared, never to be seen again. No one can tell how many loyal ships, armies and lives were lost during those dark days – the toll of death is too dreadful to contemplate.

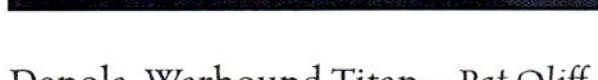

Denola, Warhound Titan – *Pat Oliff*

Void Battle – *Neil Roberts*

Helixus – *Karl Richardson*

Boradol – *Michael Phillippi*

Fire Cultists of Tharn – *Dave Millgate*

Calth Besieged

The savagery of the Word Bearers' assault left the Ultramarines reeling. Their fleet was scattered and entire planets destroyed by Lorgar's warships. Entire Chapters of Word Bearers and their allies descended upon Calth to attack the loyal warriors of the Ultramarines Legion and destroy them in the name of Horus and the Dark Gods of Chaos.

Kor Phaeron had tens of thousands of Space Marines and many times more Chaos cultists at his command. He also had aid from traitorous elements of the Mechanicum of Mars, who supplied him with a variety of giant war machines, including dozens of fearsome Titans.

The fighting on Calth was intense. At first, the Word Bearers threatened to overrun the Ultramarines defenders within a few hours. Kor Phaeron's troops massed into vast columns and charged at the loyal Ultramarines forces. Having scattered the loyalists and pinned them in place, they then pounded them with artillery and orbital bombardments. The Ultramarines were on the defensive and had no choice but to dig in and fortify their positions.

Using vast hordes of cultists as human shields, the Word Bearers were able to protect themselves from any significant Ultramarines counterattack. Kor Phaeron then deployed the war machines of the Dark Mechanicum as battering rams to punch through the defensive lines of the loyalists. Packs of screaming daemons followed up into any breaks in the lines, inflicting terrible carnage upon the defenders within. As each Ultramarines position was breached, the Word Bearers themselves followed up with vicious assaults, killing every loyal Space Marine they could find. Leading these final deadly assaults were the Dark Apostles of the Word Bearers. Chanting foul hymns to the dark gods, they spurred on the traitor Space Marines, inciting them to dreadful acts of violence and atrocity.

Remus Ventanus – *Sam Wood*

However, Kor Phaeron underestimated the tenacity and resolve of the Ultramarines. As the hours passed, the defenders began to slow and then halt the Word Bearers' assault. Eventually the Ultramarines were even able to organise some counterattacks against the traitors.

Captain Remus Ventanus of the Ultramarines was defending the Palace of Leptius Numinus on Calth. When the traitors had launched their first wave of attacks, Ventanus and his troops had been preparing to board their transport ships at the nearby Numinus Spaceport. The attacks took the Ultramarines by complete surprise. The loyal captain had lost over half of his Space Marines and had been forced to retreat to the palace.

Ventanus assessed the situation. His force now numbered less than five hundred Space Marines and a few Imperial Army companies. He had precious few tanks, maybe only a dozen or so Land Raiders, and no artillery. Against him was ranged a vast horde of human cultists, too many to accurately estimate their number, and a large group of Word Bearers, with dozens of giant war machines in their midst. Hundreds of strange, bat-winged creatures flew above the enemy ranks. The traitors had encircled the palace and were launching incessant attacks against Ventanus's defenders. The loyal captain knew his troops could not repel the attacks indefinitely. Although strong in spirit and well-armed, it was only a matter of hours before his position would be overrun and all of his troops slaughtered.

The loyal captain established comm-links with other besieged Ultramarines. His situation was not unique. In fact, all of the Ultramarines on Calth seemed to be in the same predicament. Of the fate of the Ultramarines primarch, none knew. Ventanus realised that there was no possibility of support from any of the other loyal forces left on Calth.

Erebus, first and most powerful of all of the Dark Apostles of the Word Bearers, was ecstatic. This was the culmination of all of his secret planning. The hated Guilliman's Ultramarines were being defeated! They were dying in droves. Finally, the Word Bearers would get their revenge on the Emperor's lackeys. The Time of Chaos was close!

But a message was received by Captain Ventanus: it was from Guilliman. The primarch was alive! Not only alive but organising the embattled and besieged loyal forces.

'Ventanus, your situation is desperate and I can offer you little hope of immediate reinforcement. Many of my faithful officers and men are in similar dire straits. I have a plan that offers you the chance to serve me better than simply dying where you stand. Quickly organise your force for a single concentrated assault against one point in the encircling lines. Your objective is to breakout and make for the Numinus Spaceport.'

'Sire, you would have us run like curs and quit the world of Calth?'

'Faithful captain, your goal is not to scurry away from this planet. I would have you launch as many of the transport ships as possible. You will need to assign brave pilots to each, for they are to harass the enemy ground troops and distract them for as long as possible.'

'With respect, my lord, these ships will not last long. They are weakly armoured vessels and have few guns. I fear they will be easily brought down by our foes.'

'But they will secure you precious time, time in which you can activate the spaceport's defence lasers. In their bloodlust and arrogance, the traitors were more concerned with killing our brethren than with disabling our cannons. The defence lasers of Numinus offer us a chance to win back the initiative. Do this thing for me, Ventanus, and your name will be honoured by the Ultramarines for eternity.'

'Yes, my Lord!'

Proving Grounds – *Rick Sardinha*

Bellarius – *David Hudnut*

Mountains of Twilight – *Rick Sardinha*

Invictus – *Franz Vohwinkel*

Golobar – *Dan Wheaton*

Lu-gardis – *Steve Boulter*

Olodar – *Steve Boulter*

Praetor – *John Wigley*

Gauntlet of Power – *Justin Norman*

Harbingers of Death – *Franz Vohwinkel*

Dark Heart – *John Gravato*

Palace of Leptius Numinus – *Rick Sardinha*

Rowd – *Neil Roberts*

Boarding Action – *Neil Roberts*

Roboute Guilliman – *Adrian Smith*

Balthamir's Sword – *Justin Norman*

Roboute Guilliman

Guilliman, primarch of the Ultramarines, was on the bridge of the *Macragge's Honour* when the Word Bearers struck. The attack was unexpected and the shock of it total. Guilliman's battle-barge shook as thunderous explosions ripped through its mid and aft sections. Klaxons blared as the mighty ship listed and turned slowly in space. Around it, Ultramarines ships exploded like small suns as torpedoes fired from the Word Bearers' strike craft pounded them. Below, the world of Calth rippled as gigantic plasma-quakes boiled up through the atmosphere.

Within minutes, the primarch had established the scale of the attacks upon both his fleet and the planet below. The battle-barge limped away from its attackers, and was badly damaged. Its weapon systems were non-operational and it could only manage half speed from the non-warp engines. The fleet had been savaged by the surprise assault. Fully three-quarters of the Ultramarines warships and transports had been crippled or destroyed, the rest scattered across the Veridian System as they evaded their attackers. Reports from the planet surface were even more depressing. The Word Bearers' orbital bombardment had been devastating. Tens of thousands of casualties had been inflicted on the ground troops, and many key strongholds destroyed.

Aboard the crippled battle-barge, Roboute Guilliman had already realised that he had been the victim of a deadly trap set for him by the Warmaster Horus. It was the Warmaster who had ordered him to Veridian, and it was only Horus who Guilliman had told of his plans to muster the Ultramarines fleet at Calth.

That it was the Word Bearers Legion of Lorgar that had perpetrated the cowardly attack was also a surprise to Guilliman. Although he had never liked Lorgar, he had never given him any reason to doubt his loyalty to the Emperor. In fact, it was because of Lorgar's extreme religious adoration of the Emperor that Guilliman had found him unsettling and distasteful. The fact that two of his fellow primarchs had conspired together against him filled Guilliman with deep unease. It was possible, he thought, that this was not an isolated act of treachery. The inability to send or receive any astro-telepathic communiques heightened the primarch's disquiet.

However, Guilliman's first priority was to stabilise the Ultramarines' situation. It was very clear that a mortal blow had been struck against his Legion. It would require all of his strategic and tactical brilliance to rescue them from annihilation.

Guilliman began to organise a series of hit-and-run counterattacks with the few ships able to operate. This was only possible because of the extraordinary discipline and training of the Ultramarines commanders and crews. The enemy fleet was over-confident and lacked cohesion. Time and time again the Word Bearers battleships were isolated and destroyed. After each attack, the loyal ships scattered and regrouped far from the traitor fleet. Even so, the loyalists faced a foe that outnumbered and outgunned them. Any losses weighed heavily against the Ultramarines whilst the traitors appeared to have an endless supply of fresh vessels. But Roboute would not surrender; the traitors would pay in blood for their cowardly aggression.

Even as he directed his crippled fleet, Guilliman was also sending orders planetside to his beleaguered troops on the ground. The traitors had not counted on two things. The first was the unbreakable fighting spirit and tenacity of the Ultramarines, who simply refused to give in to their desperate situation. After the initial wave of attacks, the loyal Space Marines were now dug into strongly defended positions, and from these they could not be dislodged. The second factor overlooked by Lorgar's forces was the brilliance of Guilliman's command. Each and every pocket of resistance had been assessed with lightning speed and a plan formulated to increase the success of its defence against the traitors. Clear, concise orders were being broadcast to the defenders and the Ultramarines began to fight back.

Guilliman's Fury – *Neil Roberts*

Aeonid Thiel – *Neil Roberts*

The Underworld War

The Word Bearers' assault on Calth wrecked the planet's atmosphere and ecology. The surface of the world became uninhabitable as plasma fires raged unchecked through the sky and wave after wave of caustic radiation washed down from the crippled, dying sun at the heart of the Veridian System. Millions died. The survivors fled to the refuge of Calth's underworld – loyalist and traitor alike were driven into the maze-like arcology network deep beneath the surface.

Their war did not stop. Now it turned into a bitter fight for survival in a dark, inhospitable landscape. Every useful resource was in short supply and what little food, water and space that could be found and claimed was quickly consumed.

As the days and weeks passed, those trapped in this dark and unforgiving place became ever more desperate in their efforts to survive. Natural caverns were extended in frantic tunnelling operations, as starving refugees dug with their bare hands through the rubble and dirt to reach new tunnels which held the hope of a scrap of food to eat or a drop of water to drink. The underground network was thus greatly extended by the warring factions but, with no access to building materials and only limited expertise, these new excavations were invariably of poor construction. The fanatical forces that had sworn themselves to the Ruinous Powers had no qualms about deliberately bringing down the flimsy excavations of the loyalists to sow confusion, terror and despair among their ranks.

So the Underworld War continued, and although the Ultramarines were eventually able to relieve their own forces after a year or so, the traitors dug themselves in, retreating into the darkest reaches of the network. This prompted a long guerrilla war that lasted for nearly a decade before the traitors were finally defeated. Even then, rumours persisted for many long years of there still being hideous mutants living deep within the bowels of Calth, biding their time, waiting to emerge and once again bring terror to the peoples of the Imperium.

Ventanus, Saviour of Calth – *Neil Roberts*

The Age of Darkness

Warmaster Horus – *Neil Roberts*

A Galaxy at War

To later generations of the Imperium, the events of the great conflict known as the Horus Heresy are recalled only as hoary old myths, recorded in the monumental sculptures and architecture of Imperial buildings and palaces; in the faded manuscripts of ancient archives; in crackling, static-laced and near-defunct holo-tubes; and in the oral histories passed between the brethren of the Space Marine Chapters. These myths tell of only the most dramatic and significant aspects of the legendary story, and of course all of them present Horus and his cohorts as unremitting villains. For the most part, the real details of what took place during those few short years have never been revealed to the wider citizenry of the Imperium.

Of course, the great span of centuries since that time alone would be enough to clothe the ancient war in mystery, through the loss and distortion of whatever information may have been recorded over the years. There were, however, *other* reasons for this paucity of information about the Heresy.

Quite apart from the relatively low priority given to the keeping of accurate records during such a momentous conflict – and the certainty that what was recorded would be prone to the same chance of destruction as any other aspect of human life at the time – the two sides in the war deliberately withheld information from the rest of the galaxy. From the time of the Dropsite Massacre on Isstvan V, right until the final desperate call to arms that heralded the beginning of the infamous Siege of Terra, the official records of those dark days were largely blank. It was as though the Imperium had deliberately sought to keep the Horus Heresy a great secret from its own people.

This is the time known as the Age of Darkness.

Of course records were lost. Some were deliberately destroyed, but many more were caught up in the war of propaganda and public opinion as planets and planetary systems moved back and forth from Imperial to traitor control. Many details and truths were simply forgotten, though this would later come to suit the masters of an Imperium who maybe preferred that certain facts were best lost in the shrouds of time.

Battles – and even entire campaigns – were fought and lost, and the loyalties of many factions within the Imperium wavered. The lines between those considered heroes and those damned as heretics blurred, as even the most pious and goodly did terrible deeds in the name of the Emperor. Innocents died in their millions to secure objectives that would be surrendered almost immediately in the service of a

Angel Exterminatus – *Neil Roberts*

revised strategic plan, or another desperate yet futile gamble.

Alliances were made and broken during the Age of Darkness, with some Imperial factions switching allegiance with alarming ease and frequency. Most of this dubious behaviour was exhibited by relatively minor elements of the loyalist forces, but there were some incidents of more noteworthy factions going astray. The details of these betrayals would surely shake the foundations of the Imperium were they to become more widely known after the war…

Shattered Legions

The loyal Legions of the Iron Hands, Salamanders and Raven Guard had been terribly betrayed at Isstvan V – the Dropsite Massacre had all but ruined the three Legions. Their collective losses were dreadful: a mere handful of survivors remained from three of the most powerful military organisations the galaxy had ever seen. Yet survivors there were. Despite the best efforts of the traitors, some of the loyal Space Marines not only lived but were also able to escape the scene of their betrayal.

And they were far from defeated.

Corax, primarch of the Raven Guard, somehow survived the massacre and was stealthily spirited away from Isstvan V by a surviving remnant of his loyal legionaries. This group was the largest of the remaining Raven Guard, but even so they were now massively outnumbered. Fearing for the life of their primarch and not knowing how many others of their Legion had also survived, they secretly quit the Isstvan System and retreated back to Terra, there to regroup. The remaining Raven Guard survivors may have suspected that Corax had escaped the massacre and still lived, but the secrecy of his retreat from the Isstvan System meant that they did not see him again until many long and difficult years later.

These other Raven Guard eventually joined with the survivors of the Iron Hands and Salamanders Legions, becoming an ad-hoc resistance force that came to be known as the Shattered Legions.

The Shattered Legions were led mainly by the Iron Hands who, after the death of Ferrus Manus and the annihilation of their veteran companies in the opening stages of the massacre, were still relatively strong in numbers compared to the other two Legions. The Iron Hands were absolutely resolute in their defiance of Horus; they had suffered a terrible evil at his hands and were determined to see him brought to justice. However, such was the perfidy of the betrayal they had suffered that they became suspicious of all. Trusting no one, they were unwilling even to re-submit to the rule of the Council of Terra.

The Iron Hands organised the survivors of the three Legions into groups of up to a thousand warriors each, based upon the structure of their home world clans of Medusa. These relatively small units took what space-worthy ships remained of their fleets and scattered to the four corners of the Imperium. From the depths of interstellar space, the groups would strike at Horus's forces and disrupt his supply and communication lines.

The units of the Shattered Legions were each led by a single centurion-level officer, with the various cells interacting only rarely and always in total secrecy. This meant that there was no central leadership to be removed. Furthermore, their small size meant that the traitors found it hard to track them and this lent the Shattered Legions the distinct advantages of surprise and flexibility.

The Shattered Legions scored victory after victory against Horus. The battles they fought were bloody and personal – bonds of brotherhood, stronger than those of mere Legion blood, were forged in those actions, bonds that would prevail beyond the years of the Heresy itself. Every warrior of the Shattered Legions was spurred on by the terrible tragedy that had befallen them at Isstvan V, and a desire to win justice for their betrayed comrades.

The Salamanders in particular mourned the loss of their primarch, and were convinced that their Legion would soon be nothing but a memory after searching without success for Vulkan's final resting place. Yet despite all their travails and troubles, they remained humanistic and compassionate even when faced with overwhelming odds, and with the unspeakable horrors perpetrated by the treacherous followers of Horus.

Rather than being crushed by their near-destruction at Isstvan V, the Shattered Legions were driven by a burning need for vengeance. Their unquenchable spirit and indomitable will made them a far greater threat than their numbers alone would suggest. Whilst even the other loyalist Legions might have considered them a spent force, it is possible that they were responsible for many more victories over the traitors than any could guess at, or have ever been recorded in the official records. No one can tell how many of Horus's plans were disrupted by their actions, how many more warriors or how much more materiel he might have had at his disposal had the survivors of Isstvan not been so dogged in their pursuit of their betrayers.

Scorched Earth – *Neil Roberts*

The Emperor's Benevolence – *Michael Phillippi*

Age of Darkness – *Neil Roberts*

Alcorax – Torstein Nordstrand

Darras – Torstein Nordstrand

Slearne – *Kari Christensen*

The Shadow Crusade

Lorgar, Primarch of the Word Bearers, had been tasked with a special mission by Horus. While his Legion and their dark allies were engaging the main force of Ultramarines in battle at Calth, Lorgar was to strike secretly at Ultramar – the domain of Roboute Guilliman's loyalists. Horus had demanded that Lorgar not just defeat Guilliman's Legion but destroy it utterly, to prevent it becoming a threat to his ambitions in future. Lorgar relished the opportunity to wreak his vengeance upon his old rival, although he would always deny that this was his true motivation. His ultimate ambition was clear: a direct assault against Macragge, the base of all the Ultramarines' power and influence in the sector. Without their home world, the XIII Legion would be shattered and never recover.

Lorgar had a broader goal in mind as well. He planned to consecrate whole sectors of the galaxy in blood, dedicating them to the gods of Chaos, according to a very specific series of dreadful rituals. His assault on Macragge was to be a part of that foul scheme. He had drawn Angron of the World Eaters into his madness, and together the two primarchs set world after world alight. Erebus's apocalyptic destruction of Calth turned out to be but

Phraetus – *Ben Peck*

one sacrifice amongst a host of villainy – the horrors unleashed there were repeated a hundredfold across the realm of Ultramar alone. The galaxy burned and the Dark Gods of Chaos laughed.

The foul rituals of the Word Bearers fed the Ruinstorm with blood and skulls, reinforcing its power and increasing the control exerted upon it by Lorgar. Macragge itself might have been at the mercy of Lorgar and Angron, but for the fact that the World Eaters primarch withdrew his forces, suddenly and without warning.

The Shadow Crusade collapsed. Some mysterious turn of events had saved the Ultramarines home world, and with it came a new spark of hope for the loyalists.

Argel Tal – *John Wigley*

Conqueror – *Justin Norman*

Betrayer – *Neil Roberts*

The Warfleet of the Imperial Fists

When Rogal Dorn of the Imperial Fists had chanced upon the becalmed frigate *Eisenstein*, and met with the loyal Captain Garro of the Death Guard, he had ordered his warfleet to Isstvan. His troops had been tasked with reinforcing the loyalist effort upon the third planet. Dorn had personally escorted the loyal Garro to Terra, taking with him only his elite veteran companies. The rest of Dorn's Legion had made for Isstvan. It was a significant force of arms – over thirty thousand Space Marines aboard a fleet of seventeen battle-barges and assorted cruisers, with a host of smaller supporting craft.

The Imperial Fists warfleet could deal a hammer-blow to the traitors gathered at the Isstvan System. But Horus had powerful allies in the warp and the fleet's Navigators could not penetrate the warp storms that plagued the immaterium at their behest. The days turned to weeks and the weeks to months as they tried again and again to plot a course through the maelstrom of swirling energies. Each attempt to move the fleet through the warp seemingly placed it even further away from Isstvan. Furthermore, they were unable to navigate a course back to Terra.

The violent storms also crippled their astropaths' abilities and they could not send nor receive any communication from either Terra or their primarch. But it was not in the nature of Space Marines to give up, and so the Imperial Fists stubbornly kept trying to penetrate the storms.

The Imperial Fists warfleet established a base of operations at the Phall System. The two habitable planets of Phall were unremarkable agrarian worlds, lightly populated and of no great strategic importance. In the normal course of events, there would be no reason for a backwater system like this to host such a mighty force of Space Marines and their battleships. However, for reasons they could not ascertain, the warp was calm in this region and the Imperial Fists found that they could navigate to and from the system with some surety. The Legion's commanders decided therefore to use Phall as a base for the fleet whilst they sent ships to scout the surrounding space and probe the warp for routes to either Isstvan or Terra.

The Legion quickly established a routine. Whilst regular scouting missions were launched into the warp, the Legion's astropaths busied themselves with trying to break through the warp storms and make contact with the rest of the Imperium, in particular the loyalists at Isstvan and their own primarch on Terra. The fleet was kept at full battle-stations and the Space Marines were ready to move into action as soon as communications could be re-established.

With their astropaths blind, as time wore on the Legion's commanders had grown increasingly frustrated. They knew that something terrible had happened at the Isstvan System and that loyal Space Marines were in grave danger. They were also aware that their own primarch carried news of the betrayal of Horus to the Emperor on Terra.

The attack by Perturabo was sudden and devastating. The Iron Warriors primarch commanded a fleet of over twenty large warships. Before the Imperial Fists astropaths could relay news of the rebel fleet's appearance at the warp jump points, it was firing upon the loyalist ships orbiting the second planet. Within minutes, three Imperial Fists battle-barges had been crippled, the *Hammer of Terra* exploding as a salvo of torpedoes smashed into its aft section, setting off a chain reaction in the plasma engines. A dozen smaller craft were simply ripped apart by the hail of fire from the traitor vessels.

The traitors pushed onwards, driving into the heart of the loyalist fleet, reaping death and destruction all around them. Their attack threatened to overwhelm the Imperial Fists before they could even fire back.

Perturabo's strategy was to plunge his ships into the midst of the loyal fleet, scattering its formation and then to destroy it piecemeal. His plan was dependent upon the loyal ships not being able to fight back quickly enough to break the momentum of his thrust.

However, as they recovered from the shock and suddenness of Perturabo's attack, the Imperial Fists fought back. Despite their long sojourn at Phall, the loyal fleet had been kept in a state of constant battle-readiness and this policy now paid off for the Imperial Fists. The loyal ships began firing at the traitors as soon as they broke into their formation. The Imperial Fists concentrated their fire on the leading ships of Perturabo's fleet. The impact of this was devastating to the traitors as their lead ships were torn apart in the firestorm. As the vanguard was battered, the following ships of Perturabo's fleet broke off their attack to regroup.

This gave the loyalists the chance to go on the offensive but before they did so, the fleet's astropaths relayed a critical message to the loyal commanders. Finally, they had succeeded in making contact with Terra and the Imperial Fists had urgent orders to return to there. These orders had the highest priority. They must not let anything delay them.

Unfortunately, the loyal Legion was embattled against the traitors of the Iron Warriors Legion as it received its orders to quit the Phall System and head for Earth.

The Imperial Fists had gained the initiative in the battle and managed to repel the traitors' surprise attack, despite severe losses at the start of the engagement. The loyalists had an opportunity to force the issue and launch a counterattack against Perturabo's fleet. The Imperial Fists demonstrated remarkable discipline as they resisted the urge to chase down the scattering rebels and instead set course for Terra.

As the loyalist ships broke orbit and manoeuvred to their jump points, the traitor ships turned back towards them and began a new assault. A number of Imperial Fists light cruisers moved to intercept the fresh attack. These few ships were no match for the battle-barges of Perturabo and were cut apart by laser fire from the prows of the heavier ships. Their sacrifice was well judged and delayed the traitors long enough for the rest of the loyal Legion to make the jump points, enter the warp and head for Terra.

Navarra – *Alex Boyd*

Perturabo – *Alex Boyd*

The Crimson Fist – *Neil Roberts*

The Wolf and The Khan

Jaghatai Khan and his White Scars Legion had spent the last few years campaigning in the Chondax System. The Space Marines had been battling against a large army of ork raiders originating from the moons of Throll-Henderson. After defeating the main ork force, the Legion had spent the last few months hunting down and destroying the scattered remnants of the alien army.

The Legion was in good shape, having had plenty of time to replace the losses it had suffered in the early weeks of the campaign. That it had been unable to contact Terra or make any long warp-trips because of the warp storms had not been of particular concern to the Khan. These kinds of disturbances were quite commonplace in this region of space, and he had no reason to see anything significant about it.

His attitude changed when he was finally contacted by Rogal Dorn and told of the events at Isstvan V. The Khan's immediate reaction was to request that his Legion be sent to Isstvan to participate in the attack on Horus. Dorn, however, was adamant that he return to Terra as soon as possible. The Imperial Fists primarch had been appointed commander-in-chief of all the loyal forces of the Imperium and so, reluctantly, the White Scars primarch agreed to the order and instructed his fleet to make ready for transit to Earth.

As the Khan's fleet was making final preparation for the warp-jumps, they received urgent astropathic signals from an unexpected quarter. It was the primarch of the Space Wolves, Leman Russ. The Wolf King told of his mission to Prospero, which was relatively close to the Chondax System, and of the rebellion of Magnus the Red. The Khan had been unaware of Russ's attack on Prospero and hearing of the treachery of the Thousand Sons added to his growing sense of unease. Worse still was the news that the Space Wolves had intercepted a traitor fleet bound for Chondax. Russ told Jaghatai that his fleet was now battling the rebel ships and warned him that some elements of their armada had broken away and were heading his way.

The two loyal primarchs exchanged communications and discussed the options open to them. They agreed that, combined, their two fleets could easily defeat the traitors, who Russ identified as the Alpha Legion. However, either of the loyal fleets would be at grave risk of defeat if they tried to fight alone. Russ told the Khan that he was only able to avoid being overwhelmed by adopting hit and run tactics. This was stopping Alpharius from being able to bring his greater number of ships to bear, but it was doing little to slow the advance of the traitor fleet.

Jaghatai Khan had a hard decision to make. He had been sent very specific orders to return to Terra and deploy his Legion in defence of the Imperial Palace. These orders came directly from Rogal Dorn, who spoke with the authority of the Emperor and was therefore not lightly dismissed. On the other hand, his fellow loyal primarch Leman Russ had requested his aid in combating a traitor fleet that was bound for his current position. Russ was a great friend of the Khan and the rebel ships heavily outnumbered his fleet. If the Khan did not aid him it was likely that the traitors would not be stopped or, worse, the Space Wolves fleet would be destroyed.

It was a difficult choice for the Khan to make. He sent urgent communications to Terra, requesting that Dorn amend his orders in the light of this latest revelation and allow him to support his old friend. While he was waiting for a response from Dorn, the White Scars primarch ordered his fleet to make ready to support the Space Wolves. Even as the great battle-barges swung into position, leading elements of the traitor fleet of Alpharius appeared on their scanners. Within moments, the traitor ships were upon them. The battle had come to the Khan!

The leading ships of Alpharius's fleet were small, fast cruisers and escorts. It did not appear to the White Scars that these would present too much of a threat to them and so it proved. The massed gunnery of the White Scars battle-barges ripped the smaller ships to pieces. The Khan and his officers were confused. They could not understand what the traitors were trying to achieve. As long as they attacked piecemeal and with their

Brotherhood of the Storm – *Neil Roberts*

smallest ships, the loyal fleet was virtually invulnerable. It did not make any sense.

It made even less sense to the Khan when the larger Alpha Legion warships started to appear. These vessels did not attack but held station at the edge of the system whilst their smaller comrades continued to commit suicide. As the Khan pored over the tactical charts and scanners aboard his flagship, trying to glean the intent of his foe, his officers pleaded with him to give the order to attack. The primarch resisted their calls – he did not want to commit himself to a full-scale battle with the traitors unless it was absolutely necessary.

As this was happening, the Space Wolves Legion was fighting a losing battle against the rest of the Alpha Legion fleet. Even though the ships of Russ were trying to evade the much larger traitor fleet, they were taking terrible punishment from their gunnery. Again, Russ sent furious communications to Jaghatai Khan requesting his urgent assistance.

Jaghatai Khan's reluctance to fully engage the traitor fleet of Alpharius was vindicated when he received a reply to the signal he had sent to Rogal Dorn on Terra. Dorn's new communiqué was clear and unequivocal – the Khan was instructed to move his Legion to Terra without delay, regardless of any and all other considerations. Dorn's orders also told the Khan to relay this order to Leman Russ of the Space Wolves with the added codicil that the Space Wolves Legion was to draw the enemy fleet as far as possible and that if, and only *if*, he was able to break contact with the rebels should he attempt to warp-jump to Terra.

The Khan relayed the orders to Russ as commanded and added his own personal message of apology to his old friend that he was unable to offer him any further help. With that, his fleet broke off from the harassing traitor escorts and jumped into the warp.

The Space Wolves were on their own, facing an enemy that outnumbered and outgunned them and that was intent on destroying them. Russ simply shrugged his shoulders when he received the Khan's communication. The fate of his Legion he could not foretell, but he was quite sure that his warriors and ship crews would fight as hard as they had ever fought before. The traitor Alpharius would soon remember that an injured wolf was the most dangerous foe of all.

Imperium Secundus

In the wake of the events at Calth, and after all the other atrocities of the unfolding Heresy, the warp seethed in turmoil and the sacred signal that was the Astronomican at first stuttered and stalled and then, ominously, fell silent. The ancient nightmare of isolation revisited the worlds of mankind as they first lost contact with their more distant compatriots, then with their closer neighbours. It was as though Terra had simply vanished.

Hundreds of thousands of Imperial worlds were left utterly alone in the dark – without nearby allies, their astropathic communications simply could not penetrate far enough through the aether to find and maintain any links. No world outside of the Segmentum Solar could contact Terra: the home of humanity, the seat of the Emperor and the wellspring of all Imperial power and authority was lost to them. Panic and fear gripped the far-flung peoples of the Imperium – the silence of the Astronomican was a dread portent of doom, and for many it seemed to herald the dawning of a new Age of Strife.

Roboute Guilliman and his Ultramarines were recovering from the treachery of the Word Bearers, and the attacks against the other worlds of the Ultima Segmentum, when contact with Terra and the rest of the Imperium was severed. Desperate, repeated attempts were made to re-establish communications. The entire corps of Guilliman's Astropaths were charged with the task, but all their efforts failed and eventually hopes of making contact were dashed. This was a massive setback for the mighty primarch. He thrived on information and intelligence gleaned from his enemy, relying on such to fuel his tactics and build his vaunted strategies. Without any knowledge of what had happened at Terra, he was deeply unsettled and dark misgivings quickly took shape in his imagination. He could not be certain about the cause of the Astronomican's failure, but it was all too easy for Guilliman to reason that something terrible must have occurred for the Emperor to be unable to maintain the signal. The great primarch felt the crush of grief on his soul as he eliminated one by one all the possible causes he could think of until only the sad truth remained to him that the Emperor must have fallen.

Dark, burning pain wracked Guilliman's thoughts and his massive frame shuddered and convulsed as he sobbed uncontrollably for the death of his true father. The primarch would have certainly succumbed but for the superhuman fortitude of his mind and body. It would not let him submit to the pain, would not let him become lost in blissful, ignorant oblivion. A thought occurred to him: if the Emperor had fallen, then a great many of the enemy must have died. Then he figured that if sufficient of the enemy's strength had been spent to achieve such a monumental feat then, despite this victory for them, their attempt to usurp the Emperor's power would have been set back. It was worth fighting on! It was clear to Guilliman that the war for the galaxy was by no means over. He had to carry on.

Guilliman rapidly set a new plan in motion. Mankind, he argued, needed a bastion of security and safety – a place it could call home, somewhere to look

The Unremembered Empire – *Neil Roberts*

towards in the night sky and inspire hope. A shining beacon that would be the centre of humanity's ongoing war against the forces of darkness. If that place was no longer ancient Terra then a new world must arise to fulfill that role.

He decided that Ultramar, the empire of the Ultramarines Legion – despite all the predations it had suffered at the hands of the treacherous Lorgar and Angron – would be that place. His battered realm would become a new Imperium, and he even named it 'Imperium Secundus'. In time, many of his brother primarchs were drawn to Guilliman's banner and shared in his vision.

Nothing more is known of this unremembered empire – whatever transpired in the few years that followed Guilliman's declaration has been struck from all Imperial records. Subsequent events and the retrospective knowledge of the true cause of the Astronomican's failure cast the whole episode in a less palatable light, possibly even a heretical one. Whether to protect certain individuals or to protect the whole of mankind, the truth of those days has been left forgotten and unrecorded. It now perhaps exists only within the secret and sealed vaults deep in the heart of the Ultramarines fortress on Macragge.

Blades of the Traitor – *Sam Wood*

Horus Orders his Armada to Terra

The Warmaster had ordered the Legions of Night Haunter, Perturabo and Alpharius to carry out certain missions in preparation for the attack against Terra. The rest of his forces would eventually travel to the Solar System and rendezvous at Mars. When his invasion armada was in place, Horus intended to launch an attack on the weakened Terra and lay siege to the Emperor's Palace itself.

Even with the help of Horus's allies within the warp, the journey would take some time to complete. Horus instructed that this time would be well-spent by his primarchs and commanders preparing for the coming battles. Plans for the attack were scrutinised and finessed, troops drilled and trained.

Horus was pleased with the turn of events. In a short time he would confront the Emperor, defeat him and claim lordship over all human space. It would be the dawn of a new age for mankind.

Erebus, the Dark Apostle – *Sam Wood*

Ingethel the Ascended – *Sam Wood*

The Red Angel – *Sam Wood*

Horus, the Arch-traitor – *Sam Wood*

Magnus the Red, Prince of Change – *Wayne England*

Magnus the Red contacts Horus

As the Warmaster was preparing his forces for the coming attack against Terra, he received an unexpected communication. It was from Magnus the Red, primarch of the Thousand Sons Legion. Horus knew that eventually Magnus would join him – his allies within the warp had foretold as much – but he was nevertheless surprised that he had made contact now. This was a good omen, thought Horus as he scanned the transcript of the message.

'Hail Warmaster! I offer you grim tidings of events that have destroyed fair Prospero and I offer you my services in the coming invasion of Terra. Though you and I have never been close, it now appears that we share common cause. The Emperor, who I had ever admired and loved, has spurned me and set his dogs on me as if I were but a petty criminal. The barbarians of Russ have destroyed my precious Prospero and foully murdered many of my dearest kith and kin. Only through the grace of a mutual ally was I able to escape the carnage and mine own death at the hands of the Wolf King.

'I never sought to become embroiled in your disagreement, but they have driven me to your side. I vow to make them regret that they should have treated me so. I am much changed; our mutual ally has bequeathed me power beyond any mortal means to measure. You will find me a most useful and loyal servant.

'Even as you receive this communiqué, the remnant of my Legion and I are marshalling at the moons of Fasdahn-Oryx in preparation for transit to the Solar System. We await your orders to move on Terra.'

Ahriman and the Thousand Sons – *Sam Wood*

Abaddon, First Captain – *Sam Wood*

Lords of Caliban

When the First Legion rediscovered their primarch Lion El'Jonson on the feudal planet of Caliban, they adopted their new home world's culture and traditions, and took for themselves the name of 'Dark Angels'. With the Lion leading from the front, they returned to the Great Crusade and won many glorious victories in the Emperor's name.

However, something happened during the pacification of the planet Sarosh which shook the Legion to its core. Little is known for certain, though some records suggest that there was an attempted assassination of the primarch by local dissidents – whatever the cause, the Lion decided that the Dark Angels needed to recruit and train new legionaries at a much faster rate to ensure their supremacy in future. To this end, he sent a sizeable contingent from his crusading forces back to Caliban to oversee the process, led by none other than his second-in-command, Luther.

As the Great Crusade continued without them, Luther began to feel that he and his fellow warriors had been exiled in all but name. He made a few vain attempts to recover some sense of glory by allying his forces with other Legions in the local area, but after fighting alongside the Luna Wolves on Zaramund he was confronted by his enraged primarch once more. As punishment for his disobedience, the Lion took all of Luther's fleet, ensuring that he must remain on Caliban until he was relieved of his duties.

It is there that the story of Luther and the Calibanites ended, at least officially. Dark forces had always been known to dwell in the deep forests of their home world, and it is possible that a little of this darkness had crept into Luther's soul as the decades wore on. Though they took no significant role in the Heresy, a schism had emerged between these forgotten Dark Angels and the rest of their battle-brothers – a schism that would lead to the Legion's ultimate downfall.

Fallen Angels – *Neil Roberts*

Loyalty and Honour – *Neil Roberts*

Alajos – *Michael Phillippi*

Astelan – *Sam Wood*

Hadwyn – *Michael Phillippi*

Phalanx – *Eric Polak*

Mantle of the Champion – *Sam Wood*

Betrayal – *David Rabbitte*

Descent cf Angels – *Neil Roberts*

The Doom of the Death Guard

Mortarion was typically silent on receiving his orders from Horus detailing the role his Legion would take in the coming battle for Terra. The grim primarch passed on the orders to his command staff with the minimum of ceremony. He delivered a short speech to his troops, explaining that this battle would decide the fate of the Imperium and that they had proved themselves worthy of the chance to be a part of the inevitable triumph it would be for Horus. If he had any doubts at all about their mission, he kept such thoughts to himself.

With his entire fleet, Mortarion crossed into the warp and straight into a nightmare. The Death Guard fleet was sucked into a warp storm, a deadly vortex that battered the ships to and fro and made navigation impossible. Frantic efforts by the fleet's Navigators and helmsmen to stabilise the ships were for naught, and they could do nothing save ride out the storm and hope that the fleet was not scattered within the warp.

In time the storm abated and the fleet lay becalmed, its ships slowly drifting through the immaterium, unable to find their bearings. And then the Destroyer came upon them and they were changed for all time.

For Mortarion and the Space Marines of the Death Guard, there was nothing so terrifying as the plague that rendered their legendary resilience meaningless. These were warriors who were immune to the diseases, contagions, toxins and pollutions that bedevilled normal men. The pestilence raced through the entire fleet, roiling in their guts, bloating and distending their superhuman bodies, transforming them into horrible, pustulent grotesques. They were made corrupt within and sickening to behold without. They grew sicker by the minute; their incredible constitution became their worst enemy as their bodies refused to die and they were wracked with the agony of their macabre transformation.

What the Death Guard endured was unimaginable, yet none suffered more than Mortarion himself. For the primarch, it was as though he were upon the mountaintops of Barbarus once more, surrendering to the poison, without the mercy of unconsciousness to claim him or the Emperor to come to his salvation as he had done all those years ago.

Whether he perceived, in those terrible hours, the loss of what he had once stood for, the damnation he had wrought upon himself and his Legion, the final sundering of any vestigial loyalty to the Emperor or to mankind, only Mortarion would ever know. Unable to endure the suffering any longer, the primarch offered himself and his Legion to the warp in exchange for deliverance from their torment. His call was answered by a presence in the immaterium, as though it had been waiting all along. From the stygian depths of the warp, the great entity that was Nurgle, Lord of Decay, Father of Disease, opened his arms and embraced Mortarion and the Death Guard, drawing them to his breast and making them his own.

What emerged from the warp when the Death Guard fleet broke out bore little resemblance to that which had entered. The gleaming armour of the once-Imperial champions was no more; in its stead was a sickly pall of greenish hue. Bloated corpulence replaced the sleek proud form of the Space Marine and every warrior was pock-marked with boils, scabs and putrescent sores. Maggots writhed in their unhealing wounds and the air about them was clouded with swarming flies. They bore the stink of corruption.

Even their weapons and war machines had been mutated and were now powered by the sickly sorcery of Chaos, glowing with lambent green energy and oozing gangrenous pus. The Death Guard had become creatures of Nurgle, walking pestilence carriers; they had become the Plague Marines.

Mortarion himself was also changed. He had grown taller and more gaunt, as if stretched on a rack. His power-glaive now bore the hallmarks of the reaper's scythe. In return for rescue from the torments of the plague, Nurgle had set him on the path to daemonhood and transformed him into the very image of death.

Indomitable Will – *Justin Norman*

Mortarion – *John Blanche*

Ujioj – *Franz Vohwinkel*

Holgoarg – *Alex Boyd*

Mortarion, Liberator of Barbarus – *Adrian Smith*

Mortarion, the Death Lord – *Alex Boyd*

Running on Empty – *Steve Boulter*

Father's Chosen – *Torstein Nordstrand*

Seduction of Chaos – *Franz Vohwinkel*

Kærggat – *John Wigley*

Terra

Aboard the Vengeful Spirit – *Neil Roberts*

The Palace Vaults

The Emperor had retreated to Terra, and in the vast dungeons beneath his great Imperial Palace he busied himself with his secret project. Cloistered deep within the stygian vaults, the Emperor laboured day and night. Whatever it was that he worked on, it was a mammoth undertaking. At first, dozens of tech-priests, labourers, and Imperial scientists were seconded to work alongside him within the depths of the Palace. As the days passed, more workers were recruited and sent into the vaults. Now each day saw many hundreds entering through the gargantuan iron doors that sealed the dungeons from the rest of the Palace.

For all of this time, the Emperor was seemingly oblivious to the events in far Isstvan, Calth, Signus and Prospero. He had appointed Malcador the Sigillite as Regent of the Imperium, to rule it in his stead, whilst he completed his secret project.

No one could guess at what was happening within the vaults. Few workers left the secured area and those that did either did not know themselves or would not say what they had seen within. The ever-present Custodian Guard were customarily stoic. Of all the people who did not work in the dungeons, only Malcador was allowed free and regular access, and none dared question the First Lord of Terra and Imperial Regent about the secret workings within.

The Imperial Truth – *Neil Roberts*

The Golden Throne

Malcador the Sigillite and Rogal Dorn, Primarch of the Imperial Fists Legion of Space Marines, stood before the great edifice that was the Emperor's Throne. After many long months of waiting, they had finally been granted an audience with the Master of Mankind. The order to appear before the Emperor had been timely, coming as it did just as news had reached Terra of the disaster at Isstvan V.

The two men looked up at the Emperor from bended knee. He was seated upon a huge chair, bulky and machine-like, a mass of twisted cables, wires and conduits linking it to the enormous portal over which it hung. Arcs of power crackled about the Emperor's head, his eyes were shut tight and he did not move. The air was thick with the smell of ozone and machine. The entire construct was fabricated of metal, gold in colour, and gigantic mechanised doors of the same golden metal blocked the portal shut. The huge machine-throne and the doorway beneath it filled one end of a vast, cavernous hall. This was the Emperor's main laboratory, the centre of his underground complex, his Imperial Dungeon. Within this secret vault, the Emperor had worked his science and tested his theories. Great machines and storage crates littered the hall and hundreds of red-robed technicians and labourers were occupying themselves with a myriad of tasks.

Rogal Dorn was amazed and confused. He had seen much in his time as a Space Marine primarch but he had never imagined such a place existed here on Earth, let alone beneath the Imperial Palace. The hall itself was large enough to accommodate five or six fully equipped companies of Space Marines and he was sure even a Warhound Titan of the Mechanicum of Mars would be able to walk through the portal unbowed. But he could not fathom the purpose of it. Was there another chamber beyond the portal? A still larger hall filled with more technological wonders? What was the function of the machine to which the Emperor was bound? As these and a thousand other questions filled his mind, he stared intently at the Emperor as if seeking answers.

The Emperor slowly opened his eyes and looked down at the two figures kneeling before him. As he did this, the lightning dancing on his brow abated and the machine's roaring quietened to a dull bass throbbing.

'You are here. There is much to do and time is against us, so I shall be brief.

'Beyond these golden doors lies a vast network of tunnels. These are no ordinary passageways. They were constructed eons ago by a race more ancient than our sun. The tunnels do not pass through the rock upon which my Palace is built, but instead pass through the fabric of the warp itself. The web of tunnels is so unimaginably large and complex that it is difficult to map. However, it is possible to travel to the other side of the Imperium in the blink of an eye through its arcane passageways if one can access the necessary warp-gates. The location of these doorways and the layout of the web are the greatest secrets of the aliens who built it.

'How I came to know of this lattice need not concern us now. Suffice to say, I did learn of it, and having done so I resolved to construct my own means of egress. The warp-gate before you is the fruit of many decades of labour – work I set in motion when first I set my Palace on this mount. Its construction was to have been the first stage in a bold mission to conquer the web of the warp and thus free humanity from reliance on warp-ships and astro-telepathy. Unfortunately, events have conspired to disrupt my schemes and we now face a time of crisis.

'The warp-gate I have constructed and the short section of passage beyond require constant maintenance lest they fall into ruin. At first this demanded only a small portion of my psychic might – and so I was able to command my armies and do all that was expected of me as Emperor. But the hideous monstrosities that rule the warp – the self-proclaimed gods of Chaos – have ever been my foes and they conspired to subvert my goals. To this end they tempted the naïve Magnus to warn me of the very plot they had incepted – the betrayal of Horus. Magnus sent his warning by means of powerful sorcery that wreaked havoc on the protective psychic shielding around my construct. The spell of Magnus not only allowed the foul denizens of the warp entry to the section of the web my secret army had by then conquered, it destroyed the delicate controls I had set in place. Now this warp-gate requires virtually all of my power and concentration lest it rips open a permanent doorway between our world and the warp!

'Even as I speak to you, a secret war is raging in the web – a bitter struggle between my own Custodian bodyguards and the hellish daemons of Chaos that have surged into the damaged sections. There remains a slim chance of victory. If I can repair the damage caused by Magnus and my troops within can best the daemons, then mayhap my plan can yet be accomplished.

'Yet soon I must leave this place. Horus has gathered his army of traitors and is planning to attack Terra. He seeks my crown and will not rest until he has bested me in combat. I must confront Horus in person if he is to be stopped. Someone else will have to take my place on this throne whilst I deal with the Traitor – this person will have to be one who is a powerful psyker in their own right but even so it will be a sacrificial duty, they will most likely not survive the ordeal. My first choice was to have been Magnus, but I sense that this is no longer possible. He has been duped into siding against us, and despite the consequences of his actions, he acted faithfully. Are you fit for this task, Malcador?'

Malcador was taken aback, but did not doubt that this was his destiny.

'Of course I will do it, sire! You have always known that I would lay down my life for you.'

'Thank you. There is much work to do beforehand. Dorn, you are to assume full and absolute command of all of the remaining loyal troops of the Imperium. You must make immediate preparation for the coming assault on Terra by the Warmaster. You will need all the forces you can muster. The Imperial Palace must stand firm against the traitor army. You have to stop them gaining access to my Dungeon and this warp-gate, or it will spell the end of times for all humanity. And I need time; time to do my best to fix the damage caused by Magnus and time to frustrate the Warmaster into rashness. If Horus can be stalled, he will drop his guard and offer me a moment to strike him down.

'However, I fear that in itself will not end this trouble. The actions of Horus and his cronies will have consequences far into the future – far beyond the point where my clairvoyance is clear. The Warmaster has opened up possibilities for treachery that will bedevil humanity for centuries to come. Malcador, you must draw about you men of character, skill and determination. These men are to be rigorously tested and trained to ensure that they are of the highest calibre and that their loyalty to me is unshakeable. These men will be the core of an elite group of investigators whose role is to root out heresy and treachery wherever it may hide. You must also prepare yourself for the dreadful sacrifice you will be called upon to make.

'Go now! Both of you know what needs to be done, and I must give my full attention to this machine. I will summon you when the time is upon us.'

The Eternity Gate – *John Blanche*

War in the Webway

The warp-gate in the Imperial Dungeon led to a short section of human-built warp-tunnel. Beyond this lay the vast interlocking maze of tunnels, passageways and conduits that was the alien webway. Many of the passageways were small, intimate walkways just big enough for a human to walk along. Some were so large it was possible to drive a large vehicle along them. In places there were enormous tunnels, easily big enough to facilitate the passage of large ships. At the junctions of the largest tunnels sat ancient cities; long-abandoned by their former occupants – these places had fallen into disrepair and ruin.

The Emperor's army within the webway had first secured the tunnels nearest to the warp-gate of the Golden Throne. Teams of technicians and tithed labourers of the Mechanicum were given this task and they set about constructing huge armoured seals at strategic points in the immediate vicinity of the Imperial conduit. Although the web appeared to be deserted, there was much evidence that someone or something lurked within its twisting weave. The agents of the Mechanicum were loath to work in the webway undefended. To this end, the Custodian Guard had been sent into the web to protect the workers as they completed their labours.

The consequences of Magnus the Red's warning spell to the Emperor were devastating. The Golden Throne gateway, the Imperial conduit and the alien-built web-tunnels were all both physical and psychic in nature. Wrapped around the physical component was a psychic sheath or shield. The very substance of the alien tunnels appeared to generate this shielding naturally – the Imperial engineers and technicians found no mechanisms or engines that were responsible for it. For the human-built gateway and conduit, the Emperor himself generated the protective psychic sheath. This psy-shield sealed the web from the warp and its denizens in some inexplicably arcane fashion. Magnus's spell disrupted this shield, causing great rifts to appear in it.

It was through these rifts that the creatures of the warp were able to gain egress to the tunnels. Thousands of hideous daemons poured into the webway and immediately set about attacking the Imperial forces within. The workers of the Mechanicum were slaughtered in their thousands and the Custodian Guard were hard-pressed to hold back the tide of daemonic fury that had been unleashed upon them.

As the Imperial forces within the webway were being attacked, the Emperor mustered the remainder of his Custodian bodyguard and ordered them into the tunnels. Alongside the Custodians was a contingent of the Sisters of Silence, the Emperor figuring that their unique nature would make them especially effective against creatures of the warp. This soon proved to be true as the Sisters cut a swathe through the invading horde of daemons, who shrieked as if in great pain whenever they were close to them.

The reinforcements stemmed the onrush of daemons and the battle within the webway fell into a pattern. The Custodians established a series of blockades across the tunnels. Behind these defended areas, the Mechanicum workers were repairing the damaged sections of tunnel and sealing the rifts to prevent more daemons from getting inside the webway. In front of the blockades, the Custodians and Sisters launched lightning-fast counter-attacks to keep the daemonic horde off-balance and prevent them massing in strength.

Slowly, but surely, the Imperial forces were pushing the blockades forward as the pressure from the daemons' attacks waned. Nevertheless, some daemon assaults did manage to break through the Imperial

Warp Conduit – *Dave Millgate*

defences, and on those rare occasions the attackers wreaked havoc on the Imperial workers. More than once, the daemonic insurgents were able to fight their way to the warp-gate of the Golden Throne. Desperate combats ensued as the Custodians and Sisters doubled their efforts to throw back the daemons and prevent them surging through the warp-gate and into the Imperial Dungeon beyond.

As the war raged on, new troops appeared amongst the hordes of daemons attacking the Imperial forces. The powers of Chaos sent foully corrupted Space Marines, Titans and other war machines into the webway to try and force a victory. The sanctity of the Imperial Palace, the fate of the Imperium and the very life of the Emperor depended on the Custodian Guard and the Sisters of Silence. If they couldn't defeat the daemonic horde and its corrupted allies, then humanity was surely doomed.

The Emperor's Gift – *Pat Oliff*

Frost Wolves Prosecutor Squad – *Andrea Uderzo*

Steel Foxes Vigilator Squad – *Chris Dien*

Nurgling Swarm – *Colin MacNeil*

Battle Flies – *Steve Boulter*

The Emperor's Wisdom – *Dan Scott*

Warp Breach – *Steve Boulter*

Legio Custodes – *Michael Phillippi*

Golden Throne – *Dave Millgate*

Slayer of Worlds – *Colin MacNeil*

Syrgalah, Warhound Titan – *John Zeleznick*

Abyssa – *Wayne England*

Beyond the Golden Throne

The war within the webway was going badly for the Emperor. Even though, at first, the army of the Custodian Guard and their supporters, the Silent Sisterhood, had managed to push back the daemonic invaders, they had taken many casualties. The Imperial forces had never had the advantage of numbers and each death weakened them, whereas the daemons appeared to have a numberless horde at their disposal. Despite thousands of daemons and their allies having been destroyed or banished back into the warp, there were thousands more to take their place.

As the battle within wore on, the daemons began to gain the advantage. Their assaults regularly reached deep into the Imperial defences – more than once approaching dangerously close to the human-built conduit that led to the warp-gate of the Golden Throne. On one occasion, a mighty Bloodthirster, greatest of the daemons of Khorne, fought its way through the Imperial defenders to the gate itself – only the last-minute intervention of Sister Celia Harroda of the Sisters of Silence was able to stop the beast from crashing through the gate and into the Imperial Palace dungeons. Sister Celia confronted the huge daemon, her presence chilling the air around it and stifling its otherworldly power, and silently she dispatched the monster with swift strokes from her blade of frost. The effort utterly exhausted her and with the final banishing stroke of her sword she collapsed upon the threshold between the warp and realspace, never to breathe again.

The death of Sister Celia was but one of many acts of brave sacrifice by the loyal warriors of the webway. Eventually, after many long days of bloody battle, these deaths took their toll and the defenders were forced to draw back to within sight of the Golden Throne. Here they were bolstered by the presence of the Emperor, who appeared as a brightly burning star to those within the alien conduits. The Emperor drew on his reserves of power and his star burned ever brighter; the daemons, unwilling to approach the shining nimbus, were held back.

The star of the Emperor gave the defenders respite enough that many were able to cross through the portal and retreat into the Imperial Palace. At first all of the tech-priests and workers were evacuated and then, reluctantly, the Silent Sisterhood and the Custodian Guard withdrew from the battle and into the Palace dungeons.

The gate would remain closed to the daemons for as long as the Emperor was able to power it from his throne atop the golden portal. Only the mightiest of psykers had power enough to do this, and even then most would be exhausted and fail in a short time. Only the Emperor had the might to keep the gate closed permanently and even for him, the effort got harder as the daemonic forces gathered about him. For as long as the daemon horde threatened to breach the portal, the Golden Throne would be his prison.

Webway Breach – *Dave Millgate*

Delta-Omega 03 – *Kari Christensen*

Ice Maidens Prosecutor Squad – *Chris Dien*

Terra is Reinforced

Rogal Dorn was concerned. He had recalled all remaining known loyal Legions to Terra to face the impending threat of invasion by Horus and his traitor army. Early responses to his signals suggested that the traitors had anticipated this move and were actively trying to prevent these Legions from reinforcing the defences of Terra.

The Space Wolves Legion had been attacked and thus prevented from travelling to the Solar System. The loyal defenders of Terra would miss the strong arm of Russ and his Legion. However, their actions at least allowed the White Scars Legion of Jaghatai Khan to make headway for Earth. Even allowing for the vagaries of warp travel, Dorn expected the Khan and his fleet to arrive within days. He pressed Malcador to maintain the Astronomican beacon at peak efficiency to give them as much aid as possible and reduce their chance of mis-navigation.

The Blood Angels had sent communications to Dorn, but warp disturbances had garbled the content and it was unclear to Dorn if, and when, they would be able to get back to Terra. The Legion of Sanguinius was one of the strongest, and their presence would be a tremendous boost to the loyalists. Dorn fervently prayed that they would arrive soon.

Rogal Dorn's own Legion had been split earlier in the war. His veteran companies had accompanied the primarch to Terra to break news of Horus's treachery to the Emperor. These companies had been severely mauled during the Mars battles and were down to less than half strength. The greater part of Dorn's Legion had been despatched on a futile mission to the Isstvan System. It was clear from what communications had been received from them that this mission had failed. The Imperial Fists primarch was deeply concerned about the state of his Legion.

Dorn's anxiety about the Imperial Fists increased when more news was received from the Legion. They had been becalmed for some months, unable to communicate or navigate through the warp. Suddenly they had been able to make contact with Terra, but were being subjected to an attack by a traitor fleet led by Perturabo of the Iron Warriors. Frantic signals from their fleet indicated that the Imperial Fists were attempting to break off from their attackers and make the warp-jump back to Terra. These were the last messages received from the fleet, and so Dorn could do nothing but wait in hope for them to arrive.

Of the Ultramarines and the Dark Angels, Rogal Dorn had received no information. If these Legions were heading for Terra, or intended to do so, he couldn't know. Dorn again impressed upon Malcador the importance of making contact with these Legions, but the Sigillite could offer him no answers. Dorn resolved to plan the defence of Terra without those two mighty Legions.

At long last, Dorn's wait was over as, first, the Imperial Fists fleet broke warp near the Uranus jump point and then the White Scars and the Blood Angels fleets appeared on long-range scanners. It was with some relief that signals were sent to the fleet commanders detailing their deployment patterns around Terra. Dorn requested that Sanguinius and Jaghatai Khan transport directly to the Imperial Palace for an immediate summit. Even as the loyal ships moved into Earth orbit, reports were received of traitor ships assembling near the space-docks of Mars. It appeared that Horus had begun mustering his armies for the invasion of Terra.

The loyal primarchs quickly assessed their forces. In addition to their three Legions of Space Marines, the loyalist defenders included nearly one and a half million troops of the Imperial Army and three

Senitorus – *James Ryman*

entire Titan Legions of the Mechanicum. All of these would be deployed in defence of the Imperial Palace complex on Terra. The loyal fleets were stationed as a first line of defence in orbit above the Earth. A string of Mechanicum orbital gun platforms, missile stations and clouds of space mines reinforced this ring of battleships. The Traitor would not find Terra a weak target.

News from within the Imperial Palace gave Dorn and his command staff some additional solace. The Custodian Guard had been redeployed in the upper levels of the Palace, apparently under the direct orders of the Emperor. If the Emperor himself were able to lead them then Horus would indeed have cause to regret his actions, thought Dorn.

Publoron – *Ed Cox*

Artulon – *Andrea Uderzo*

Xetsa – *Al Eremin*

Vaddark – *Abrar Amjal*

The Agony and the Ecstasy – *David Deen*

The Siege of Terra

On the thirteenth day of Secundus, the bombardment began. From orbit, the Warmaster's ships laid down an unrelenting barrage of missiles and deadly energy beams. Horus's aim was to cripple the defences around the Emperor's Palace and make possible a massive invasion of the Earth. Striking from Mars, the traitor ships had destroyed the lunar bases, smashed Terra's orbiting defences and scattered the protecting loyal fleets.

Horus's attack was a call to arms to all of his followers, and on countless worlds across the galaxy forces loyal to the Warmaster rose up and attacked those still sworn to the Emperor. The Emperor's realm was in turmoil, and some of the greatest battles humanity had ever known were being fought. The Imperium was bathed in flames as the bitter civil war enveloped the stars but it was on Earth, Holy Terra, that the fate of the galaxy – and of humanity – would be decided.

The skies of Earth were black with dust and ash thrown up by the barrage. The land was split with gigantic fissures and the tectonic plates groaned with stress. Mountain chains shivered and seas evaporated to become barren deserts. Rains of blood and ash dripped from the darkening sky. Astropathic choirs sang of evil portents and men went mad with fear. The fleet of Horus hung in orbit over the ravaged world. Shielded by the cunningly-wrought defences of the tech-priests, the pitifully few defenders of Terra stood ready to repel the invaders.

The loyal defenders of the Imperium gathered their thoughts and prepared to meet the onslaught. Within the Imperial Palace itself, the Emperor's personal bodyguard, the Custodians, stood ready to fight. At their side was the Blood Angels Legion with their primarch, the Angel Sanguinius. Beyond the Palace walls, the White Scars Legion of Jaghatai Khan was arrayed, and beneath the ruins of the Imperial Basilica, the Imperial Fists Legion of Rogal Dorn made final preparations for the coming battle.

As the earth shuddered under the bombardment, tank divisions roared across the tortured landscape to take up positions against the coming invasion. Defence lasers swivelled to face the turbulent, threatening sky. Suddenly, the night was streaked by the plasma contrails of drop pods.

The pods touched the ground and from them erupted a mass of traitor Space Marines who charged at the Imperial defenders, guns ablaze with fire, roaring the name of Horus. At head of the invading army were the primarchs Angron, Mortarion and Lorgar.

Mighty Angron bellowed orders to his blood-crazed followers, the World Eaters, driven insane by the buzzing of the neural implants surgically grafted to their brains. Brandishing his great runesword, crackling with newly acquired arcane power, Angron led his troops against the defenders of the Eternity Wall spaceport. Around his red-armoured warriors, bolter shells whined. Unflinchingly they advanced, determined to take the fortified construct and put its defenders to the sword.

At Mortarion's rasping command, the Death Guard emerged silently from the festering cocoons of their warped drop pods and advanced upon their terror-stricken foes. The dread runes on Mortarion's scythe glowed eerily in the night as he gestured for the Plague Marines to move forward.

The giant figure of Magnus the Red glared triumphantly about him with his one watchful eye before ordering the mage-warriors of the Thousand Sons to hurl their spells of death and destruction at the enemy.

A hail of deadly bolter fire cut down dozens of the Emperor's Children Legion.

Castason – *Tiernan Trevallion*

Riders of Tzeentch – *Wayne England*

Snow Condors Prosecutor Squad – *Andrea Uderzo*

Undeterred, they ploughed forwards singing the praises of their primarch Fulgrim. The traitor Legion surged onwards, carving a path of devastation through their foes.

As the battle raged, perhaps some defenders went mad with fear. Perhaps the corruption of Chaos that Horus had unleashed ran deeper than any might have suspected. Perhaps some were foolish enough to think that they could negotiate with the enemy. Whatever the reason, one last vile treachery was to take place. Many units of the Imperial Army that had pledged loyalty to the Emperor now turned against him, even as the traitor Space Marines made their landfall. It was almost as if it were a pre-arranged signal for them to act as they turned their weapons against their fellow warriors and cut them down with withering fire. This was surely one of the basest acts of treachery in the history of humanity. The Lions Gate spaceport fell to the invaders. As the traitors chanted the name of Horus and mad prayers were howled out, the air shimmered and a host of slavering daemons emerged from the warp to spread terror and dismay.

If there was ever doubt as to which masters Horus served, then the appearance of the daemonic horde dispelled them. For the defenders, it seemed as if this truly was the end of all that had been – that they were witnessing the last days of mankind.

The Warmaster ordered the rest of his army to the battle, and at his signal the troop transports of his fleet began to make planetfall. A veritable host of great ships drifted down through the atmosphere of Earth, hoping to overwhelm the defenders by sheer weight of numbers. Unlike the drop pods that had carried the traitor Space Marines, these vast bloated ships presented fine targets for the weapons of the defenders. Thus the battle for Terra began in earnest.

Defence lasers blasted many renegade ships from the sky, sending thousands of tons of fused metal death raining down onto the ground below. Crippled vessels crashed into buildings or were vaporised in flight by the lancing energy beams of the huge Terran guns. As quickly as the surviving ships landed, they disgorged their cargoes and tens of thousands of traitor troops surged forth to attack the bastions of the defenders. The traitors' first objective was to silence the defence lasers that were still firing at the descending fleet and causing such havoc amongst the attackers.

The loyal defenders of Terra fought back tenaciously. Across the wide swathe of the Imperial plateau, a hundred or more battles were being waged as the traitors repeatedly assaulted the strongholds that comprised the Palace complex and the loyalists doggedly repulsed them.

The defenders of the Eternity Wall spaceport couldn't resist the attacking forces and were swept aside by the merciless assault. The hordes of the Warmaster were in total possession of the space field. More and more drop-ships descended from orbit, towering above the landing ground like nightmarish skyscrapers, dark runes on their hulls glowing evilly in the gloom.

Hundred-metre high doors opened along the flanks of the monstrous ships and from within their stygian holds the Titans of Chaos emerged. They were warped giants, the armour of their carapaces fused and moulded into new macabre designs by the power of Chaos. Some of the Titans had been equipped with strange and potent weapons, while others had become a bizarre hybrid of the organic and the machine. Metal tentacles lashed and spiked tails whipped back and forth. Engines roared like the bellowing of ancient beasts. Banners unfurled bearing the foul runes of Chaos, and the Titans of the Storm Lords and the Flaming Skulls Legions marched to war.

Screamers of Tzeentch – *J D Smith*

Lambda-Zeta 01 – *Kari Christensen*

Kumblai – *John Gravato*

At the Lions Gate spaceport, the traitors heralded the arrival of the towering black engines of the Khornate host. Monsters, mutants and cultists seethed like angry ants around the bases of the mighty war machines.

The traitors swept onwards. Reinforced by the arrival of the Chaos Titans and death-dealing war machines of Khorne, they pushed through the demoralised and exhausted loyal troops until they faced the walls of the Emperor's Palace itself.

The raging World Eaters raced towards the marble and steel outer ring of the Palace façade. The unstoppable Thousand Sons marched relentlessly forwards, their bolter fire raking the defenders. The Emperor's Children Legion swept aside the Imperial Army divisions facing them and approached the Saturnine Gate. All around the walls, bitter fighting ensued as the Imperial defenders sallied forth, trying to drive back their attackers before the traitors could bring their main force to bear.

From their pillbox emplacements along the Palace walls, loyal gun crews rained death down on the relentless attackers. Again and again, the plazas and walkways outside the Palace were cleared of traitors. Again and again, new foes stepped forward to take their place.

Within a few scant hours, the forces of Horus had seized control of the Palace complex's spaceports, destroying thousands of Imperial war machines and killing many tens of thousands of loyal warriors. Now the hordes of the Warmaster pressed forward against the Palace walls. Even as his army laid siege to the Emperor's Palace, Horus ordered even more of his waiting fleet to land and disembark their troops.

The number of traitor soldiers was so great that huge columns stretched from the Lions Gate and Eternity Wall spaceports to the Emperor's Palace. As well as Space Marines, the great army of Horus included many Titans, traitor Imperial Army units, cultists, mutants and daemons. Thunderhawk gunships flew overhead and the massed tank brigades that drove on towards the Palace threw up great clouds of dust.

The Palace was surrounded by the Warmaster's army and around its entire circumference they attacked, driven on by the urgent commands of the traitor primarchs and by Horus's own mad ambition.

Meanwhile, in the depths of the Imperial Palace, the Emperor sat on his Golden Throne and brooded on the events occurring far above him. The great edifice of machinery upon which he sat had become his prison. His psychic might was needed to keep the warp-portal tightly shut against the hordes of Chaos that pounded at the doorway from within the webway beyond. If he relented and let slip his focus, then the daemonic forces of Chaos would be able to pile through the gateway and into his Palace.

But the Emperor knew he must soon relinquish his hold on the Throne and confront Horus in person. The Warmaster could only win the victory he sought by vanquishing the Emperor – everything he had done and was doing was intended to bring about that goal. The battle above was merely a sideshow – a deliberate act of provocation whereby Horus was attempting to goad the Emperor into dropping his guard and facing him.

The Emperor was patient. He would meet Horus soon enough. For now he waited and bided his time. Horus would become impatient and act rashly – then, and only then, would the Emperor face him.

Day by day the siege of the Palace wore on, casualties rising from the thousands to tens of thousands to hundreds of thousands. Chaos Titans blazed at the walls, specially

The Imperial Reaper – *Dan Scott*

Punishers – *Torstein Nordstrand*

Mellerus – *Tiernan Trevallion*

Angron, Prince of Blood – *Alex Boyd*

constructed missiles ripping great chunks from the masonry. The Titans of the Fire Wasps answered with their volcano cannons. The smell of burning flesh filled the air as the corpses of the dead were incinerated in funeral pyres a hundred metres high. Obscene ash parched the throats of the defenders. The World Eaters, now driven irrevocably insane, built a pyramid of scorched skulls in Temple Square. By night, the chants of degenerate cultists echoed through the darkness and daemonic entities flitted among the ruins of Earth.

Slowly, foot by torturous foot, the defenders were forced back. The great Palace walls were riddled with endless corridors and bulkheads, and within this maze there was constant skirmishing and bitter hand-to-hand fighting. The passages were becoming blocked with bloated corpses as the fighting intensified.

Horus ordered his army to push on. They must take the wall, he commanded. The Death's Head Titan Legion was commanded to break the walls. The fell Titans began to demolish entire sections of the bastion. The defenders inflicted dreadful carnage upon them – three, four then five massive Titans were destroyed in as many minutes. But the Chaos Titans would not relent and they kept hammering away at the walls.

The Siege of the Emperor's Palace had gone on for many days. Days of countless assaults, counter-attacks, sallies, shelling and death. The battle raged on and on. Slowly, very slowly, the walls were beginning to crumble and the defenders' fire was waning.

The daemon that was Fulgrim was bored by it. His plots and schemes had not been designed so that he could simply spend time waiting around for petty mortals to break down a wall. He craved action, he yearned for something to happen. Yet still the defenders of the Palace repulsed the attackers. No matter how many troops were thrown at the walls, the daemon thought, still they stood. The daemon decided he could bear it no longer and that there must be easier prey on the planet.

With this, the daemon Fulgrim gathered his Legion about him and set off on an orgy of destruction across the Earth. With so much of the loyal efforts directed towards defending the Emperor, they found the rest of Earth largely unprotected and weak. The carnage they inflicted upon the population of the planet was immense – the violence completed the Emperor's Children Legion's descent into Chaos.

While the traitor army had been battering at the Palace walls, Jaghatai Khan and his White Scars Legion had been harassing their flanks in a series of hit-and-run attacks. Now the Khan changed his plans. Rather than continue futile attempts to draw the traitors away from the Palace, he launched a lightning raid against the Lions Gate spaceport. The attack was launched during the night hours, under cover of darkness. The Khan's force included his own White Scars Space Marines, the remnants of the First Terran Tank Division and a large number of surviving loyal Imperial infantry regiments. The loyalists easily defeated the traitor garrison and reclaimed the spaceport in the name of the Emperor. The Khan threw a defensive perimeter around the space field and, despite furious attempts by the Warmaster's army to counter-attack, was able to hold the position. The Khan ordered the defence lasers to be re-manned and they soon fired at the rebel drop-ships that were still attempting to land. The Khan's actions stemmed the flow of warriors and war machines from the spaceport to the Palace.

Buoyed by this success, other loyalists began to attack the Eternity Wall spaceport, but here the forces of the Warmaster were better prepared. Traitor Space Marines ambushed the loyalist attackers; thousands of loyal warriors were killed and they were driven back in confusion. The spaceport remained in the hands of the Warmaster. Their lines of communication secured, the traitors once more turned their full attention towards the Palace.

Fulgrim, Prince of Pleasure – *Wayne England*

Khorma – *Tiernan Trevallion*

The Walls of the Palace Break

The walls of the Emperor's Palace finally broke under the onslaught by the Death's Head Titan Legion – the huge Warlord Titans of the Legion smashed their way through the last few metres of the bastion and unleashed a flood of traitors into the inner courtyard of the Palace.

The invading traitors were met by the loyalist troops defending the Palace, and battle raged across what was once the Emperor's private garden. The fine statues and ornaments of the inner gardens were wrecked as the fighting intensified. The smell of burning mingled with the acrid stench of weapon fire and the foul pestilent exhaust fumes of the giant Titans, as the traitors attempted to put the Palace to the torch.

The defending warriors dug in and soon the entire parkland was a maze of trenches and earthworks. There was little space in the inner gardens for the Chaos Titans to operate efficiently and they became easy targets for the heavy weapons of the Emperor's troops.

Both sides fought with unimaginable ferocity. Loyalist and traitor alike sensed that the end was drawing close, and so they attacked each other in desperate attempts to win the day.

Even as the battle raged, within the Palace the commanders of the Emperor's besieged army met to plan their final strategies of the war. Sanguinius was the most senior commander present; Dorn and the Khan were waging their own battles beyond the Palace wall. With the Blood Angels primarch were a number of high-ranking Custodians and Malcador the Sigillite.

Sanguinius instructed the Custodians to counter-attack against the invaders in the inner gardens. They were tasked with occupying the traitors long enough for the defence of the Palace to be reinforced by the Legions of the Khan and Rogal Dorn. He and his Legion would take up position around the key entrances to the Palace building itself – they were the last line of defence should the traitors resist the Custodians. He asked Malcador to signal the Khan and Dorn to get their Legions to the Palace.

Malcador left the assemblage to organise the signals and to attend the Emperor – he had finally received the order he had been dreading. The Emperor was preparing to leave the Golden Throne and confront Horus and Malcador knew his own life was now forfeit to victory.

Sanguinius took up his position above the Ultimate Gate – the main entrance to the Imperial Palace. Below him, wounded troops were ushered through the great portal by his Blood Angels. From his vantage point, the primarch could see the huge mass of traitors pressing forward through the breaches in the bastion wall. Through sheer weight of numbers, they were overwhelming the defenders.

He watched as the Custodians launched their counter-attacks. The Emperor's bodyguard fought with brutal efficiency and none of the traitorous horde could stand against them – but they were too few in number and their attacks only slowed the tide. The Custodians did not relent and attacked again and again. But each attack was less effective than the last and they were inched back towards the Palace.

A huge shape rose up from amongst the army of Horus. The creature was tall, taller than any around it, and as it rose up it unfolded its great leathery wings and took to the air. It was a Bloodthirster, greater daemon of Khorne, the most fearsome and dangerous of the Blood God's followers. The daemon flew towards Sanguinius and he recognised it instantly – its name was Ka'bandha and he had fought the creature before.

Atop the Ultimate Gate, the two mighty figures clashed in aerial combat. Both were winged – the Angel's wings were pure white and shone brightly through the smoke and

Eternity Gate – *Brad Williams*

smog of war, while the other was a creature of nightmare, its daemonic wings dark. As they wheeled about each other in the air, the warring troops below seemed to pause to watch the unfolding drama.

'Know this, creature of darkness – I will take my revenge on you for past evil,' the Angel said as he plunged his sword into the daemon's face, spearing one of its eyes. The daemon shrieked as if in pain, but wheeled about, lashing at the primarch with its whip and chopping at him with its great axe. The daemon's whip stung Sanguinius's wing and he faltered in the air slightly. As he did so, the Bloodthirster grabbed him by the throat with its massive taloned fist. Sanguinius cut with his sword against the daemon's flank – the beast flinched but did not release its hold.

'Now you are finished, pathetic little bird,' rumbled the daemon, throwing the primarch down onto the gate below. The granite stonework splintered as the Angel's body smashed into it. The traitor horde watching roared their approval. The primarch lay still upon the broken stone as the daemon landed next to him and prepared to deal the deathblow. The monstrous creature threw back its head and let loose a howl of exultation.

'Blood for the Blood God! A Skull for the Skull Throne!'

As the daemon howled in triumph over him, Sanguinius drew on his last reserves of strength and power. With a massive effort, he painfully rose to face Ka'bandha for the last time.

'Your cry of victory is mistimed, daemon. I am not finished. My vengeance has yet to be taken. I shall not fall at this hour, nor to your bloodied hand.' At this, Sanguinius leapt at the daemon and, seizing it by the wrist and ankle, he raised the beast up high and smashed it down across his knee. The crack of its back breaking shook the masonry upon which they stood and echoed across the Palace grounds, the hordes below watching in silence.

Sanguinius, now terrible in aspect, lifted the carcass of the daemon above his head. An arc of power danced on his brow as he swung the body around and hurled the broken behemoth into the midst of the daemon's followers. The traitors beat their chests and wailed in dismay. The Blood Angels cheered and the Ultimate Gate was shut tight against the ravening hordes.

Even as Sanguinius defeated the daemon atop the Ultimate Gate, the Imperial Fists and their primarch Rogal Dorn returned to the Palace. They rode in aboard the great Sky Fortress – a massive fortified gunship. Dorn had received the signal from Malcador and was determined to stand, and if necessary, die side by side with the Emperor in the final hour. The Imperial Fists disembarked quickly and the Sky Fortress raced away from the Palace to reach the Khan and bring him and his White Scars to the Emperor's side.

The traitor Titans of the Death's Head Legion spied the great ship and with a hail of fire from their mammoth weapons, they shot it down. As the ship fell from the sky, the loyal command crew bravely struggled to crash the crippled vehicle amongst Horus's attacking army.

To those watching from the Palace towers, it seemed as if a new sun had been born on Earth as the Sky Fortress's reactor exploded. The glare from the orb of plasma fire seared their eyes and the shockwave in its wake knocked them from their feet. The explosion ripped a huge crater in the land fully three kilometres across. Despite this huge blow to the army of Horus, the defenders now realised that they were completely cut off from the rest of the loyalists on Earth. Only a miracle could save them.

Malcador faced the Emperor. He had received the call and now prepared to perform his final duty to the man he had followed for the greater part of his life.

'Malcador, the time is upon us. Horus thinks me blinded by his psychics, but I am more

Torgaddon – *John Hodgson*

Macaddon – *Ralph Horsley*

Ballatoron – *Andrea Uderzo*

Ice Dragons Vigilator Squad – *Andrea Uderzo*

powerful than he can possibly imagine. The Space Wolves have had help from an unexpected quarter and, having turned the tables on their pursuers, are now bound for Earth. The Ultramarines have likewise triumphed and also head this way, as does the fleet of the Dark Angels. Horus knows that these Legions are coming and will want to finish affairs here before they arrive. He can only do this by confronting me in person. This will force him to act rashly, against the counsel of his closest advisors. I must be ready to take advantage of his mistake. Are you prepared to take the Throne?'

'Of course, my lord. I have always been ready to repay the debt I owe you. Since first we met, my life has been yours.'

'Thank you, old friend. You will be remembered for your sacrifice.'

Before Malcador the Sigillite ascended to the Golden Throne, he had one last duty to perform. As he stood before the Emperor he was accompanied by a group of twelve hooded attendants. Malcador looked up at the Emperor and at the machine to which he was bound.

'Sire, when last we met you commanded me to gather together a group of people whose loyalty to you and to the Imperium was unquestioning. This I have done. I have worked long and hard to find those I thought would suit. I have personally overseen every aspect of the exhaustive tests to which they have been subjected and can vouch for their character, loyalty and strength of mind. They have many skills and will serve you well.'

Malcador gestured to the hooded figures behind him. As he did so, four of them stepped forward and knelt before the Emperor. The Emperor nodded an acknowledgement of their show of fealty to him.

'Sire, these others are known to you. Each of them is a Space Marine. They have cast aside their allegiance to primarch and Legion and pledged themselves anew to you, their Emperor and father. I have chosen these eight since, allied to their unflinching loyalty, they each are blessed with paranormal skills, kept dormant in respect of your previous commands. However, these skills are most apt in combating the horrors that have recently emerged from the warp and I know they will be needed in the coming years.'

'Malcador, you have judged well. These eight Space Marines do indeed have a vital role to play in the future of the Imperium, though veiled in secrecy will they be.'

The final siege of the Emperor's Palace had begun. The traitors piled reinforcements through the great breaches in the outer walls and into the expansive courtyards that surrounded the Palace building. Giant Chaos Titans and other war machines of the Dark Mechanicum pounded at the towering edifice with their massive array of cannons, guns, missiles and bombs. The hordes of Horus swarmed around the building, firing up at the battlements and smashing at the gates and doorways through which they would enter. Overhead, gunships swooped down on the Palace from the darkening skies and unleashed their deadly payloads upon its roofs.

The Palace walls were thick, its defences well-designed. The relatively small numbers of loyal troops within were able to maintain a stout and brave defence. They dealt a terrible toll of death on the attackers. They did not surrender and would not submit to either Horus or despair; they just kept fighting, though they knew they had only days remaining.

Horus felt that he was so close to victory he could taste it. He began to make ready to teleport down onto the surface from the *Vengeful Spirit* to personally supervise the last days of the siege and to finally confront his former lord and master, the Emperor.

Ula, Doom of Heroes – *John Gravato*

Tales of Heresy – *Neil Roberts*

As Horus was about to make his teleport, he was approached by Erebus, the Dark Apostle of the Word Bearers. Erebus told the Warmaster that important information had just been received that he must hear.

Erebus reported to Horus that their warp-based allies had espied a number of loyal fleets heading for Terra. The Space Wolves under Leman Russ had somehow evaded the Alpha Legion of Alpharius and had set course for Earth. Likewise, a huge loyal fleet had departed from Ultramar carrying the apparently victorious Ultramarines Legion. Horus's daemonic allies said that they were but scant hours from reaching the Solar System. Furthermore, the Dark Angels of Lion El'Jonson were also Earth-bound, though the daemons could not say when they would arrive.

Horus was furious at this news. The Space Wolves on their own would pose no great threat to his impending triumph, though their presence would be an irritating distraction. However, the news of the Ultramarines and Dark Angels heading for Terra was a disaster for the Warmaster. Despite their war against the Word Bearers at Calth, the Warmaster assumed that Roboute's Legion was still the largest and most powerful Legion and he had no reason to doubt the fighting strength of the Dark Angels. These three Legions together would at best delay his victory; at worst they would deny it him altogether.

Horus had gambled everything on being able to defeat the forces of Terra before the Emperor could muster help from all of his still-loyal Legions. With time seemingly against him, it now appeared as if this gamble had failed.

Horus was the first among the fallen, with the power of a god and the cunning of a daemon. He resolved to try one final gambit. He could still kill the Emperor. He immediately ordered all comm-net communications to be blocked so that the defenders on Terra could receive no word from their rescuers. He concentrated on his own psychic powers to cloud the Emperor's psy-senses and prevent him knowing of the approaching fleets. He turned to his waiting minions, his head ablaze with psychic fire, and gave his fateful command.

'Maloghurst, if I cannot get to the Emperor through the walls of his Palace-fortress then I shall tempt him to come to me. Shut down all the shields!'

'But, sire, with the shields lowered, the *Vengeful Spirit* will be unprotected. Our foes will be able to blast this ship to oblivion,' Maloghurst replied.

Erebus also spoke. 'My lord, this is folly. You must teleport to the surface and lead the final assault against the Palace. Without shields, we are easy prey. With respect, you must rescind this order.'

'No. The order stands! The Emperor will not let this ship be fired upon. He will see this action as an invitation and a personal challenge. I am offering him the chance to finally confront me and finish this one way or the other. He will not be able to resist this opportunity. We must prepare for his attack!'

Epsilon-Alpha 63 – *John Gravato*

Tormaggedon – *Adrian Smith*

Sarpati – *John Wigley*

Verklosh – *John Gravato*

Wrath of the Blood Angels – *Alex Boyd*

The Punisher – *Eric Ren*

Abisha – *James Ryman*

Appollus – *Tony Parker*

Khalophis, Warlord Titan – *James Brady*

Metallis – *John Wigley*

The Undying – *David Deen*

Sor Talgron – *Alex Boyd*

Hydra's Eyes – *John Wigley*

Delvarus – *Tiernan Trevallion*

Press the Advantage – *John Wigley*

Horus's Vengeance – *Adrian Smith*

The Lord of Flies – *Neil Roberts*

Spectre of Death – *Justin Norman*

Feron's Militia – *Torstein Nordstrand*

Lorgar – *Michael Phillippi*

Maloghurst the Twisted – *Sam Wood*

Mikaelor Cobernus – *Adrian Smith*

Imperial Fists – *Alex Boyd*

Syrius – *Adam Denton*

Malnor – *Karl Kopinski*

Kinmourn, Warhound Titan – *Wayne England*

Voluntary Sacrifice – *John Gravato*

The Throne Room – *John Gravato*

Malcador's Sacrifice

Malcador the Sigillite ascended to the Golden Throne, replacing the Emperor who now stood before the edifice with his loyal captains Rogal Dorn and Sanguinius. The great confusing mass of machinery around the Throne throbbed with power. Arcs of static energy leapt across the cables and conduits and the air was thick with the smell of ozone. Malcador could not speak, such was the concentration he had to bring to bear in order to control the tempestuous forces at his call.

'Behold the greatest sacrifice of our age!' the Emperor directed the two mighty primarchs. 'Malcador is Sigillite no more. Henceforth he shall always and only ever be Malcador the Hero!' At this, the three figures retired from the Palace vault and make ready to teleport onto the battle-barge of Horus.

The Warmaster had lowered his battle-barge's shields. It was a clear invitation to the Emperor, and was the mistake that the Master of Mankind had been waiting for.

'I must accept the Warmaster's challenge and aboard his ship. There I will face him and this business shall be ended,' the Emperor said to his cohorts. 'You must remain here and prepare for the aftermath of my confrontation – whatever its outcome, I must be returned to the Throne. Malcador buys us only time and we have precious little of that commodity left to us.'

The Emperor instructed his loyal primarchs to wait in the Palace for his return from the *Vengeful Spirit*. Dorn and Sanguinius would not countenance this. For possibly the first and only time they refused to obey the command of their liege lord.

It was Sanguinius who spoke first. 'My lord, I will not idle here whilst you risk all aboard the fell ship of Horus. Weakened though I am by my battle with the great daemon, I still have power enough to aid you. You will have my sword at your side.'

Dorn was equally adamant. 'Whatever we can achieve here will count for naught if you fail. I simply will not let you do this thing alone. The traitor is sly and you must have every protection we can offer in case he has some tricks yet to play.'

'Very well, you shall both accompany me!' said the Emperor. 'But know you both that my prescience fails me and I cannot fathom how this will resolve. I believe that this is the one chance I have to meet Horus and end his madness. Death stalks the *Vengeful Spirit*, this much I do know. Mayhap it will claim the Warmaster, but its hunger is great and I doubt we shall all return.'

The Emperor's comments did not deter the primarchs and so the three, together with a detachment of the Emperor's own Custodian bodyguard, teleported up to the battle-barge of Horus.

Tangahi – *Tiernan Trevallion*

Tolkhata – *Alex Boyd*

Halbrecht – *Tiernan Trevallion*

Deriuz – *Dan Scott*

Argonus – *Adrian Smith*

Scrodha – *John Gravato*

Fabius's Enhanced Warriors – *Dan Wheaton*

Centurion – *Adrian Smith*

The Final Battle

A flash of light and a feeling of coldness enveloped the Emperor and his two loyal primarchs, Rogal Dorn and Sanguinius. They had teleported into the Warmaster's flagship, the *Vengeful Spirit*. The Emperor took an instant to re-orientate himself and realised that something had gone wrong. He stood in a vast, warped chamber with only a handful of his Custodian Guard in attendance. The other Custodians and the primarchs were not present. How was this possible, he wondered? Could Horus have disrupted the teleport beam? Had he become so powerful?

Insane voices gibbered madly inside his mind. There were figures trapped within the stone walls of the vast room. Inhuman hands reached out for him, grasping at him with rock-like strength. He shrugged them off easily.

His comrades were not so lucky. Bolters chattered and flashed as the Custodians attempted to fight off their daemonic assailants. One screamed as he was drawn into the dark and slimy walls. As he vanished, ripples spread out from his point of disappearance. The other Custodians were grabbed and struggled to avoid the fate of their comrade. The Emperor's sword lashed out, severing limbs, freeing those trapped. He summoned his psychic energies. A nimbus flickered around his head as he unleashed but a fraction of his power. A tidal wave of destruction ripped through the daemons, destroying them utterly, yet left his own men unscathed.

The Emperor scanned about him, seeking the primarchs, but the walls of the Warmaster's battle-barge were resistant to his mindsight. He gestured for the surviving Custodians to follow him as he made his way to the command centre of the ship.

They wandered through a vessel hideously distorted beyond all recognition by the warping power of Chaos. Great sphincter-doors distended from walls of flesh-like stone. Transparent veins bore rivers of blood along conduits in the floor. Carpets of mucus covered a road of tongues. Winged and distorted things that might once have been human flitted through archways of bone and perched on ledges of rib. The Custodians gasped in horror. The Emperor exerted himself to calm them, psychically soothing their fear of the dreadful place. All the while, he scanned the area looking for the spoor of Horus. He knew the nature of the pact the Warmaster had made with the Ruinous Powers and the dreadful consequences should he win his victory.

They passed pits that gaped like glistening gullets in the floor and echoed the beat of a distant giant heart. They were showered by waterfalls of stinking yellowish liquid that cascaded down cliffs of carved cartilage. Sometimes they heard weapons fire but when they arrived at the source they found nothing. Mists of foetid vapour drifted across their field of vision, obscuring corridors of carnivorous stone. Clouds of insects swarmed over their faceplates and choked the external ports of their armour.

Scuttling skull-faced things garbed in the armour of Space Marines ambushed them. They fought hordes of mutated beasts. The Emperor's bodyguard fought well, but one by one the Custodians died. In the end, the Emperor stood alone. Then, and only then, was he allowed to enter the presence of Horus.

The Emperor entered the command deck of the *Vengeful Spirit* and beheld Horus. The Warmaster bestrode the body of a broken angel. Behind him, the tortured planet filled the viewport, a bauble for Horus to seize with one clawed hand. Corpses of massacred Custodians lay everywhere.

Face glowing with internal bloodlight, Horus turned to the Emperor and spoke. 'Poor Sanguinius. I offered him a position of power in the new order. He could have sat

The Horus Heresy – *Adrian Smith*

at the right hand of a god. Alas, he chose to align himself with the losing side. He gave me little alternative but to kill him. With my bare hands I throttled the life from him.'

The Emperor stood transfixed by the grim tableau: one son dead, the other his hideously transformed murderer. He tried to force words from his frozen tongue. In the end he could only whisper, 'Why?'

Mad laughter rang out. 'Why? You ask me why? Have all those millennia taught you nothing? Weak fool, your timidity prevented you from binding the forces of Chaos. Rather than tame your enemy, you merely antagonised them. You meekly refused to take ultimate power. I have done that which you would not do. I have bound the Ruinous Powers to my will and I shall lead humanity into a new age of galactic supremacy. I have done this, I, Horus, Master of Chaos, Lord of Mankind, True Emperor of Humanity.'

The Emperor looked at his former favourite and shook his head. He knew well the trap that had ensnared Horus. 'No man who ever lived can master Chaos,' he said quietly. 'You believe me weak to have not followed this course. You have deluded yourself. You are the servant of Chaos, not its master.'

A look of rage transfigured the Warmaster. He stretched out a hand and a bolt of psychic force leapt forth. The Emperor screamed as agony wracked his body. 'Feel the true nature of my power, then tell me I am deluded,' roared Horus, his voice that of an angry god.

Beads of sweat stood out on the Emperor's forehead, but he steeled himself against the pain. He could sense the taint of Chaos infused through the power that Horus wielded. He recognised the touch of the four great Ruinous Powers. 'You are deluded,' he said.

Once again Horus gestured and lances of pure poison seared through the Emperor's veins. 'I let you come here, father, so you could witness my triumph. Kneel before me and I will spare you. Acknowledge the new Master of Mankind.'

Desperately, the Emperor summoned his strength and power and lashed out at his miscreant son. Lightning flickered between the combatants. The stench of ozone filled the air. The Emperor leapt forward, sword raised. Weapons clashed as battle was joined on every level, physical, spiritual and psychic.

Bolts of force flashed back and forth as the demi-gods clashed, balancing the fate of the galaxy on every blow. Runesword and lightning claw rang against each other with a sound like thunder. Energies potent enough to level planets were unleashed. The chamber was filled with fire and brimstone and the *Vengeful Spirit* shook from prow to stern.

A backhand swipe from Horus knocked the Emperor through a stone bulkhead. His counterstroke tore a supporting column out of the ceiling as the Warmaster ducked.

The Emperor could sense the Chaos powers in the warp. They howled in glee and rage as they fed their pawn more power. They had waited long for this chance to strike at their most ardent foe. The Lord of Humanity stood alone against their massed might and knew that he was losing. Somehow, he could not make himself bring his full force to bear on Horus; the Warmaster might be a traitor, but deep within him was still the favoured son, the finest of the primarchs, the beloved scion.

Horus showed no such restraint. A lightning claw cut the Emperor's armour as if it were cloth, shearing through flesh and bone. The Emperor riposted with a psychic stroke intended to disrupt the Warmaster's nervous system. Horus laughed as he deflected it easily. His claws raked the Emperor across the throat, crushing windpipe and severing jugular. The Emperor gasped for breath as his blood spurted forth. He staggered, clutching desperately at his neck. Another blow severed the tendons of his wrist, causing his sword to drop from nerveless fingers.

Insane laughter echoed around the chamber. Horus broke several ribs with an almost playful punch. A surge of energy seared the Emperor's face, melting flesh till it ran, bursting an eyeball, setting hair alight. The Emperor stifled a moan and wondered how he could be losing. Blackness threatened to engulf him.

Horus grabbed his wrist, splintering bones. Blood pumped from the Emperor's throat. The Warmaster lifted his foe above his head and brought him down across his knee, breaking his spine. For a second, the Emperor knew only darkness; then a flare of agony brought him back to consciousness as Horus ripped his arm from its socket. The Warmaster howled with bestial triumph.

Suddenly, the battering stopped. Through his good eye, the Emperor saw that a solitary Imperial soldier had entered the room. Without hesitation, the loyal warrior charged towards the Warmaster, his blade in hand. Horus looked at him and laughed. For a moment he stood triumphant, allowing the bodyguard to see what he had done to his Emperor.

The Emperor instantly realised what was going to happen next, saw the gloating triumph on Horus's face, knew that his loyal servant was about to die. There was no trace of his beloved son left in Horus. Whatever humanity he once possessed had been all but eradicated, and now there was only a daemon driven by insane destructive fury.

The Warmaster turned his burning gaze on the soldier and his armour was blasted apart. His flesh flaked away to reveal his skeleton, then even that was gone, reduced to dust. It was over in moments.

The Emperor was stung by the death. He had known this warrior for centuries. This was not a fitting reward for such duty and loyalty. That Horus should so callously and casually kill him, without ceremony, without mercy, jolted the Emperor. It finally showed him that the Horus he had known and loved had gone, irrevocably destroyed by the madness of Chaos and the power that he had embraced. He had hoped that he could somehow rescue the Warmaster from the thrall of the Ruinous Powers, cleanse him of the sickness of ambition, bring him back into the fold and end the conflict forever. Now he knew that there was only one way he could end this. The grip of the Chaos gods was too strong, their claws sunk too deeply into Horus's soul. The Emperor must kill his favoured son to break their hold on him. He must strike one deadly blow. He knew he would get no other chance.

The Emperor used the brief respite won for him by the death of his bodyguard to gather his wits. Mustering every iota of his concentration, he focused his psychic might into a bolt of pure force, more coherent than a laser, more destructive than an exploding sun. He hurled the bolt at Horus, a lance of power destined for the madman's heart. Horus sensed the upsurge of energy and turned to face the Emperor, his look of surprise turning to one of horror as he realised the strength of the attack and the doom it brought.

The Emperor's psychic bolt struck the Warmaster. Horus screamed as destruction rained down upon him, and he twisted and writhed in titanic agony. He strove frantically to counter the Emperor's deathblow, but his struggles became ever more feeble as the lethal energies played over him. Driven by all the force of his rage, pain and hatred, the Emperor willed Horus's death. He sensed the forces of Chaos retreat, disengaging themselves from their pawn. As they did so, sanity returned to the Warmaster. The Emperor saw the realisation of the atrocities he had committed flicker across Horus's face. Tears glistened there.

Through the torrent of the Emperor's psychic assault, Horus howled in pain and remorse. He painfully uttered his last words: 'I have been… a fool. I was so wrong… Everything is ruined. I have betrayed you… my father. I do not ask for forgiveness… End my torment… Kill me now! I am too weak to resist them… They call to me… Please end this.'

Horus was free, but the Emperor knew that he himself was dying and that the powers of Chaos might once again possess the Warmaster – and that he would not be able to stop them a second time. It was too great a risk. Horus must die. Yet, for a brief moment, looking into his old friend's face, he hesitated, unable to do the deed. Then he thought of the slaughter that still went on outside, that might go on forever. Resolve hardened within him. He forced all mercy and all compassion from his mind, emptied it of all knowledge of friendship and camaraderie and love. His remaining eye locked with Horus's and he saw understanding there. Then, with full cold knowledge of what he was doing, the Emperor destroyed the Warmaster.

The Custodian Guard – *Neil Roberts*

The Final Battle – *Neil Roberts*

Horus and the Emperor – *Adrian Smith*

Horus versus the Emperor – *Michael Phillippi*

The Emperor's Victory

Rogal Dorn knew something was wrong. He had materialised on one of the lower decks of the great battle-barge that was the flagship of Horus. The Emperor was not with him. Nor was the Angel Sanguinius. The Custodian Guard, the Emperor's sworn bodyguard, surrounded him and instantly adopted a defensive posture.

'What has happened?' one of them asked Dorn. 'Where is the Emperor?'

'It seems we have been tricked. Horus has worked some fell magic to separate us,' the primarch replied. 'We must locate the Emperor at all costs, and do it quickly,' he added.

As the words left his mouth, the small band was attacked. From within the labyrinthine passageways of the *Vengeful Spirit*'s corridors and chambers, a vast horde charged at the loyal warriors. Dorn and the Custodians had never seen their like before. Mutants, monsters and hideously transformed Space Marines shot and clawed and spat and lashed at them. The air was filled with flame and noise; shots ripped at their armour; blood-flecked talons tore at their flesh.

The attackers would easily overwhelm and destroy normal opponents, but even though some Custodians died, the rest fought back. With the primarch Dorn leading them, the band of loyal Custodians were indefatigable. They scythed down their attackers with bolter shell, power blade and willpower. Hundreds were killed in the ensuing firestorm. The Chaos horde was not only stopped by the ferocity and bravery of their defence, it was routed.

As the horde retreated, Dorn ordered the Custodians forward. They had no time to waste; they must find the Emperor. And so they went on, tracking their way through the bowels of the great fetid vessel. At every turn they were attacked by fresh enemies, and every time they fought them back. Occasionally, the ship itself seemed to attack them – foully corrupted tentacles extruded from the walls to grasp at them, spines burst forth from scabrous pores to spear at them, gaseous clouds of evil vapours were vented from weeping sores to choke them. Some of them died, but Dorn and the Custodian Guard fought on through everything that was placed between them and their goal.

Eventually, after what seemed like an age of fighting, the attacks ceased and the ship was still. Rogal Dorn and the last few remaining Custodians rushed to the command centre of the *Vengeful Spirit*, the great chamber within which the Emperor and Horus had fought, and despair overcame them.

Dorn entered the chamber, saw the mutilated form of the Emperor and the shrivelled husk inside the Warmaster's armour and horror gripped his soul. He cursed himself for taking so long to fight through the Chaos hordes. He knew now why their attacks had ceased and why the ship was quiescent. Horus was dead, he thought, he hoped, he knew, he must be dead: he couldn't bring himself to even think of the alternative. But the Emperor – what of him?

'Does he live? Our liege lord, does he live?' cried the Custodians as they rushed towards the stricken form of the Emperor.

Dorn hesitated for a moment. He was not sure what he would do if his beloved master and father were dead. That was a world he couldn't conceive of, a place only of darkness and despair. The Custodians were silent as they encircled their fallen master, and openly wept tears of sadness and anger.

'Our lord yet lives!' one said. 'Though his breath is shallow and his heartbeat faint.'

Dorn gathered himself and went to the Emperor's side.

'My lord,' he asked quietly. 'What orders are we to follow?'

The Emperor's voice was frail and pained. 'The Throne… Golden Throne… Take me there now!'

Dorn activated his teleport homing signal and two of the Custodians gently lifted the Emperor. The transport beam washed over them and they were back in the Imperial Palace.

Jaghatai Khan was waiting for them. He was caked in blood and gore, and his armour was pitted and torn. Faint sounds of battle could be heard from outside the Palace, slowly receding into the distance. The Khan and Dorn exchanged cursory greetings. Dorn was grim, the Khan more cheerful until he saw the Emperor's unmoving body.

'Rogal, the Palace is saved, mayhap all of Terra. The traitors retreat in haste before the ravening Blood Angels. Even now they are fleeing to their ships and their fleets scattering. What of the Emperor?' The Khan feared the answer.

'Friend Khan, the Emperor is in peril still. Alone against the arch-traitor Horus did he battle, and though he triumphed o'er him, now lies close to death. We must get him to the Golden Throne – 'tis the only device that can save him.'

'Then let us tarry not here. To the Throne at once!'

At that they went straight to the Golden Throne, where Malcador sat tortured and wasted. Plumes of energy lashed about the shrivelled body of the former Sigillite, arcs of power scythed across the cables and conduits of the great machine to which he was bound. Malcador was all but dead, only the slimmest vestige of life still lingering within him, only the supremest effort of will stopping him relinquishing it.

'How can such a device save the Emperor? It will more likely finish him. It is madness to bind him to it. This cannot be the thing to do!' the Khan exclaimed.

'The Emperor's word is law. His order is to bind him once more to the machine that is his Throne of Gold. We know not the full mysteries of this fabulous artefact, built as it was by the Emperor's own hand. We must trust him as we have ever trusted him and bind him to it, forthwith!' Dorn insisted.

The waiting tech-priests were directed to make the exchange. Malcador's husk was carefully disengaged from the complexities of the machine and the Emperor ascended to his Golden Throne once again, this time for eternity. As Malcador was removed, the last flicker of life left him. He died, and the dust of his corpse blew across the stone floor. At the instant of Malcador's death, the Emperor awakened, as if somehow he had been boosted with a powerful salve or medicine.

The Emperor, still frail and weak, spoke. 'Poor, brave Malcador the Hero. He reserved a fragment of his strength for me. It gives me a little time to pass final orders to you all. If you do as I ask then I shall not wholly die; my spirit at least will survive. My injuries are severe, more so than I had hoped but less so than I had feared. My psychic powers will return to me in time, but my body will never heal. I shall never walk amongst you again. I am now bound to this machine for all time. My faithful bodyguard and attendants know what is required. You must do as they request!

'Dorn and Jaghatai, you have much work to do. Though the head of the serpent has been destroyed, its coils still choke the safety of mankind. You and your loyal brothers must fight on. Cleanse the taint of treachery from our stars. Never again must we allow the Ruinous Powers of Chaos to have such a chance.

'Now, all of you go! You know your duties. Execute them well. The universe has many horrors yet to throw at us. This is not the end of our struggle. This is just the beginning of our crusade to save humanity. Be faithful! Be strong! Be vigilant!'

The Emperor spoke no more.

Hall of the Gods – Brad Williams

The Traitors are Routed

The commanders of the Blood Angels Legion knew that their beloved primarch Sanguinius had teleported with the Emperor to confront Horus. They had pleaded to go with him, but the Angel had refused. He asked instead that they do their duty and defend the Imperial Palace. This they had done, and with bravery and honour, fighting alongside the Custodian Guard and the Imperial Fists, they had kept the hordes of Chaos at bay.

Suddenly, without warning, each and every Space Marine of the Blood Angels Legion was struck with a searing vision – a nightmare scenario in which they were Sanguinius, and Horus, the arch-traitor, was throttling them to death with his bare hands. As they experienced the last moments of death, they knew the vision to be truth. A deep rage grew within their breasts, the darkness that had touched their souls on Signus revisited them and they went berserk. Casting aside all thoughts of danger and duty, they hurled themselves at the horde beyond the walls. Utterly consumed by anger, they smashed into the surrounding forces, killing and killing again. Awash with blood, the Angels of Sanguinius vented their fury on the Warmaster's army.

The Blood Angels' actions were as much of a surprise to their loyal allies as they were to the traitors. Even though the ferocity and speed of their assault pushed back the encircling hordes, the other defenders could see no possibility that it alone could win the battle and lift the siege. The other loyalists tried to call them back to the safety of the Palace, but their cries were in vain as the Blood Angels heedlessly continued their rampage.

The Custodians and Imperial Fists despaired – if the forces of Horus regrouped and attacked the Palace again, they doubted they would be able to hold them back without the Blood Angels at their side. Was this some evil plan of the Warmaster? Some kind of foul spell to draw out the defenders one by one and defeat them piecemeal? Suddenly it was clear that this was no plan of Horus's.

The Warmaster was dead. The psychic shock wave of his passing surged across the warp and enveloped the Earth. The great powers of Chaos retreated from their mortal pawn, and as they did so the daemon horde on Terra was vanquished. Chaos daemons screamed in anger and frustration as they were reabsorbed into the fabric of the immaterium and vanished without trace. The traitor primarchs were dumbfounded and confused. With their leader dead and their cause turned to dust, the Warmaster's army disintegrated. The besieging horde lost all sense of cohesion as each primarch looked only to the needs of his own Legion. The traitors retreated in disarray before the berserkers of the Blood Angels Legion who were quickly joined by the warriors of Rogal Dorn and Jaghatai Khan.

The resurgent loyalists slaughtered thousands as they pushed back the fleeing traitors. Even the mighty war machines of the Chaos Titan Legions could not stand against them and one by one the massive walking mechanical monsters were felled and destroyed. The retreat quickly turned into a rout and the demoralised forces of the rebellion fled the Earth in utter defeat.

The Traitor Legions took to their ships. As he was about to board his vessel, Angron, now daemon-primarch of the World Eaters, looked back at the glittering dome of the Imperial Palace that he had come so close to conquering and shook his fist. He growled angrily then shrugged his shoulders and left. He and his fellow rebels had an eternity to seek revenge.

The fleets of the Traitor Legions left the Solar System and scattered across the galaxy. The *Vengeful Spirit* and its tragic cargo, the ashen remains of Horus, disappeared into the void of the warp. The Siege of Terra was over. The Horus Heresy was ended.

Sagittarus – *Adrian Smith*

Defence Satellites – *Tiernan Trevallion*

Jubal Khan – *Tiernan Trevallion*

Fallen Leader – *Wayne England*

Aftermath

The Immortal Emperor – *John Blanche*

In the decades that followed the Horus Heresy, the Imperium faced many challenges. Rebellion, inspired by Horus's actions and by the machinations of the Dark Gods of Chaos, was rife across the worlds of humanity. Horus had unleashed a tide of treachery and betrayal – many would attempt to follow in his path. The Traitor Legions and their twisted primarchs continued to fight: no longer for the Imperium, but for their own survival. War was so incessant that, at times, the safety and sanctity of the Imperium was almost as great as during the Heresy.

The loyal forces of the Emperor dedicated themselves to ridding the galaxy of the traitors and their allies. The wars of the Scouring lasted many years, and the effort nearly exhausted the forces of Terra. They fought and fought and eventually hounded the traitors to the Eye of Terror – the strange area of space where the warp and realspace comingled. It became the prison and stronghold of the traitors. Guardian fleets patrolled its borders, and nearby planets became garrison worlds – ever ready to combat raiding forces from the Eye.

As if the traitors were not enough for the badly mauled Imperium to deal with, this time also marked the rise of the aliens. With so much of its strength siphoned off to fight the civil war, humanity found itself at the mercy of a new wave of aggressive xenos races. Sensing that the Imperium was weak, a plethora of alien races appeared or returned to plague the worlds of mankind. Orks were on the move, as vast hordes of the greenskin menace established powerful empires close to the heartlands of the Imperium – it would take centuries of war to contain them.

The Dark Confederation of Hykos, the cannibalistic Thrual, the mechanically enhanced warriors of Jorgall, the shape-shifting Lacrymoles, the savage hordes of the Kalardun, the enigmatic Eldar, the fearsome raiders of Grundbaj, to name but a few; all now preyed upon a shattered mankind. Humanity became ever more strident in its xenophobia as tales of these alien horrors percolated around the Imperium.

The Emperor was trapped on his Golden Throne, its arcane engineering barely able to keep his physical being from simply rotting away, communicating only through psychic mysteries, a thousand psykers a day sacrificed to keep his spirit charged.

During this period, the hierarchy of the Imperium underwent fundamental changes. Only through the mystic light of the great Astronomican beacon, was the Emperor now known to this new Imperium. The peoples of the worlds of humanity worshipped him still, not as their leader and king, but as their god. Lorgar of the Word Bearers would no doubt be greatly angered by the irony of this particular turn of events.

The Council of Terra was reformed and became the 'High Lords of Terra', who spoke for the Emperor and whose word was law. New organisations were created to govern the Imperium and combat the ever-present threat of Chaos. The Space Marine Legions, under the guidance of Roboute Guilliman, were reformed into smaller, more flexible, 'Chapters' to better combat the myriad threats to the Imperium – the legendary 'Second Founding' of the Space Marines. Though potent enough, these new Chapters were not as powerful as the Legions had been. The Space Marines were recast as an elite strike force. No longer would a single man wield the awesome power of one hundred thousand Space Marines. Fettered by the petty dreams of lesser men, never again would the Space Marines conquer the galaxy.

The Ultramarines – *Adrian Smith*

Alpharius – *John Blanche*

Although long-lived, the primarchs were not immortal, but it is hard to ascertain fact from the legends that surround such god-like beings. Certainly, each spearheaded a host of victories and heroic deeds across the galaxy, leaving behind innumerable tales of mythic proportion. Who knows if Leman Russ, Primarch of the Space Wolves, really did best a mighty draxbeast single-handedly? And if Ferrus Manus didn't forge the Iron Pyramids of Medusa, then who did?

One by one, they fade from the annals of history, the last of their kind reputedly disappearing sometime during M32. Whether the many extraordinary - and sometimes contradictory - accounts of the primarchs hold any truth or are just apocryphal tales, they are preserved in the lore of each Space Marine Chapter. Others are still remembered on the primarchs' adopted home planets.

Today, the primarchs are worshipped as gods themselves, and pilgrimages are made along the trails that they blazed across the stars, often ending at tombs or great memorials - places of ancient history that hold revered relics of their bones or wargear. Many still insist that the primarchs will arise again, in the time of the Imperium's most dire need, for one final battle...

Artwork Index

Deliverance Lost – *Neil Roberts*

The Emperor

The Primarchs

Luna Wolves/Sons of Horus

Word Bearers

Salamanders

Raven Guard

Alpha Legion

The Legio Custodes

The Sisters of Silence

The Mechanicum

Imperial Personnel

Agents of the Sigillite

Dan Abnett and Neil Roberts

MACRAGGE'S HONOUR

The vengeance of Ultramar

The Battle of Calth continues in this exclusive five-page, full artwork extract from the first ever Horus Heresy graphic novel

[mark: 20.27.17]

THE WORD BEARERS battle-barge *Infidus Imperator* turns in the debris-rich belt of Calth nearspace, ships dying in flames behind it. It engages its drive and begins a long, hard burn towards the outsystem reaches.

As it accelerates away, raising yield to maximum, the *Macragge's Honour* turns in pursuit, its main drives lighting with an equally furious vigour.

It is the beginning of one of the most infamous naval duels in Imperial history...

– Dan Abnett, *Know No Fear*